CRITICAL ACCLAIM FOR REGINALD HILL AND HIS DALZIEL/PASCOE MYSTERIES:

"Stylish and superior."

—*Kirkus Reviews*

"An exemplar of its genre."

—*Publishers Weekly*

"The real joy of the Dalziel-Pascoe books is the writing and the characterizations. Mr. Hill has such disparate writers as Trollope, Beerbohm, Sayers and Shaw in his blood."

—*The New York Times*

"Hill's polished, sophisticated novels are intelligently written and permeated with his sly and delightful sense of humor."

—*The Christian Science Monitor*

"A lot of people write classic detective stories, but Reginald Hill is one of the elite few who write *classy* classics."

—*The Baltimore Sun*

Books by Reginald Hill

A CLUBBABLE WOMAN

FELL OF DARK

AN ADVANCEMENT OF
    LEARNING

A FAIRLY DANGEROUS
    THING

RULING PASSION

A VERY GOOD HATER

AN APRIL SHROUD

ANOTHER DEATH IN
    VENICE

A PINCH OF SNUFF

PASCOE'S GHOST

A KILLING KINDNESS

DEADHEADS

EXIT LINES

TRAITOR'S BLOOD

WHO GUARDS A PRINCE

THE SPY'S WIFE

NO MAN'S LAND

CHILD'S PLAY

THE COLLABORATORS

UNDERWORLD

THERE ARE NO GHOSTS
    IN THE SOVIET UNION

BONES AND SILENCE

ONE SMALL STEP

RECALLED TO LIFE

BLOOD SYMPATHY

PICTURES OF
    PERFECTION

BORN GUILTY

THE WOOD BEYOND

ASKING FOR THE MOON

ON BEULAH HEIGHT

ARMS AND THE WOMEN

DIALOGUES OF THE
    DEAD

REGINALD HILL

A

Pinch

of

Snuff

A DALZIEL/PASCOE MYSTERY

A Dell Book

Published by
Dell Publishing
a division of
Random House, Inc.
1540 Broadway
New York, NY 10036

Dell® is a registered trademark of Random House, Inc., and the colophon
is a trademark of Random House, Inc.

ISBN: 0-440-16912-7

Reprinted by arrangement with the author

Printed in the United States of America

Published simultaneously in Canada

August 1990

19 18 17 16 15 14

OPM

"If you find you hate the idea of getting out of bed in the morning, think of it this way—it's a man's work I'm getting up to do."

Marcus Aurelius, *Meditations*

One

All right. *All right!* gasped Pascoe in his agony. It's June the sixth and it's Normandy. The British Second Army under Montgomery will make its beachheads between Arromanches and Ouistreham while the Yanks hit the Cotentin Peninsula. Then . . .

"That'll do. Rinse. Just the filling to go in now. Thank you, Alison."

He took the gray paste his assistant had prepared and began to fill the cavity. There wasn't much, Pascoe observed gloomily. The drilling couldn't have taken more than half a minute.

"What did I get this time?" asked Shorter, when he'd finished.

"The lot. You could have had the key to Monty's thunderbox if I'd got it."

"I obviously missed my calling," said Shorter. "Still,

it's nice to share at least one of my patients' fantasies. I often wonder what's going on behind the blank stares. Alison, you can push off to lunch now, love. Back sharp at two, though. It's crazy afternoon."

"What's that?" asked Pascoe, standing up and fastening his shirt collar, which he had always undone surreptitiously till he got on more familiar terms with Shorter.

"Kids," said Shorter. "All ages. With mum and without. I don't know which is worse, Peter, can you spare a moment?"

Pascoe glanced at his watch. "As long as you're not going to tell me I've got pyorrhea."

"It's all those dirty words you use," said Shorter. "Come into the office and have a mouthwash."

Pascoe followed him across the vestibule of the old terraced house which had been converted into a surgery. The spring sunshine still had to pass through a stained-glass panel on the front door and it threw warm gules like bloodstains onto the cracked tiled floor.

There were three of them in the practice: MacCrystal, the senior partner, so senior he was almost invisible; Ms. Lacewing, early twenties, newly qualified, an advanced thinker; and Shorter himself. He was in his late thirties, but it didn't show except at the neck. His hair was thick and black and he was as lean and muscular as a fit twenty-year-old. Pascoe, who was a handful of years younger, indulged his resentment at the other man's youthfulness by never mentioning it. Over the long period during which he had been a patient, a pleasant first-name relationship had developed between the men. They had shared their fantasy fears about each other's professions and Pascoe's revelation of his Gestapo-torture confessions under the drill had given them a running joke, though it had not yet run them closer together than sharing a table if they met in a pub or restaurant.

Perhaps, thought Pascoe as he watched Shorter pouring a stiff gin and tonic, perhaps he's going to invite me and Ellie to his twenty-first party. Or sell us a ticket to the dentists' ball. Or ask me to fix a parking ticket.

And then the afterthought: What a lovely friend I make!

He took his drink and waited before sipping it, as though that would commit him to something.

"You ever go to see blue films?" asked Shorter.

"Ah," said Pascoe, taken aback. "Yes, I've seen some. But officially."

"What? Oh, I get you. No, I don't mean the real hardporn stuff that breaks the law. Above-the-counter porn's what I mean. Rugby Club night-out stuff."

"*The Naughty Vicar of Wakefield.* That kind of thing?"

"That's it, sort of."

"No, I can't say I'm an enthusiast. My wife's always moaning they seem to show nothing else nowadays. Stops her going to see the good cultural stuff like *Deep Throat.*"

"I know. Well, I'm not an enthusiast either, you understand, but the other night, well, I was having a drink with a couple of friends and one of them's a member of the Calliope Club—"

"Hang on," said Pascoe, frowning. "I know the Calli. That's not quite the same as your local Gaumont, is it? You've got to be a member and they show stuff there which is a bit more controversial than your *Naughty Vicars* or your *Danish Dentists.* Sorry!"

"Yes," agreed Shorter. "But it's legal, isn't it?"

"Oh yes. As long as they don't overstep the mark. But without knowing what you're going to tell me, Jack, you ought to know there's a lot of pressure to close the place. Well, you will know that anyway if you read the local rag. So have a think before you tell me anything that could involve your mates or even you."

Which just about defines the bounds of our friendship, thought Pascoe. Someone who was closer, I might listen to and keep it to myself, someone not so close, I'd listen and act. Shorter gets the warning. So now it's up to him.

"No," said Shorter. "It's nothing to do with the club or its members, not really. Look, we went along to the show. There were two films, one a straightforward orgy job and the other, well, it was one of these sex and violence things. *Droit de Seigneur* they called it. Nice simple story line. Beautiful girl kidnapped on wedding night by local loony squire. Lots of nasty things done to her in a dungeon, ending with her being beaten almost to death just before hubby arrives with rescue party. The squire then gets a taste of his own medicine. Happy ending."

"Nice," said Pascoe. "Then it's off for a curry and chips?"

"Something like that. Only, well, it's daft, and I hardly like to bother anyone. But it's been bothering me."

Pascoe looked at his watch again and finished his drink. "You think it went too far?" he said. "One for the vice squad. Well, I'll mention it, Jack. Thanks for the drink, and the tooth."

"No," said Shorter. "I've seen worse. Only in this one I think the girl really did get beaten up."

"I'm sorry?"

"In the dungeon. The squire goes berserk. He's got these metal gauntlets on, from a suit of armor. And a helmet, too. Nothing else. It was quite funny for a bit. Then he starts beating her. I forget the exact sequence but in the end it goes into slow motion; they always do, this fist hammers into her face, her mouth's open—she's screaming, naturally—and you see her teeth break. One thing I know about is teeth. I could swear those teeth really *did* break."

"Good God!" said Pascoe. "I'd better have another of these. You're saying that . . . I mean, for God's sake, a mailed fist! How's she look at the end of the film? I've heard that the show must go on, but this is ridiculous!"

"She looked fine," said Shorter. "But they don't need to take the shots in the order you see them, do they?"

"Just testing you," said Pascoe. "But you must admit it seems daft! I mean, you've no doubt the rest of the nastiness was all faked?"

"Not much. Not that they don't do sword wounds and whip lashes very well. But I've never seen a real sword wound or whip lash! Teeth I know. Let me explain. The usual thing in a film would be someone flings a punch to the jaw, head jerks back, punch misses of course, on the sound track someone hammers a mallet into a cabbage, the guy on the screen spits out a mouthful of plastic teeth, shakes his head and wades back into the fight."

"And that's unrealistic?"

"I'll say," said Shorter. "With a bare fist it's unrealistic, with a metal glove it's impossible. No, what would really happen would be dislocation, probably fracture of the jaw. The lips and cheeks would splatter and the teeth be pushed through. A fine haze of blood and saliva would issue from the mouth and nose. You could mock it up, I suppose, but you'd need an actress with a double-jointed face."

"And this is what you say happened in this film."

"It was a flash," said Shorter. "Just a couple of seconds."

"Anybody else say anything?"

"No," admitted Shorter. "Not that I heard."

"I see," said Pascoe, frowning. "Now, why are you telling me this?"

"Why?" Shorter sounded surprised. "Isn't it obvious? Look, as far as I'm concerned they can mock up anything they like in the film studios. If they can find an audience, let them have it. I'll watch cowboys being shot and nuns being raped, and rubber sharks biting off rubber legs, and I'll blame only myself for paying the ticket money. No, I'll go further, though I know our Ms. Lacewing would pump my balls full of novocaine if she could hear me! It doesn't all have to be fake. If some poor scrubber finds the best way to pay the rent is to let herself be screwed in front of the cameras, then I won't lose much sleep over that. But this was something else. This was assault. In fact the way her head jerked sideways, I wouldn't be surprised if it ended up as murder."

"Well, there's a thing," murmured Pascoe. "Would you stake your professional reputation?"

Shorter, who had been looking very serious, suddenly grinned. "Not me," he said. "I really *was* convinced that

John Wayne died at the Alamo. But it's bothered me a bit. And you're the only detective-inspector I know, so now it can bother you while I get back to teeth."

"Not mine," said Pascoe smugly. "Not for six months."

"That's right. But don't forget you're due to have the barnacles scraped off. Monday, I think. I've fixed you up with our Ms. Lacewing. She's a specialist in hygiene, would you believe?"

"I also gather that she too doesn't care for what goes on at the Calliope Kinema Club," said Pascoe.

"What? Oh, of course, you'd know about that. The picketing, you mean. She's tried to get my wife interested in that lot, but no joy there, I'm glad to say. No, if I were you I'd keep off the Calli while she's got you in the chair. On the other hand I'm sure she'd be fascinated by any plans Bevin might have for harnessing female labor in the war effort."

"Shorter," said Detective-Superintendent Andrew Dalziel reflectively, "does your fillings in a shabby mac and a big hat, does he?"

"Pardon?" said Pascoe.

"The blue film brigade," said Dalziel, scratching his gut.

"I managed to grasp the reference to the shabby mac," said Pascoe.

"Clever boy. Well, they need the big hats to hold on their laps."

"Ah," said Pascoe.

"Of course it's a dead giveaway when they stand up. Jesus, my guts are bad!"

Scatophagous crapulence, diagnosed Pascoe, but he kept an expression of studied indifference on his face. On his bad days Dalziel was quite unpredictable and it was hard for his inferiors to steer a path between overt and silent insolence.

"I reckon it's an ulcer," said Dalziel. "It's this bloody diet. I'm starving the thing and it's fighting back."

He thumped his paunch viciously. There was certainly less of it than there had been a couple of years earlier when the diet had first begun. But the path of righteousness is steep and there had been much backsliding and strait is the gate and it would still be a tight squeeze for Dalziel to get through.

"Shorter," reminded Pascoe. "My dentist."

"Not one for us. Mention it to Sergeant Wield, though. How's he shaping?"

"All right, I think."

"Shown his face at the Calli, has he? That's why I picked him, that face. He'll never be a master of disguise, but, Christ, he'll frighten the horses!"

This was a reference to (a) Sergeant Wield's startling ugliness and (b) the Superintendent's subtle tactic for satisfying both parties to a complaint. The Calliope Kinema Club had opened eighteen months earlier, and after an uneasy period as a sort of art house it had finally settled for a level of cine-porn a couple of steps beyond what was available at Gaumonts, ABCs and on children's television. All might have been well had the Calli known its place, wherever that was. But wherever it was, it certainly wasn't in Wilkinson Square. Unlike most centrally situated monuments to the regency, Wilkinson Square had not relaxed and enjoyed the rape of developers and commerce. Even the subtle advances of doctors' surgeries, solicitors' chambers and civil servants' offices had been resisted. It was true that some of the larger houses had become flats and one had even been turned into a private school which for smartness of uniform and eccentricity of curriculum was not easily matched, but a large proportion of the fifteen houses which faced on the Square remained in private occupation. Even the school was forgiven as a necessary antidote to the creeping grayness of postwar education based on proletarian envy and Marxist subversion. No parent of sense with a lad aged six to eleven could be blamed for supporting this symbol of a nation's freedoms, whatever the price. The price included learning to add in pounds, shillings and pence and being subjected to Dr. Haggard's interesting theories on corporal punishment, but it was little to pay for the social kudos of having a Wilkinson House certificate.

What inefficiency and pedophobia could not achieve, inflation and a broken economy did, and in the mid-'seventies so many parents had a change of educational conscience that the school finally closed. The inhabitants of Wilkinson Square watched the house with interest and suspicion. The best they could hope for was expensive flats, the worst they feared was NALGO offices.

The Calliope Kinema Club was a shattering blow cushioned only by the initial incredulity of those receiving it. That such a coup could have taken place unnoticed was shock enough; that Dr. Haggard could have been party to

it defied belief. But it had and he was. His master stroke
had been to change the postal address of the building.
Wilkinson House occupied a corner site and one side of
the house abutted on Upper Maltgate, a busy and noisy
commercial thoroughfare. Here, down a steep flight of
steps and across a gloomy area, was situated the old
tradesmen's entrance through which postal and most other
deliveries were still made. Dr. Haggard requested that his
house be henceforth known as 21A Upper Maltgate.
There was no difficulty, and it was as 21A Upper Maltgate
that the premises were licensed to be used as a cinema
club while the vigilantes of the Square slept and never felt
their security being undone.

But once awoken, their wrath was great. And once the
nature of the entertainments being offered at the club became clear, they launched an attack whose opening bar-
rage in the local paper was couched in such terms that
applications for membership doubled the following week.

Legally the club was in a highly defensible position.
The building satisfied all the safety regulations and the
local authority had issued a license permitting films to be
shown on the premises. The films did not need to be cer-
tificated for public showing, though many of them were,
and even those such as *Droit de Seigneur* which were not
had so ambiguous a status under current interpretation of
the obscenity laws that a successful prosecution was most
unlikely.

In any case, as the Wilkinson Square vigilantes bitterly
pointed out, Haggard clearly had strong support in high
places and they had to content themselves with appeal-
ing against the rates and ringing the police whenever a

car door slammed. Most of them hadn't known whether to raise a radical cheer or a reactionary eyebrow when WRAG, the Women's Rights Action Group, had joined the fray. Sergeant Wield, who had been given the job of looking into complaints from both sides, was summoned by Haggard; and later three members of WRAG, including Ms. Lacewing, Jack Shorter's partner, were fined for obstructing the police in the execution, etc. This confirmed the vigilantes' instinct that the rights of women and the rights of property owners had nothing in common, and a potentially powerful alliance never materialized. But the pressures remained strong enough for Sergeant Wield to be currently engaged in preparing a full report on the Calli and all complaints against it. Pascoe felt a little piqued that his own contribution was being so slightingly dismissed.

"So I just ignore Shorter's information?" he said.

"What information? He thinks some French bird got her teeth bust in a picture? I'll ring the Sûreté if you like. No, the only thing interests me about Mr. Shorter is he likes dirty films."

"Oh come on!" said Pascoe. "He went along with a friend. Where's the harm? As long as it doesn't break the law, what's wrong with a bit of titillation?"

"Titillation," repeated Dalziel, enjoying the word. "There's some jobs shouldn't need it. Doctors, dentists, scoutmasters, vicars—when any of that lot start needing titillation, watch out for trouble."

"And policemen?"

Dalziel bellowed a laugh. "That's all right. Didn't you know we'd been made immune by Act of Parliament?

Two

Pascoe was surprised at the range of feelings his visit to the Calliope Kinema Club put him through.

He felt furtive, angry, embarrassed, outraged and, he had to confess, titillated. He was so immersed in self-analysis that he almost missed the teeth scene. It was the full frontal of a pot-bellied man wearing only a helmet and gauntlets that triggered his attention. There was a lot of screaming and scrabbling, all rather jolly in a ghastly kind of way, then suddenly there it was: the mailed fist slamming into the screaming mouth, the girl's face momentarily folding like an empty paper bag, then her naked body falling away from the camera with the slackness of a heavyweight who has run into one punch too many. Cut to the villain, towering in every sense, with sword raised for the coup de grace, then the door bursts open and enter the hero, by some strange quirk also naked and clearly a match for tin-head. The girl, very bloody but no longer bowed, rises to greet him, and the rest is retribution.

When the lights were switched on, Pascoe, who had arrived in the dark, looked around and was relieved to see not a single large hat. The audience numbered about fifty, almost filling the room, and were of all ages and both sexes, though men predominated. He recognized several faces and was in turn recognized. There would be some speculation whether his visit was official or personal, he guessed, and he did not follow the others out of the viewing room but sat and waited till word should reach Dr. Haggard.

It didn't take long.

"Inspector Pascoe! I didn't realize you were a member."

He was a tall, broad-shouldered man with a powerful head. His hair was touched with gray, his eyes deep-set in a noble forehead, his rather overfull lips arranged in an ironic smile. Only a pugilist twist of the nose broke the fine Roman symmetry of that face. In short, it seemed to Pascoe to display those qualities of authoritarian, intellectual, sensuous brutality which were once universally acknowledged as the cardinal humors of a good headmaster.

"Dr. Haggard? I didn't realize we were acquainted."

"Nor I. Did you enjoy the show?"

"In parts."

"Parts are what it's all about," murmured Haggard. "Tell me, are you here in any kind of official capacity?"

"Why do you ask?" said Pascoe.

"Simply to help me decide where to offer you a drink. Our members usually foregather in what used to be the staff room to discuss the evening's entertainment."

"I think I'd rather talk in private," said Pascoe.

"So it *is* official."

"In part," said Pascoe, conscious that this was indeed only a very small part of the truth. Shorter's story had interested him, Dalziel's lack of interest the previous day had piqued him, Ellie was representing her union at a meeting that night, television was lousy on Thursdays, and Sergeant Wield had been very happy to supply him with a membership card.

"Then let us drink in my quarters."

They went out of the viewing room, which Pascoe guessed had once been two rooms joined together to make a small school assembly hall, and climbed the stairs. Sounds of conversation and glasses as from a saloon bar followed them upstairs from one of the ground-floor rooms. The Wilkinson Square vigilantes had made great play of drunkards falling noisily out of the club late at night and then falling noisily into their cars, which were parked in a most inconsiderate manner all around the square. Wield had found no evidence to support these assertions.

Haggard did not pause on the first-floor landing but proceeded up the now somewhat narrower staircase. Observing Pascoe hesitate, he explained, "Mainly classrooms here. Used for storage now. I suppose I could domesticate them again, but I've got comfortably settled aloft that it doesn't seem worth it. Do come in. Have a seat while I pour you something. Scotch all right?"

"Great," said Pascoe. He didn't sit down immediately but strolled around the room, hoping he didn't look too like a policeman but not caring all that much if he did. Haggard was right. He was very comfortable. Was the room rather too self-consciously a gentleman's study? The rows of leather-bound volumes, the huge Victorian desk, the miniatures on the wall, the elegant chesterfield, the display cabinet full of snuffboxes, these things must have impressed socially aspiring parents.

I wonder, mused Pascoe, pausing before the cabinet, how they impress the paying customer now.

"Are you a collector?" asked Haggard, handing him a glass.

"Just an admirer of other people's collections," said Pascoe.

"An essential part of the cycle," said Haggard. "This might interest you."

He reached in and picked up a hexagonal enameled box with the design of a hanging man on the lid.

"One of your illustrious predecessors, Jonathan Wild, thief taker, himself taken and hanged in 1725. Such commemorative design is quite commonplace on snuffboxes."

"Like ashtrays from Blackpool," said Pascoe.

"Droll," said Haggard, replacing the box and taking out another, an ornate silver affair heavily embossed with a coat of arms. "Mid-European," he said. "And beautifully airtight. This is the one I actually keep snuff in. Do you take it?"

"Not if I can help it."

"Perhaps you're wise. In the Middle Ages they thought that sneezing could put your soul within reach of the devil. I should hate you to lose your soul for a pinch of snuff, Inspector."

"You seem willing to take the risk."

"I take it to clear my head." Haggard smiled. "Perhaps I should take some now before you start asking your questions. I presume you have some query concerning the club?"

"In a way. It's a bit different from teaching, isn't it?" said Pascoe, sitting down.

"Is it? Oh, I don't know. It's all educational, don't you think?"

"Not a word some people would find it easy to apply to what goes on here, Dr. Haggard," said Pascoe.

"Not a word many people find it easy to apply to much of what goes on in schools today, Inspector."

"Still, for all that . . ." tempted Pascoe.

Haggard regarded him very magisterially. "My dear fellow," he said, "when we're much better acquainted, and you have proved to have a more than professionally sympathetic ear, and I have been mellowed by food, wine and a good cigar, *then* perhaps I may invite you to contemplate the strange fluttering of my psyche from one human vanity to another. Should the time arrive, I shall let you know. Meanwhile, let's stick with your presence here tonight. Have my neighbors undergone a new bout of hysteria?"

"Not that I know of," said Pascoe. "No, it's about one of your films. One I saw tonight. *Droit de Seigneur*."

"Ah, yes. The costume drama."

"Costume!" said Pascoe.

"Did the nudity bother you?" said Haggard anxiously.

"I don't think so. Anyway it was the assault scene I wanted to talk about, where the girl gets beaten up."

"You found it too violent? I'm astounded."

"The scene was brought to my attention—"

"By whom?" interrupted Haggard. "Has he not seen *A Clockwork Orange*? *The Exorcist*? *Match of the Day*?"

"I would like you to be serious, Dr. Haggard," said Pascoe reprovingly. "What do you know about the making of these films?"

"In general terms, very little. You probably know more yourself. I'm sure the diligent Sergeant Wield does. I am merely a showman."

"Of course. Look, Dr. Haggard, I wonder if it would be possible to see part of that film again. It'll help me explain what I'm doing here."

Haggard finished his drink, then nodded. "Why not? I'm intrigued. You could always gatecrash again, of course, but I suppose that might compromise your reputation. Besides, we only have that film until the weekend, so let's see what we can do."

Downstairs again, Haggard left Pascoe in the viewing room and disappeared for a few moments returning with a small triangular-faced man with large hairy-knuckled hands, one of which was wrapped around a pint tankard.

"Maurice, this is Inspector Pascoe. Maurice Arany, my partner and also, thank God, my projectionist. I am mechanically illiterate."

They shook hands. It would have been easy, thought Pascoe, to develop it into a test of strength, but such games were not yet necessary.

As well as he could he described the sequence he wished to see, and Arany went out. Haggard switched off the lights and they sat together in the darkness till the screen lit up. Arany hit the spot with great precision and Pascoe let it run until the entry of the vengeful husband.

"That's fine," he said and Haggard interposed his arm into the beam of light and the picture flickered and died.

"Well, Inspector?" said Haggard after he had switched on the lights.

"My informant reckons that was for real," said Pascoe diffidently.

"All of it?" said Haggard.

"The punch that knocks the girl down."

"How extraordinary. Shall we look again? Maurice!"

They sat through the sequence once more.

"It's quite effective, though I've seen better," said Haggard. "But on what grounds would you claim it was real, if by real you mean that some unfortunate girl really did get punched?"

"I don't know," admitted Pascoe. "It has a quality . . . I've seen a few fights, and that kind of . . ."

He tailed off, uncertain if he was speaking from even the narrowest basis of conviction. If he had seen the film without Shorter's comments in his mind, would he have paid any special attention to the sequence? Presumably hundreds of people (thousands?) had sat through it without unsuspending their disbelief.

"I've seen people burnt alive, decapitated, disemboweled and operated on for appendicitis, all I hasten to add in the commercial cinema," said Haggard. "So far as my own limited experience of such matters permitted me to judge, I was completely convinced of the verisimilitude of these scenes. I shouldn't have thought dislodging a few teeth was going to present the modern director with many problems."

"No," said Pascoe. He was beginning to feel a little foolish, but under Dalziel's tutelage he had come to ignore such social warning cones.

"Can I see the titles, please?" asked Pascoe.

Haggard addressed Maurice Arany again and as the titles rolled, Pascoe made notes. There wasn't a great deal of information. It was produced by a company called Homeric Films and written and directed by one Gerry Toms.

"A name to conjure with," said Pascoe.

"It must be his own," agreed Haggard.

"You don't know where this company is located, do you?"

"It's a mushroom industry," said Haggard. "It probably no longer exists."

"But there have been other films from the same people?"

Haggard admitted there had.

"Perhaps your distributor could help."

"I wouldn't bank on it, but you're welcome to the address."

Upon this cooperative note, they parted. Pascoe sat in his car in the square for some time until other members of the audience began to leave. There were no overt signs of drunkenness, no undue noise in the way they entered and started their cars, and certainly no suggestion that anyone was about to roam around the square all night in search of some luckless resident to assault and ravish.

When he got home, Ellie was sitting in front of the television eating a dripping sandwich.

"Good meeting?" he asked.

"Useless," she said. "Why don't you declare a police state and shoot the bastards? You know what they said? Higher education might be a luxury this authority could no longer afford!"

"Quite right," he said, regarding her affectionately. She was worth his regard. Friends at university, they had met again during an investigation at Hohn Coultram College, where Ellie was a lecturer. After some preliminary skirmishing they had become lovers and then, the previous year, got married. It was not an easy marriage, but nothing worthwhile ever was, thought Pascoe with a swift descent into *Reader's Digest* philosophy.

"You know who they've brought in to chair our liaison committee? Godfrey bloody Blengdale, that's who."

"Is that bad?" asked Pascoe, yawning. He sat down on the sofa next to Ellie, took a bite of her sandwich and focused on the television screen.

"It's sinister," said Ellie, frowning. "He's the right-wing hatchet man on that council. I've never really believed there was a chance they could seriously consider closing the college down, but now . . . Shall I switch this off?"

"No," said Pascoe, watching with interest as James Cagney prepared to sort out a guy twice his size. "I may learn something."

"About dealing with suspects?"

"About dealing with women. Is this the one where he pushes the grapefruit in whatsername's face?"

"I don't know. I haven't really been watching. It's just been something to take my mind off those pompous bastards. Where've you been anyway? Boozing with Yorkshire's Maigret?"

"No. I've been to the pictures, which is what makes this so nice."

Briefly he explained. Ellie listened intently. He didn't often discuss the details of his work with her, but this wasn't a case, just a speculation; and Pascoe, who would have welcomed her clarity of thought on many occasions, was glad to invite it now.

To his surprise, like Dalziel she dismissed as irrelevant the question of the broken teeth.

"It's not very likely, is it?" she said. "It's this chap Haggard you want to be interested in. I've heard of him. Before his school folded, he was a thorn in everyone's side. No official standing, of course, and he had ideas that made the Black Papers shine at night. But he knew how to get to people, push them around."

"He obviously hasn't lost his charming ways," said Pascoe. "The neighbors are almost solidly against him, but it's getting them nowhere."

"So you *have* a complaint to investigate? Great! Can't you fit him up? Slip a brick in his pocket or something?"

Pascoe sighed. Ellie made police jokes like some people make Irish jokes, and at times they began to wear a bit thin.

"It's nothing to do with me. Sergeant Wield's looking after things there. I'm only here for the teeth."

"So you say. Sounds odd to me. And this dentist of yours, he sounds a bit odd too."

"Christ," said Pascoe. "You sound more like Dalziel every day."

He bit into Ellie's dripping sandwich again and watched James Cagney bust someone right on the jaw. The recipient of the blow staggered back, shook his head admiringly, then launched a counterattack.

This, thought Pascoe, is what fighting ought to look like. When the Gerry Toms of this world could produce stuff like this, then they might climb out of the skin-flick morass. This appealed to man's artistic sense, not his basic lusts.

Guns had appeared now. Cagney dived for cover and came up with a huge automatic in his hand.

"Great," said Pascoe, his artistic sense thoroughly appealed to. "Now kill the bastard!"

Three

Sergeant Wield's ugliness was only skin deep, but that was deep enough. Each individual feature was only slightly battered, or bent, or scarred, and might have made a significant contribution to the appeal of any *joli-laid* hero from Mr. Rochester on, but combined in one face they produced an effect so startling that Pascoe, who met him almost daily, was still amazed when he entered his room.

"Thanks for the membership card," said Pascoe, tossing it on the desk. "Maurice Arany, what do you know about him?"

"Hungarian," said Wield. "His parents brought him out with them in 'fifty-six. He was thirteen then. They settled in Leeds and Maurice started work in a garage a couple of years later. He has no formal qualifications but a lot of mechanical skill. He got interested in the clubs and for a while he tried pushing an act around, part time. Bit of singing, juggling, telling jokes. Trouble was he couldn't sing and his jokes never quite made it. Arany spoke near perfect English, but he couldn't quite grasp the subtleties of our four-letter words. So he packed it in and got involved in other ways, lighting and sound to start with, but eventually a bit of dealing, a bit of management."

"Who'd he manage?"

"Exotic dancers mainly. No, it wasn't like that. Most of these girls have mum to mind them, so there's no room for a ponce. Arany just smoothered the way, made contacts, arranged bookings. Now he's got his own agency. Small, just an office and a secretary, but he does a lot of business."

"And how'd he get involved with Haggard?"

Wield shrugged. "God knows. He just appeared, as far as I can make out. There's no trace of a previous connection, but then we never had any cause to keep a close watch on either of these two."

"Kept his nose clean, has he?"

"Oh yes. Everyone keeps a bit of an eye on the club circuit, that's how we know as much as we do about him, but he's never been on the books."

"Clever or clean," said Pascoe. "How's it going anyway, Sergeant?"

"Slowly and nowhere. No one's breaking the law and there isn't any public nuisance to speak of. I don't know why we bother? But Mr. Dalziel says to keep at it, so keep at it I will! You didn't get anything, did you, sir?"

He spoke with a kind of reproachful neutrality. Pascoe had offered only the most perfunctory of explanations for his visit to the Calliope Club. He had passed on Shorter's

comments on *Droit de Seigneur*, of course, but the
sergeant obviously suspected that there was some other
motive for his interest. Was there? wondered Pascoe. All
he could think of was obstinacy, because everyone else
seemed to be so dismissive of the dentist's claim, but he
was not by nature an obstinate man. On the other hand
here he was with enough work to keep two MP's, or six
shop stewards, or a dozen teachers, or twenty pop groups,
or a hundred members of the Jockey Club, or a thousand
princesses, going for a year and he was reaching for the
phone and ringing Ace-High Distributors, Inc., of Stret-
ford, Manchester.

A girl answered. Quickly assessing that the word "police" was more likely to inhibit than expedite information,
he put on his best posh voice, said he was trying to contact
dear old Gerry Toms, last heard of directing some masterpiece for Homeric Films, and could she help? She could.
He noted the address with surprise, said thank you kindly
and replaced the receiver.

"Mike Yarwood, beware," said Dalziel from the doorway. "There's laws against personation, you know that?
Sergeant Wield tells me you went to the pictures last
night. Asked a few questions I dare say?"

Pascoe nodded, feeling like a small boy caught
trespassing.

"Jesus wept." Dalziel sighed. "What do I have to say to
get through to you, Peter? You must be bloody slack at the
moment, that's all I can say. Well, we'll soon put that right.
My office, five minutes."

He left and Pascoe resumed his feeling of surprise that

such a respectable place as Harrogate should house such a *prima facie* disreputable company as Homeric Films.

At least it was relatively handy.

He dialed again. Another girl. This time he put on his official voice and asked to speak to the man in charge.

After a pause, another female voice said, "Hello. Can I help?"

"I asked for the man in charge," said Pascoe coolly.

"Did you indeed?" said the woman in sympathetic motherly tones. "Were you perhaps shell-shocked in the First World War? They let us women out of the kitchen now, you know, and we've even got laws to prove it."

"I'm sorry," said Pascoe. "You mean you're in charge?"

"You'd better believe it. Penelope Latimer. Who're you?"

"I'm sorry, Miss Latimer. My name's Pascoe; I'm a detective-inspector with Mid-Yorkshire CID."

"Congratulations. Forget my shell-shock crack. You've just explained yourself. What can I do for you, Detective-Inspector?"

She sounded amused rather than concerned, thought Pascoe. But then why should she be concerned? Perhaps I just want people to be concerned when I give them a quick flash of my constabulary credentials.

"Your company produced a film called *Droit de Seigneur*, I believe."

"Yes." More cautious now?

"I'm interested in talking with the director, Mr. Toms, and I wondered if you could help?"

"Gerry? How urgent do you want him?"

"It's not desperate," said Pascoe. "Why?"

"He's in Spain just now, that's why. If you want him urgent, I can give you his hotel. We're expecting him back tonight, though."

"Oh, that'll do," said Pascoe. "You say you're expecting him back. That means he's still working for Homeric?"

"He better had be," said Penelope Latimer. "He owns a third of the company."

"Really? And he wrote and directed the film?"

"You've seen it? Yes, he wrote it. Not very taxing on the intellect though, you agree? What's with this film anyway? Some local lilywhite giving trouble?"

Pascoe hesitated only a moment. She sounded cooperative and bright. At the worst he might pick something up from her reaction. He told her Shorter's theory.

Her reaction was an outpour of pleasantly gurgly laughter.

"I'm sorry," he said. "I didn't catch that."

"Funny," she said. "You think we pay actresses to get beaten up? Who can afford that kind of money?"

"If you beat them up enough, I suppose they come cheap," said Pascoe with great acidity, tired of being made to feel foolish.

"Oh-ho! Snuff films we're making now? When can we expect you and the dogs?"

"I'm not with you," said Pascoe. "What was that you said! Snuff films?"

"I thought the police knew everything. It's when someone really does get killed in front of the camera. They snuff it—get it?"

"And these exist?"

"So they say. I mean, who wants to find out. Look, you're worried about the leading lady being duffed up, right? So if you could have a little chat with her, you'd be happy? All right. I'll dig out her address on one condition. You see her, ask about the film, nothing more. No follow-up just to make your bother worthwhile."

"You've lost me again," said Pascoe.

"Do I have to spell it out? This is lower-division stuff. I mean it won't be Julie Andrews you're going to talk to. This girl might—I don't say she *is*, but she *might* be on the game. Or she might have a bit of weed about the place. Or anything. Now I don't want to stick the police on her. So I want your word. No harassment."

"How do you know you can trust me?" asked Pascoe.

"For a start you wouldn't be pussyfooting around about promising if it didn't mean anything," she answered.

"A psychologist already," mocked Pascoe. "All right. I promise. But all bets off if she's just stuck a knife into her boyfriend or robbed a bank. OK?"

"Now we're talking about *crimes*," said Penelope Latimer. "Hold on."

While he waited, Pascoe picked up his internal phone and got through to Wield. "You ever heard of something called a snuff film?" he asked.

"Yes," said Wield.

"Don't keep it to yourself, Sergeant," said Pascoe in his best Dalziel manner.

"In the States mainly," said Wield. "Though there are rumors on the Continent. No one's ever picked one up as far as I know, so obviously there's no prosecution recorded yet."

"Yes, but what are they?"

"What they're *said* to be is films made of someone dying. Usually some tart from, say, one of the big South American seaports who no one's going to miss in a hurry. She thinks it's a straightforward skin flick. By the time she finds out wrong, it's too late. The scareder she gets, the more she tries to run, the better the picture."

"*Better!* Who for?"

"For the bent bastards who want to see 'em. And for the guys who make the charge."

"Jesus!"

"Hello? You there?" said the woman's voice from the other phone.

"Thanks, Sergeant," said Pascoe. "Yes, Miss Latimer?"

"It's Linda Abbott. Address is twenty-five Hampole Lane, Borage Hill. That's a big new estate about twelve miles south of here, just north of Leeds."

"Local, eh?"

"What do you think, we fetch them from Hollywood."

"No, but I reckoned you might cast your net as far as South Shields, say, or Scunthorpe."

Penelope Latimer chuckled. "Come up and see us sometime, Inspector," she said throatily. " 'Bye."

"I might, I might," said Pascoe to the dead phone. But he doubted if he would. Harrogate, Leeds, they were off his patch and Dalziel didn't sound as if he was about to let him go drifting west on a wild-goose chase. No, he'd have to get someone local to check that this woman Linda Abbott had all her teeth. On the other hand, he'd promised Penelope Latimer that he'd handle it with tact. What he needed was an excuse to find himself in the area.

The phone rang.

"Have you got paralysis?" bellowed Dalziel.

Thirty seconds later he was in the fat man's office.

"There's a meeting this afternoon. Inter-divisional liaison. Waste of fucking time, so I've told 'em I can't go, but I'll send a boy to observe."

"And you want me to suggest a boy?" said Pascoe brightly.

"Funny. It's four-thirty. Watch the bastards. Some of them are right sneaky."

"One thing," said Pascoe. "Where is it?"

"Do I have to tell you everything?" groaned Dalziel. "Harrogate."

Four

Pascoe had no direct experience of the polygamous East, but he supposed that, with arranged marriages thrown in, it was possible for a man to know a woman only in wedding dress and total nudity. But would he recognize her if he met her in the street? Pascoe doubted it. He regarded the gaggle of women hanging around outside the school gates and mentally coated each in turn with blood. It didn't help.

He'd come to see Linda Abbott hoping that the law-breaking forecast by Penny Latimer would not be too blatant. Now he wished that he'd found the woman leaning against a lamppost smoking a reefer and making obscene suggestions to passersby. Instead he'd found himself at the front door of a neat little semi, talking to an angry Mr. Abbott, who had been roused from the sleep of the just and the night-shift worker by Pascoe's policeman's thumb on the bell push.

Having mentally prepared himself to turn a blind eye to Mrs. Abbott's misdemeanors, Pascoe now became the guardian of her reputation and pretended to be in washing machines. Mrs. Abbott, he learned, had a washing machine, didn't want another, wasn't about to get another, and cared perhaps even less than Mr. Abbott to deal with poofy commercials at the door. But he also learned that Mrs. Abbott had gone down to the school to collect her youngest, and, having noticed what he took to be the school two streets away, Pascoe had made his way there to intercept.

He spotted Linda Abbott as the mums began to break off, clutching their spoil. A bold face, heavily made up; a wide loud mouth remonstrating with her small boy for some damage he'd done to his person or clothes. The camera didn't lie after all.

"Mrs. Abbott?" said Pascoe. "Could I have a word with you?"

"As many as you like, love," said the woman, looking him up and down. "Only, my name's Mackenzie. Yon's Mrs. Abbott, her with the little blond lass."

Mrs. Abbott was dumpy, untidy and plain. Her daughter on the other hand was a beauty. Another ten years, if she maintained her present progress, and . . . I'll probably be too old to care, thought Pascoe.

"Mrs. Abbott," he tried again. "Could I have a word?"

"Yes?"

"Mam, is this one of them funny buggers?" asked the angelic six-year-old.

"Shut up, our Lorraine," said Mrs. Abbott.

"Funny . . . ?" said Pascoe.

"I tell her not to talk with strangers," explained Mrs. Abbott.

" 'Cos there's a lot of funny buggers about," completed Lorraine happily.

"Well, I'm not one of them," said Pascoe. "I hope."

He showed his warrant card, taking care to keep it masked from the few remaining mums.

"You might well hope," said Mrs. Abbott. "What's up?"

"May I walk along with you?" he asked.

"It's a free street. Lorraine, don't you run on the road now!"

"It's about a film you made," said Pascoe. *"Droit de Seigneur."*

"Oh aye. Which was that one?"

"Can't you remember?"

"They don't often have titles when we're making them, not real titles, any road."

Briefly Pascoe outlined the plot.

"Oh, that one," said Mrs. Abbott. "What's up?"

"It's been suggested," said Pascoe, "that undue violence may have been used in some scenes."

"What?"

"Especially in the scene where the squire beats you up, just before the US cavalry arrive."

"You sure you're not mixing it up with the *Big Big Horn*?" said Mrs. Abbott.

"I don't think so," said Pascoe. "I was speaking figuratively. Before your boyfriend rescues you. You remember that sequence? Were you in fact struck?"

"I don't think so," said Mrs. Abbott. "It's six months ago, of course. How do you mean, *struck*?"

"Hit on the face. So hard that you'd bleed. Lose a few teeth even," said Pascoe, feeling as daft as she obviously thought he was.

"You *are* one of them funny buggers," she said, laughing. "Do I look as if I'd let meself get beaten up for a picture? Here, can you see any scars? And take a look at them. Them's all me own. I've taken good care on 'em."

Pascoe looked at her unmade-up and unblemished face, then examined her teeth, which, a couple of fillings apart, were in a very healthy state.

"Yes, I see," he said. "Well, I'm sorry to have bothered you, Mrs. Abbott. You saw nothing at all during the making of the film that surprised you?"

"You stop being surprised after a bit," she said. "But there was nowt unusual, if that's what you mean. It's all done with props and paint, love, didn't you know?"

"Even the sex?" answered Pascoe sharply, stung by her irony.

"Is that what it's all about then?" she said. "I might have known."

"No, really, it isn't," assured Pascoe, adding, in an attempt to reingratiate himself, "I've been at your house by the way. I said I was a washing-machine salesman."

"Why?"

"I didn't want to stir anything up," he said, feeling noble.

"For crying out loud!" said Mrs. Abbott. "You don't reckon I could do me job without Bert knowing?"

"No, I suppose not," said Pascoe, discomfited.

"Bloody right not," said Mrs. Abbott. "And I'll tell you something else for nothing. It's a job. I get paid for it. And whatever I do, I do with lights on me, and a camera, and a lot of technicians about who don't give a bugger, and you can see everything I do up there on the screen. I'm not like half these so-called real actresses who play the Virgin Mary all day, then screw themselves into another big part all night. Lorraine! I told you to keep off of that road!"

"Well, thank you, Mrs. Abbott," said Pascoe, glancing at his watch. "You've been most helpful. I'm sorry to have troubled you."

"No trouble, love," said Mrs. Abbott.

He dug into his pocket and produced a ten-pence piece which he gave to Lorraine "for sweeties." She waited for her mother's nod before accepting, and Pascoe drove off feeling relieved that after all he had not been categorized as a "funny bugger," and feeling also that at the moment Jack Shorter would top his own personal list.

He needn't have worried about his meeting. It started late because of the non-arrival of one of the senior members and was almost immediately suspended because of the enforced departure of another. Reluctantly Pascoe found a phone and rang Ellie to say that his estimate of a seven-o'clock homecoming had been optimistic.

"Surprise," she said. "Will you eat there?"

"I suppose so," he said.

"I was hoping you'd take me out. You get better service with a policeman."

"Sorry," said Pascoe. "Better try an old boyfriend. See you!"

He replaced the receiver and went back to the conference room, where Inspector Ray Crabtree of the local force told him they were scheduled to restart at seven.

"Fancy a jar?" asked Crabtree. He was a man of forty-plus who had gone as far as he was likely to go in the Force and had a nice line of comic bitterness which usually entertained Pascoe.

"And a sandwich," said Pascoe.

"Where do you fancy? Somewhere squalid or somewhere nice?"

"Is the beer better somewhere squalid?"

"No."

"Or the food cheaper?"

"Not so's you'd notice."

"Then somewhere nice."

"That's a sharp mind you've got there, Pascoe," said Crabtree admiringly. "You'll get on."

"Somewhere nice" was the lounge bar of a large, plush and drafty hotel.

Crabtree ordered four halves of bitter. "And two rounds of ham, Cyril," he added. "Tell 'em it's me and I like it cut with a blunt knife."

"They only serve halves in here," he said as they sat down. "Bloody daft. You've got to get them in twos. Wouldn't do for Sitting Bull."

"Who?"

"Dalziel. Your big chief. You know, I could have had his job."

"I didn't know that," said Pascoe.

"Oh yes. We were up before the same promotion board once. I thought I'd clinched it. They asked, 'Are you as thick as Prince Philip?' 'Oh yes,' says I. 'Twice as thick.' "

"And what did Dalziel say?"

"He said, 'Who's she?' "

The sandwiches arrived, filled with thick slices of succulent ham, and Pascoe understood the advantages of a blunt knife.

"Do you know a company called Homeric Films?" he asked for the sake of something to say.

Crabtree paused in his chewing. "Yes," he said after a moment and took another bite.

"End of conversation, is it?" said Pascoe.

"You could ask if I'd seen any good films lately," said Crabtree.

"All right. Have you?"

"Yes, but none of 'em were made by Homeric. They're a skin-flick bunch, but if you know enough to ask about them, you probably know as much as me."

"Why the pause for thought, then?"

"I said you'd a sharp mind. Mebbe I was just chewing on a bit of gristle."

"It seems to me," said Pascoe, "that they have more sense here than to serve you gristle."

"True. No, truth is you just jumped in front of my train of thought. What's your interest?"

"No interest. They just cropped up apropos of something. What was your train of thought?"

Crabtree finished his first half and started on his second. "See in the corner to the left of the door?" he said into his glass.

"Yes," said Pascoe, glancing across the room. Three people sat around a table in animated conversation. Two were men. They looked like brothers in their fifties, balding, fleshy. The third was a woman, gross beyond the wildest dreams of gluttony. Surely, thought Pascoe, no deficiency of diet could have produced those avalanches of flesh. She wore a kaftan made from enough shot silk to have pavilioned a whole family of Tartars in splendor, and girded quite a few of them into the bargain. Dalziel would love her. It is not enough (Pascoe paraphrased) to lose weight; a man must also have a friend who is grotesquely fat.

"Homeric films," said Crabtree. "They put me in mind."

"How?" asked Pascoe, but before Crabtree could answer, the huge woman rose and rolled across the room toward them.

"Raymond, my sweet," she said genially. "How pleasant and how opportune. I hope I'm not interrupting anything?"

Pascoe stared in amazement. It was not just that on closer view he realized how much he'd underestimated the woman's proportions. It was the voice. Seductive, amused, hinting at understanding, promising pleasure. He recognized it. He'd heard it on the phone that morning.

"Inspector Pascoe," said Crabtree rising, "I'd like you to meet Miss Latimer. Miss Latimer is managing director of Homeric Films."

"Why so formal, Ray? I'm Penelope to all Europe and just plain Penny to my friends. But soft awhile. Pascoe?"

"We spoke this morning."

"So! When a girl says come up and see me, you let no grass grow!"

"It's an accident," said Pascoe unchivalrously. "But I'm glad to meet you."

"Join us, Penny?" said Crabtree.

"Just for a moment."

She redistributed herself around a chair and smiled sweetly at Pascoe. She had a very sweet smile. Indeed, trapped in that flesh like a snowdrop in aspic, a small, pretty, girlish face seemed to be staring out.

"Will you have a jar?" asked Crabtree.

"Gin with," said the woman.

"It's my shout," said Pascoe.

"It's my patch," said Crabtree, rising.

"How's the case, Inspector?" asked Penny Latimer.

"No case," said Pascoe. "People tell us things, we've got to look into them."

"And you've looked into Linda Abbott?"

"Do you know her? Personally, I mean," countered Pascoe.

"Only as an actress. Socially I know nothing, which was why we struck our little bargain, just in case. How were her teeth?"

"Complete."

"Don't sound so disappointed, dear. What now? Would you still like to see Gerry?"

"I don't know. Not unless I really have to. But you never know."

"You could spend an interesting day on the set," she said. "Really, I mean it. Do you good."

"How?"

"For a start, it'd bore you to tears. You might find it distasteful but you wouldn't find it illegal. And at the end of the day you might even agree that though it's not your way of earning a living, there's no reason why it shouldn't be somebody else's."

Pascoe downed his second half in one and said, "You're very defensive."

"And I know it. You're bloody aggressive, and I don't think you do."

"I don't mean to be," said Pascoe.

"No. It's your job. Like one of your cars stopping some kid on a flash motorbike. His license is in order, but he's young, and he's wearing fancy gear, and he doesn't look humble, so he gets the full treatment. Finally, reluctantly, he gets sent on his way with a warning against breathing, and the Panda car tracks him for the next ten miles."

"I grasp your analogy," said Pascoe.

"Chance'd be a fine thing," she answered. Their gazes locked and after a moment they started to laugh.

"Watch her," said Crabtree, plonking down a tray with a large gin, with whatever it was with, and another four halves. "She'll have you starring in a remake of the Keystone Cops—naked."

"I doubt it," said the woman. "The Inspector don't approve of us beautiful people. Not like you, Ray. Ray recognizes that police and film people have a lot in common. They exist because of human nature, not in spite of it. But Ray has slain the beast, ambition, and now takes comfort in the arms of the beauty, philosophy. You should try it, Inspector."

"I'll bear it in mind" was the smartest reply Pascoe could manage.

"You do. And don't forget my invitation. Homeric's the company, Penelope's the name. I'll be weaving and watching for you, sailor. 'Bye, Ray. Thanks for the drink." She rose and returned to her companions.

"Interesting woman," said Crabtree, regarding Pascoe with amusement.

"Yes. Is she like that through choice or chance?"

"Glandular, they tell me. Used to be a beauty. Now she has to live off eggs and spinach and no good it does her."

"Tough," said Pascoe. "Tell me, Ray, what's a joint like Homeric doing in a nice town like this?"

Crabtree shrugged. "They have an office. They pay their rates. They give no offense. The only way that most people are going to know what their precise business is would be to see their films, or take part in one of them. Either way, you're not going to complain. Things have changed since I was a callow constable, but one thing I've learned in my low-trajectory meteoric career. If it's all right with top brass, it's all right with me."

"But why come here at all? What's wrong with the Big Smoke?"

"Dear, dear," said Crabtree. "I bet you still think Soho's full of opium dens and sinister Orientals. Up here its cheaper, healthier and the beer's better. Do you never read the ads?"

"Everyone's talking smart today and putting me down," said Pascoe. "Time for another?"

"Hang on," said Crabtree. "I'll phone in."

He returned with another four halves. "Plenty of time," he said. "It's been put back again."

"When to?"

"Next week."

"Oh shit," said Pascoe.

He regarded the half pints dubiously, then went and rang Ellie again. There was no reply. Perhaps after all she had rung an old boyfriend.

"Left you, has she?" said Crabtree. "Wise girl. Now, what do you fancy—drown your sorrows or a bit of spare?"

He arrived home at midnight to find a strange car in his drive and a strange man drinking his whiskey. Closer examination revealed it was not a strange man but one of Ellie's colleagues, Arthur Halfdane, a historian and once a sort of rival for Ellie's favors.

"I didn't recognize you," said Pascoe. "You look younger."

"Well thanks," said Halfdane in a mid-Atlantic drawl.

"On second thoughts," said Pascoe belligerently, "*you* don't look younger. It's your clothes that look younger."

Halfdane glanced down at his denim suit, looked ironically at Pascoe's crumpled worsted and smiled at Ellie. "Time to go, I think," he said, rising.

Perhaps I should punch him on the nose, thought Pascoe. Man alone with my wife at midnight . . . I'm entitled.

When Ellie returned from the front door Pascoe essayed a smile.

"You're drunk," she said.

"I've had a couple."

"I thought you were at a meeting."

"It was canceled," he said. "I rang you. You were out. So I made a night of it."

"Me too," she said.

"Difference was, my companion was a man," said Pascoe heavily.

"No difference," said Ellie. "So was mine."

"Oh," said Pascoe, a little nonplussed. "Have a good evening, did you?"

"Yes. Very sexy."

"What?"

"Sexy. We went to see your dirty film. Our interest was socio-historical, of course."

"He took you to the Calli?" said Pascoe indignantly. "Well, bugger me!"

"It was all right," said Ellie sweetly. "Full of respectable people. You know who I saw there? Mr. Godfrey Blengdale, no less. So it must be all right."

"He shouldn't have taken you," said Pascoe, feeling absurd and incoherent and nevertheless right.

"Get it straight, Peter," said Ellie coldly. "Dalziel may have got you trained like a retriever, but I still make my own decisions."

"Oh yes." Pascoe sneered. "It's working in that elephants' graveyard that does it. All that rational discourse where the failed intellectuals go to die. The sooner they close that stately pleasure dome down and dump you back in reality, the better!"

"You've got the infection," she said sadly. "Work in a leper colony and in the end you start falling to bits."

"Schweitzer worked with lepers," countered Pascoe.

"Yes. And he was a fascist too."

He looked at her hopelessly. There were other planets somewhere with life forms he had more chance of understanding and making understand.

"It's your failures I put in jail," he said.

"So, blame education, is that it? All right, but how can it work with kids when intelligent adults can still be so thick!" she demanded.

"I didn't mean that," he said. He suddenly saw in his mind's eye the girl in the film. The face fell apart under the massive blow. It might all be special effects but the reality beneath the image was valid nonetheless. If only it could be explained . . .

"There is still, well, evil," he essayed.

"Oh God. Religion, is it, now? The last refuge of egocentricity. I'm off to bed. I'm driving down to Lincolnshire tomorrow, so I should prefer to pass the night undisturbed." She stalked from the room.

"So should I," shouted Pascoe after her.

Their wishes went unanswered.

At five o'clock in the morning he was roused from the unmade-up spare bed by Ellie pulling his hair and demanding that he answer the bloody telephone.

It was the station. There had been a break-in at Wilkinson House, premises of the Calliope Kinema Club. The proprietor had been attacked and injured. Mr. Dalziel wondered if Mr. Pascoe, in view of his special interest in the place, would care to watch over the investigation.

"Tell him," said Pascoe. "Tell him to . . ."

"Yes?" prompted the voice.

"Tell him I'm on my way."

Five

The Calli was a wreck.

As far as Pascoe could make out, person or persons unknown had entered by forcing the basement area door which fronted on Upper Maltgate. They had then proceeded to wreck the house and beat up Gilbert Haggard, not necessarily in that order. That would be established when Haggard was fit enough to talk. A not very efficient attempt to start a fire had produced a lot of smoke, but fortunately very little flame, and a Panda patrol checking shop doorways on Maltgate had spotted the fumes escaping from a first-floor window.

When they entered the house, they had found Haggard on the second-floor landing, badly beaten around the face and abdomen. A combination of the blows and fumes had rendered him unconscious.

Pascoe wandered disconsolately around the house accompanied by a taciturn Sergeant Wield and an apologetic fire officer.

"Was there any need to pump so much water into the place?" asked Pascoe. "My men say there was next to no fire."

"Can't be too careful, not where there's inflammable material like film about," said the FO, smiling wanly at the staircase, which was still running like the Brook Kerith. "Sorry if we've dampened any clues."

"Clues!" said Pascoe. "I'll need frogmen to bring up clues from this lot. Where did the fire start?"

"In a storeroom on the first floor. There's a couple of filing cabinets in there, and that's where they kept their cans of film as well. Someone scattered everything all over the place, then had the bright idea of dropping a match into it on their way out."

"Can we get in there without a bathysphere?" asked Pascoe.

The FO didn't answer but led the way upstairs.

There was a sound of movement inside the storage room and Pascoe expected to find either a policeman or a fireman bent on completing the destruction his colleagues had begun. Instead, in the cone of light from a bare bulb which had miraculously survived the visiting firemen, he found Maurice Arany.

"Mr. Arany," he said, "what are you doing here?"

"I own half of this," said Arany sharply, indicating the sodden debris through which he appeared to have been picking.

"I don't like the look of your half," said Pascoe. "You got here quickly."

Arany considered. "No," he said. "You got here slowly.
I live quite close by. I have a flat above Trimble's, the bak-
ers, on Lower Maltgate."

"Who called you?" asked Pascoe.

"No one. I am a poor sleeper. I was awake when I heard
the fire engine going up the street. I looked out, became
aware they were stopping by the Square, so I dressed and
came out to investigate. After the firemen had finished, I
came in. No one stopped me. Should they have done so?"

"Perhaps," said Pascoe. "I should have thought you
would be more concerned with Mr. Haggard's health than
checking on damage here."

"I saw him being put in the ambulance. He looked all
right," said Arany indifferently. "I tried to ring through a
moment ago. The phones seem not to be working."

"Check that," Pascoe said to Wield. "See what's wrong
with them. Probably an excess of moisture."

Turning back to Arany, he said, "It would be useful,
Mr. Arany, if you could check if there's anything missing
from the house."

"That's what I'm doing," said Arany, dropping the
goulash of charred paper and shriveled celluloid he held
in his hands. "Of course, I cannot answer for Gilbert's
apartments. But on this floor and in the club rooms I think
I can help."

"Well, start here," said Pascoe. "Anything missing?"

"Who can tell? So much is burned. We kept old files of
business correspondence here. Nothing of importance."

"And the films?"

"And the films. Yes, they are finished. Still, the insurance will cover that."

"Someone's going to be disappointed," said Pascoe, looking at the mess. "They won't show these again."

"There are plenty of prints," said Arany indifferently. "I'll go and check the other rooms."

He went out as the sergeant returned. Wield waited till he was gone before saying, "The phone wire was cut, sir."

"Inside or out?"

"Inside. By the phone in the study. Both the other phones in the house are extensions."

"Let's look upstairs," said Pascoe.

Haggard had been found lying outside his bedroom door, which was two doors down the landing from the study. In between was a living room which had been comfortably if shabbily furnished with two chintz-covered armchairs and a solid dining table. Now the chairs lay on their sides with the upholstery slashed. The table's surface was scarred and a corner cabinet had been dragged off the wall.

"What's through there?" asked Pascoe, pointing at a door in the far wall.

"Kitchen," said Wield, pushing it open.

It was a long narrow room, obviously created by walling off the bottom five feet of the living room at some time in the not-too-distant past. The furnishings were bright and modern. Pascoe walked around opening cupboards. One was locked, a full-size door which looked as if it might lead into a pantry.

"Notice anything odd?" he asked in his best Holmesian fashion.

"They didn't smash anything in here," said Wield promptly.

"All right, all right. There's no need to be so clever," said Pascoe. "Probably they just didn't have time."

The bedroom was in a mess too, but it was the study which really caught his attention, perhaps because he had seen it before the onslaught.

Everything that could be cut, slashed, broken or overturned had been. Only the heavier items of furniture remained unmoved, though drawers had been dragged from the desk and the display cabinet had been overturned. Pascoe's attention was caught particularly by the shredded curtains and he examined them thoughtfully for a long time.

"Anything, sir?" asked Wield.

"Something, perhaps, but I really don't know what. They must have made some noise. Who lives next door?"

"Just two old ladies and their cats. They sleep on the floor below, I think, and they're both as deaf as toads. They've lived there all their lives, the youngest is just under seventy, the other just over. I gather the vigilantes were dead keen to recruit them for their anti-Calli campaign, but it was no go."

"Didn't they mind the club, then?"

"They are, or were, very thick with Haggard. The elder, Miss Annabelle Andover, acted as a part-time matron while the school was on the go, and I get the impression that he's been at pains to keep up the connection. You know, chicken for the cats, that kind of thing. If it ever did come to a court case, it'd be useful for him to be able to prove his immediate neighbors didn't object to the club."

"Which they don't? It's a bit different from a school!"

"I can't really say, sir," said Wield. "Old ladies, old-fashioned ideas, you'd say. But you never know."

"Well, we'd better have a chat in case they did notice anything. But at a decent hour. Let's check on Haggard first. Then I reckon we've earned some breakfast."

At the hospital they learned that Haggard, though intermittently conscious, was not in a fit state to be questioned, so they had bacon sandwiches and coffee in the police canteen before returning to the club.

Arany was still there.

"Anything missing yet?" asked Pascoe.

"Not that I have found," said Arany. "Some drink from the bar, perhaps. It is hard to say, so much is broken."

"Well, keep at it. Perhaps you could call down at the station later, put it down on paper."

"What?" inquired Arany. "There is nothing to put."

"Oh, you never can tell," said Pascoe airily. "First impressions when you arrived, that kind of thing. And by the way, would you bring a complete up-to-date list of members with you? Come on, Sergeant. Let's see if the Misses Andover are up and about yet."

The Misses Andovers were, or at least their curtains were now drawn open. Pascoe pulled at the old bell toggle and the distant clang was followed by an equally distant opening and shutting of doors and the slow approach of hard shoes on bare boards. It was like a *Goon Show* sound track, he thought. Eventually the door opened and a venerably white-haired head slowly emerged. Timid, birdlike eyes scanned them.

"Miss Andover?" said Pascoe.

The head slowly retreated.

"Annabelle!" cried a surprisingly strong voice. "There are callers inquiring if you are at home."

"Tradesmen?" responded a distant voice.

"I thought you said they were deaf," murmured Pascoe.

"They are. They switch their aids off at night," answered Wield.

The head re-emerged, accompanied by a hand which fitted a pair of pince-nez to the little nose in order to scan the two policemen. When it came to Wield's turn, the head jerked in what might have been recognition or shock and withdrew once more.

"Mr. Wield is one of them, Annabelle."

"Then admit them, admit them, you fool."

The door swung full open and they stepped into the past. Nothing in here had changed for two generations, thought Pascoe looking around the dark paneled hall. Except the woman who stood before him smiling. She must have been young and pretty and full of hope when the men delivered that elephant's-foot umbrella stand. Now the folds of skin on her neck were almost as gray and wrinkled as those on the huge foot which had been raised for the last time on some Indian plain and set down (no doubt to the ghostly beast's great amazement) here in darkest Yorkshire.

"Miss Andover will be down presently," announced the woman, her eyes darting nervously from one to the other.

"Thank you, Miss Alice," said Wield.

"Miss Alice Andover?" said Pascoe.

Wield smiled.

"Then you too are Miss Andover," Pascoe stated brightly.

"Oh no," said the woman, shocked. "I am Miss Alice Andover. *This* is Miss Andover." She indicated the figure of (Pascoe presumed) her elder sister descending the gloomy staircase.

The sisters were dressed alike in long flowered skirts which might have been antiques or the latest thing off C & A's racks. From the starched fronts of their plain white blouses depended the receivers of two rather old-fashioned hearing aids. Annabelle, however, was several inches the taller and wore her even whiter hair in a simple pageboy cut, while her sister had hers pulled back into a severe bun. Her face had probably never been as pretty as her sister's, but she had an alert, intelligent expression missing from the younger woman's.

"My dear," said Miss Alice, "this is Mr. Wield, as you know, but I'm afraid the other gentleman has not been presented."

"My fault entirely," said Pascoe, entering into the spirit of the thing. "Perhaps I may be allowed to break with convention and present myself?"

"Whoever you are," said Miss Annabelle, "there's no need to treat us both like halfwits even if m' sister asks for it. Alice, stop being a stupid cow, will you, dear? She saw Greer Garson in *Pride and Prejudice* on the box the other week and she's not been the same since. Let's go in here."

She led the way into a bright Habitat-furnished sitting room with the largest color television set Pascoe had ever seen lowering from one corner.

"Well?" said Miss Andover impatiently, taking up a

stance in front of the fireplace and lighting a Park Drive. "As you're with the sergeant, I presume you're a cop, and from the way he's hanging back behind you, you must have some rank. Unless you're a princess and he's just married you."

The quip amused her so much that she laughed till she coughed.

Pascoe waited till she'd finished both activities and introduced himself in a brusque twentieth-century fashion.

"The house next door, Dr. Haggard's house, was broken into last night and a deal of damage done. I wondered if either of you heard anything?"

Miss Alice gasped in fright and seemed to shrink into herself, but her sister just whistled in surprise, then shook her head, pointing to her hearing aid.

"An advantage of this thing is that I need hear only what I want to. It's very useful at night and when I'm with extremely boring people."

"So you heard nothing?" persisted Pascoe.

"I've said so."

"Miss Alice?"

"Oh no. I switched off too," said Alice, evidently retrieved to the present moment by her sister's command.

"Which side of the house do you sleep?" asked Pascoe, causing a time slip in Miss Alice, who put her hand to her mouth in horror at his indelicacy.

"First floor on the Wilkinson House side," said Miss Annabelle. "Alice is at the back, I'm at the front."

"It's a very large house," said Pascoe. "May I have a look upstairs just to get an impression of where you'd be in relation to next door?"

"By all means," said Miss Annabelle. "Follow me."

They set off in procession up the gloomy stairs, the older woman leading the two men close behind and the younger sister trailing.

On the first floor they halted and Miss Annabelle flung open doors. "These are our bedrooms. Mine here and that's Alice's. As you can see, they abut on to Wilkinson House, but we weren't disturbed. Over there are another couple of rooms, used to be our parents' bedroom and dressing room. We don't use them now. Bathroom, box room. We use this as a sewing room, or rather Alice does. Me, I was never a hand with the needle. But Alice is an expert. Makes all our clothes in here. Gets the best light, you see."

Pascoe peered in. The room was full of material, some of it draped around a dressmaker's dummy. On a smooth polished table stood an ancient foot-operated sewing machine and a work basket with all the tools of the art—needles, cotton reels, buttons, pinking shears, edging tape, everything.

"A hive of industry," he said brightly. "It's a big house. You live here alone?"

"Not quite," said Miss Annabelle and, flinging back her head, she cried, "Una! Duessa! Medina! Acrasia! Archimago! Satyrane! Guyon! Britomart!"

A moment later the room was filled with cats. They were all Siamese, of various ages and pointings, but all possessing in common an extremely loud voice.

"Apart from these we live alone," said Miss Annabelle. "Do you want to go higher?"

"If I may."

They set off again.

"Careful," said Miss Annabelle. "The carpet's a bit tatty here. Well, here we are. Nothing much to see. These were servants' rooms. Empty now. The age of the servant is past, I fear."

"And this one?"

"Ah, yes, That's our old nursery."

She pushed open the door. Spring sunlight fell through a dusty casement window into the long, quiet room, bringing life and color once more to the shabby old-fashioned wallpaper with a design of rather menacing fairies. Everything was still there. A rockinghorse, white and scarlet piebald. An antique playpen. A four-foot-high doll's house with detachable front, which Pascoe was certain would be worth a small fortune in an antique shop. A stack of picture books. A gaggle of dolls.

"Makes you wonder what on earth happened, doesn't it?" said Miss Annabelle.

Pascoe glanced around. Miss Alice was hanging back, not even looking through the door. He felt a pang of desperate pity for her. The past must call her like a drug, but she was trying to turn away from it, probably because there were strangers present.

"Well, thank you very much," he said, walking from the room into the corridor once again. "Now, let me get my bearings. Wilkinson House is there, right? Now, let me see."

There was a narrow corridor between the two servant bedrooms. At the end was a door. He approached it and turned the handle, but it was locked.

"Now I bet that goes into Mr. Haggard's kitchen," he said half to himself. "How interesting."

"Right you are," said Miss Annabelle. "It's been there years. It was very useful when I helped out in the school. How's Dr. Haggard taking it, by the way?"

Pascoe looked at Wield, realizing he had not mentioned Haggard's injuries. Wield's face was impassive.

"I'm sorry," said Pascoe. "I should have said. Dr. Haggard was attacked. He's in hospital."

Miss Alice screamed and even Miss Annabelle looked shaken.

"We'll be seeing him at the hospital soon. We'll take him your best wishes, ladies," said Wield, suddenly genial like a beacon on Skiddaw.

"Please do," said Miss Annabelle while her sister, clinging to her for comfort, nodded accord.

"We will, we will," said Pascoe. "I'm sure he'll feel all the better for knowing that you were not disturbed by the unpleasantness."

Which unlikely hypothesis was never to be put to the test.

For when they reached the infirmary they discovered that Haggard was dead.

Six

"**D**ead?" said Dalziel. "Oh shit!"

Pascoe waited patiently to see if this was an expression of grief or something else.

"Last thing I need's a murder inquiry," continued the fat man. "Bloody doctors. Couldn't they have injected him or connected him to something?"

"He'd been very badly beaten. His face was a mess. Nose broken, teeth loosened. Several ribs smashed. Evidently it was internal hemorrhaging that killed him, probably caused by a kick in the gut. They thought they'd got it under control, but his heart packed in."

"Heart, eh?" For a moment Dalziel looked uneasy.

"Yes," said Pascoe. "And there was one other injury. Or perhaps I should say six. He'd been caned. Very hard. On the backside. They counted the weals."

"Six of the best!" said Dalziel. "Well, well."

"They made the jokes too," said Pascoe. "The doctor told me that there was no way of timetabling the various injuries outside of saying they all occurred at least an hour before he was admitted and not earlier than six hours before that."

"That's about as helpful as most of what they tell us." Dalziel sneered.

"I think he was suggesting that the caning and the beating-up may not have been done at the same time or for the same reason."

"Haggard's got a kink, you mean? Christ, I don't need any wog medicine man to tell me that—he was one of your erudite Asians, I suppose? They usually are after midnight."

"You mean, something's known about Haggard?"

Dalziel grinned like an advert for *Jaws*. "In this town something's known about every bugger," he said. "If I could get half the sods I drink with in the Rugby Club bar into CID, the crime rate'd be halved tomorrow. Or into jail for that matter."

"I know I'm a soccer man," said Pascoe, "but if you could see your way . . ."

Dalziel settled back in his chair and scratched his right groin sensuously. "I'd have thought you and Wield, being so interested in the Calli, would have known all there was to know about Gilbert," he said in ponderous satire. "He was an interesting fellow. Like you, Peter."

"Like me?" said Pascoe, alarmed.

"Educated, I mean. University. A real university, though. Oxford. And a real subject. Classics."

Having seen his own university and discipline dismissed

as illusory, or at best mimic, Pascoe felt a need to reestablish himself.

"Was he a *real* doctor too? I mean, he wasn't brown or yellow or black, which puts him halfway there already, doesn't it?"

"A doctor of philosophy, oh yes," said Dalziel delighted at having provoked a response. "You ever thought of trying it?"

"Taking a research degree?" said Pascoe in surprise.

"No. I meant philosophy," said Dalziel. "It helps you keep your temper, they tell me. Well, he did a spell in the Foreign Office. He was out in Africa or West India, somewhere hot and black. Then he went to Europe, Vienna, I think. My more intellectual contacts—"

"Old scrum-halves," interrupted Pascoe.

"You're learning. They tell me getting from the mosquitoes into Europe would be a step up. Things going well. Then, about 1956, he left."

"Why?" asked Pascoe.

"How should I know why?"

"I thought the Rugger CIA knew everything."

"A man abroad's like a team on tour," said Dalziel. "What you do there doesn't count. Any road, when he got back to England he started teaching, down in Dorset or some such place."

"What kind of school?"

"One of them what-they-calls-it, prep schools."

"A bit of a come-down after the governor's palace," said Pascoe.

"Well, not all that much," said Dalziel. "He started as headmaster."

"Good God? With no experience? I knew these places were low level, but surely . . ."

"Ah yes," said Dalziel. "But he'd *bought* it. I mean, it was his. He's not going to sit around being third Latin teacher in charge of tuck boxes, is he? Not when it all belongs to him."

"He had money then?"

"Not when he went to foreign parts, they say. But when he came back, he had enough. After three years he sold the school and moved on. He bought another place near Cambridge. Two years there, then on to Derbyshire. Next stop—here. You'll have noticed a progression?"

"North," said Pascoe.

"Good," said Dalziel. "I'll be able to send you out to post letters before you're much older."

"It looks like he was moving on all the time," said Pascoe, "when it would make more sense to stay in one place and consolidate a school's reputation. So presumably there was a reason."

"I know nowt about reasons," said Dalziel, reaching the end of his scratch. "Only . . ."

"Yes?" prompted Pascoe.

"Some slanderous sod once told me, and I wouldn't normally listen but we were drinking and it was his next shout, that it was just a simple organizational error that caused the trouble. Kind of thing that could happen to any man."

"Yes?" repeated Pascoe. He could see that Dalziel was enjoying himself. It was like being in a cage with a frolicsome brown bear.

"Oh yes. Every now and then it seems that Haggard,

when he had to punish some lad, would get him in his study and say, 'I'm sorry, boy, this means six of the best, you realize that? Go and fetch the cane.' And the boy would go to the cupboard and pick a cane and bring it back. Then, and here's where this error crept in, then Haggard would bend down and the boy would lay into *him!*"

Dalziel rocked with laughter as he spoke, while Pascoe looked on with fascinated horror. After a while the fat man became aware his inspector wasn't laughing.

"What's up with you then?" he said, modulating his long bellowings into intermittent chortles. "You're looking like you've messed your pants."

"I didn't think it was very funny, that's all," said Pascoe.

"Not funny. Boy canes headmaster? It's like man bites dog!"

"Yes. I can see that. Only, the whole situation, well, it's pretty nasty, isn't it?"

"Nasty?" said Dalziel, amazed. "I thought you were one of these freewheeling whatever-turns-you-on types? You're noted for soft-pedaling on these squatters and six-in-a-bed communes. What's bothering you here?"

"Well, it's the children. The effect something like that must have on a child . . ."

"Come off it!" exclaimed Dalziel. "Caning teacher? It's every kid's dream. Mind you, I wouldn't like any lad of mine in a school like that. Oh no. And once word got out, the schools folded pretty quickly and Haggard moved on even quicker. But as for harming the boys! As long as he didn't touch 'em (which he didn't), how could he harm them? That's like saying . . ." He paused to search out an analogy.

"Like saying that using a truncheon on policemen could be bad for criminals?" suggested Pascoe.

"Go and get stuffed," said Dalziel, very much put out at the failure of his humorous anecdote.

"And was there anything like this while Haggard was running his school here?" asked Pascoe.

"On my patch? You've got to be joking!" said Dalziel indignantly. "He sometimes whacked the poor little sods a bit too hard, but hardly anyone complained."

"Except, presumably, the poor little sods."

"It wasn't their money," said Dalziel. "Anyway, there's two theories for you."

"Two?"

"Either Gilbert Haggard had been getting up to his old tricks with some cooperative friend who took things too far. Or some poor little sod came back for a bit of eye-for-an-eye. OK?"

"Thank you very much," said Pascoe fulsomely.

"Well, we'd better get this show on the road," said Dalziel. "A man like that, you'd think he'd have his heart checked regularly, wouldn't you?"

"It can happen to the best of us," said Pascoe.

"That's all right then. Well, don't hang around here. Go and do something. You'd best find out who was there last night, who left last, that sort of thing."

Dalziel was never afraid of telling his underlings to do the obvious.

"Arany's coming in to make a statement," said Pascoe. "He'll know."

"Good. I'll get Sergeant Wield to organize a house-to-house round the Square. He knows who's who after listening to all their complaints. And we'd best pick up a few likely tearaways and bounce them off the wall a bit. That's favorite, I think: yobbos looking for mucky pictures and loose change; Haggard disturbs them; bang!"

"Oh dear," said Pascoe. "What about those two super theories you gave me?"

"You shove off and get some work done," said Dalziel grimly.

"I'm going, I'm going."

"And Peter . . ."

"Yes?" said Pascoe at the door.

"Next time you tell me my stories aren't funny, you call me sir."

"Yes, sir," said Pascoe.

Wield had returned to the Square to set his team of detective-constables on their round of house-to-house inquiries. He himself at Pascoe's request came back to the station, bringing Arany with him.

The Hungarian seemed indifferent to the news of Haggard's death. Pascoe remarked on this.

"We were business associates, not friends," said Arany. "It is a distressing thing, but not a remarkable one. Old men die. Death comes out of a clear sky. I hope you find who did it, though when you do, what will happen to him? A little rest, then freedom again. In this country, there are no punishments."

"I'm sorry you've found us so deficient," said Pascoe. "I won't keep you too long. It's just a question of a statement."

"I have made my statement."

"Oh?" Pascoe looked up at Wield, who regarded him impassively.

"To the sergeant. I told him what I know, which is nothing; what I saw, which was nothing; what is missing, which so far as I can assess is nothing." Arany emphasized his speech by moving his head from side to side like a fox in a cage.

"Well, we'd best get it down on paper. Sergeant."

"Sir?"

"Why don't you fetch Mr. Arany's file."

"Yes, sir," said Wield. "I'll see if the Superintendent's finished with it." He turned on his heel in a very military fashion and left. Pascoe observed Arany carefully to see his reaction to all this gobbledy gook. It seemed to him that for a moment the man looked uneasy, then his features resumed their watchful blankness. There was something rather un-English about it, thought Pascoe. Even the native criminal classes were not so frightened of anything that they needed to hide behind neutrality. It was a comfortable chauvinist thought.

"You're a naturalized citizen, I believe," said Pascoe conversationally.

"Yes."

"Ever go back to Hungary? I mean, would it be possible now that things have had twenty years to quieten down?"

"I would not care to try, Inspector."

"You still have relations there?"

"Everybody has relations," said Arany.

"But no one you keep in touch with?"

"No one."

"How long have you known Mr. Haggard?" said Pascoe, switching direction.

"Four years. Five. Does it matter?"

"I'm just interested in your business relationship, Mr. Arany."

"Does it matter?" repeated Arany. "Is it relevant?"

"It depends on why he was attacked," said Pascoe.

"Why? Vandals, surely. Teenagers, breaking in for a lark. Mr. Haggard would fight with them."

"He was that kind of person?"

"Oh yes. Fearless. Of the old school," said Arany.

Was there a note of irony in his voice? wondered Pascoe. "Perhaps you're right," he said. "Still, we must take a look at your members, I'm afraid."

"I have a list. It is up to date," said Arany. He produced a brown envelope from his inside pocket and handed it over.

"Most efficient," said Pascoe. 'Now I wonder if you could also draw up a list of those present at the performance last night, so far as you can recall." He pushed a sheet of paper and a ballpoint across the table to Arany.

The Hungarian thought a moment, then started writing.

Pascoe meanwhile started looking through the membership list. He recognized many of the names, just as he had recognized faces on his visit two nights earlier. Ellie's escort, Arthur Halfdane, was there. Trendy radicals could afford to belong to such clubs, but local politicians obviously had to be a bit more careful. Godfrey Blengdale might have enjoyed the show but his name wasn't on the list. Pascoe wasn't surprised. He knew the man mainly through the papers and the less-than-Leica impartiality of Ellie's appraisal. When the family timber yard had fallen into Blengdale's care at the age of twenty-six, it had been (like many old-established businesses run on outmoded principles such as value for money and honest dealing) on the verge of bankruptcy. Blengdale had wheeled and dealed and diversified into producing ready-to-assemble whitewood furniture which compensated for its difficulty of assembly by its ease of collapse. But his prices were competitive, his delivery dates held to, and his standards of manufacture (after a minor lawsuit or two) as reasonable as anyone else's in the field. Blengdale's had prospered and Godfrey Blengdale had become a figure of some importance, entertaining lavishly at his converted farmhouse a couple of miles from Holm Coultram College, supporting good works generously and finally offering himself to the electorate with the kind of aplomb and *savior-faire* beloved by working-class Tories the world over.

He thinks that God is short for Godfrey, proclaimed Ellie, which, if not original, was certainly apt.

And God might view the cavortings of post-lapsarian Adam and Eve with some amusement, but he wouldn't let his name be carved on a tablet of members of a celestial Ultra-Paradise Club.

Further down the list Pascoe came across Jack Shorter's name. So Shorter's "friend" had been mythic. A pointless bending of the truth, but understandable.

At least *he* could understand it. Dalziel would probably seize upon it as evidence of his worst suspicions.

As Arany finished writing, Wield returned. He handed a bulky cardboard wallet to Pascoe, saying, "Sorry to be so long, sir. I had to go to Central Records."

"Thank you, Sergeant."

Pascoe opened the wallet and peered in. It was full of old newspapers. There was a single typewritten sheet accompanying them. This he withdrew. It contained details of Arany's background, and home and business addresses. Pascoe studied it thoughtfully.

Wield meanwhile had been looking at the sheet Arany had been writing on and Pascoe was surprised to see a strange expression attempting to come to grips with his face, a kind of deferential embarrassment. Like a werewolf turning into Jeeves.

He saw the reason when he himself looked at the list. Heading the names was Mrs. P. Pascoe. Second was Arthur Halfdane. There were about thirty other names. And last of all was Godfrey Blengdale.

I wonder, thought Pascoe. Would that name appear at all if Ellie hadn't been there? Probably, for there would be others who would remember his presence. But its position on the list seemed to hint at a reluctance to put it there.

"Thank you, Mr. Arany. Now, perhaps you can help us further. What time was it when you left the club?"

"Eleven. Eleven-fifteen."

"Now, were you the last to leave, or was there anyone else on the premises, apart from Mr. Haggard, that is?"

Arany looked at him, his face so blank that Pascoe wondered if he'd understood the question. But he did not repeat it.

"I saw no one. The club room was empty," said Arany finally.

"Where was Mr. Haggard?" asked Pascoe.

"He had gone to his quarters."

"At what time?"

"Ten-thirty. The show finished at ten. He had a drink downstairs, then left."

"Alone?" asked Pascoe.

Again the silence. Suddenly Wield moved forward, just half a pace. Pascoe regarded his face, which was set like a traitor's head, and thought what a boost it would have been to the Inquisition, worth two or three confessions without touching the rack.

"I think Mr. Blengdale went with him."

"I see," said Pascoe. "And you think Mr. Blengdale may still have been there when you left."

"It is possible. I cannot say definitely."

"Well, thank you, Mr. Arany. That will do for now," said Pascoe. "The sergeant here will help you prepare your statement and have it typed up for you to sign. It shouldn't take a minute."

Arany banged both hands on the table. "Inspector, I am not a bloody stupid foreigner. I can speak and write English probably much better than half of your policemen. I shall write my own statement without Mr. Wield having to translate."

"As you please," said Pascoe. "We'll be next door if you need any help."

Outside the door he hefted the cardboard wallet and grinned at Wield. "You overdid this a bit, didn't you?" he said. "He'll be complaining to Amnesty!"

"It isn't all padding," protested Wield.

"No? You mean he's made the papers?"

"In a way. The clubland columns in the local rag. You know the thing, 'Club and Pub' with Johnny Hope."

"Oh yes. Incisive criticism. 'Old Wrinkle and the

Retainers were at the Green Swan last night and kept the customers happy.' Did Arany?"

"Not according to Johnny Hope," said Wield. "He records his move to management with great enthusiasm."

"You're a very thorough man, Sergeant," said Pascoe appreciatively. "Well, back to the grind. See that Arany's OK, will you? He's more frightened of you than me."

He glanced at his watch. It was eleven-thirty. "I suppose I'd better try to have a chat with Godfrey Blengdale. He's not going to like being mixed up in this."

"I don't suppose he is," said Wield.

Something in his tone caught Pascoe's attention. "Do you know him?"

"I make it my business to know anyone who's a big man in this town, sir," said Wield. "You never know when you may find yourself dealing with them."

"Oh dear," said Pascoe, thinking he recognized another crusader. He only hoped they were heading for the same holy war.

Seven

Back in his office, Pascoe looked up Blengdale's home number and dialed. There was no reply, so he tried the business number. A voice so tired that it could have been used on a medium's tape told him that Mr. Blengdale had left the country. Further questioning produced the information that this meant he had flown to Northern Ireland on business but should be returning on Sunday.

Disgruntled, Pascoe replaced the receiver, then on impulse picked it up again and rang Ellie's parents' number in Lincolnshire.

"Just thought I'd check you'd arrived safely," he said.

"Kind of you." She still sounded cool.

"Mum and Dad well?"

"Yes. Well, not really. Dad's a bit under the weather. Nothing specific, just old age, I guess. But I thought I might stop overnight. Would you mind?"

"Love, with the kind of contact we've been having lately, what difference will it make?" He tried to say it lightly, but it didn't work.

"It takes two to make contact," she answered sharply.

"Yes. Yes. I'm sorry. What time will you be back tomorrow."

"I'm not sure. Take me when I come, will you. We've got an important liaison committee on Monday morning and there's a bit of a council of war at college on Sunday night. I thought I'd better drop in on my way home."

"Out of your way home, you mean. Yes, I'm sure they couldn't do anything without you. Well, enjoy yourself."

He banged the phone down, feeling angry and hurt; and also foolish because he knew he had no mature adult reason for feeling angry and hurt.

He glanced at his watch. The Black Bull would be open. He'd been up since five o'clock. He surely deserved an early lunch.

It says much for the humanizing influence of bitter beer that after only half a pint Pascoe was beginning to regard himself ruefully as some kind of vindictive sexist. He got himself another half and had fallen deep into a reverie about the state of his life when a hand smote captainlike upon his shoulder and a voice said, "That stuff will rot your teeth."

It was Jack Shorter. With him, though in some indefinable way not quite *of* him, was a woman whom he introduced as his wife.

Pascoe looked at the spreading pool of beer Shorter's greeting had caused him to spill, then he stood up awkwardly because Mrs. Shorter looked like the kind of woman who would expect it—the up-standing, that is, not the awkwardness. Indeed her face registered "no reaction" to the beer slopped over the table in a way which Pascoe found more disapproving than a cry of "clumsy bugger!"

"How do you do, Mr. Pascoe?" she said, holding out a white-gloved hand. Dalziel would have wiped his own paw ostentatiously on his jacket front before pumping the woman's up and down, the whiles assuring her that he was grand and how was herself? Not for the first time Pascoe admitted the attractions of action over analysis.

"John has told me a great deal about you," said Mrs. Shorter.

"John?"

"Jack. Emma and my mother stick at John," said Shorter. "All right if we join you, Peter? I'll top you up. Most of yours seems to be on the table."

He made off to the bar. Mrs. Shorter sat down with studied grace. Above medium height, slim and elegant, she reminded Pascoe of models of the pre-Shrimpton and Twiggy era whose cool gazes from his mother's magazines had provided an early visual aid in his sex education. No longer, he thought sadly. Gone were the days when *Woman* was good for a flutter, the *Royal Geographical Magazine* provided rich spoils for the assiduous explorer, and *Health and Efficiency* was like an explosion in the guts.

But she was good-looking once you got past the perfection of her hair-do and her expensively simple powder-blue suit. She would have graced any Conservative Party platform.

"We're not interfering with your business, I hope," she said.

"No. Not at all," said Pascoe, puzzled.

"I thought that detectives visited bars merely in order to observe criminals and meet informants," she went on.

She was essaying a joke, he realized.

"There are some of my colleagues who waste their time like that," he said. "Me, I just drink."

"You're not talking shop, I hope," said Shorter as he rejoined them. "Emm, please. You know what it's like when people come up to me at parties and start flashing their fillings."

"There's a difference between teeth and crime," said his wife.

"Thank you, Wittgenstein," said Shorter. "There's also a connection. Talking of which, Peter, any word on what I said to you earlier in the week?"

Peter glanced at Emma Shorter, and her husband laughed. "It's all right. I told Emm. I don't have to get my card marked when I go to see a dirty picture, you know."

"You could always try staying at home and watching them on television, though," said the woman.

"I've checked it out," said Pascoe, thinking as he used the phrase that *he* must have been watching too much television. "Nothing in it, I'm glad to say. The special effects department must be getting better and better."

He thought of referring to the previous night's events at the Calli—they would, after all, be in the evening paper—but decided against the "from-the-horse's-mouth" intimacy that would imply.

"Oh," said Shorter. "I suppose I ought to be relieved, but I feel, well, not disappointed exactly, but a bit stupid, I suppose."

"You ought to try apologizing," said Mrs. Shorter. "It's not your time that's been wasted."

"Oh Lord. Peter, I'm sorry. I hope you didn't spend a lot of time—"

"Hardly any at all," interrupted Pascoe. "It's all right. I'm glad you mentioned it. If people didn't pass their suspicions on to us, we'd get nowhere."

Again Mrs. Shorter's expression did not change, but he felt she was raising her eyebrows at his public relations cliché. He felt annoyed. She could please herself what she thought about his manners, but further than that she could get stuffed. Dalziel again. I'll be scratching my groin next, he thought in alarm. Hastily he finished his drink. "I'm sorry, I have to dash," he said.

"But I've got you a pint," said Shorter.

"You drink it," said Pascoe. "It's bad for my fillings, remember?"

"And you remember our Ms. Lacewing's going to scrape you out on Monday."

"How could I forget? Nice to meet you, Mrs. Shorter." He wondered whether he should offer his hand.

"You too, Mr. Pascoe," she said. "You must come to see us some time."

"Great, great," said Pascoe, eager to be off before she could thaw into an invitation. "Cheerio now. 'Bye, Jack."

Outside the pub he found he was in almost as bad a temper as when he'd left the office. He felt somehow manipulated, though that was absurd. But come to think of it, in all the years he'd been frequenting the Black Bull, he'd never known Jack Shorter to use the pub.

It was still early, and instead of returning to the station he strolled around to Wilkinson Square.

There should have been a constable on duty at the door, but the front steps were empty. Nor, he discovered, when he pushed the door open, had the policeman taken refuge inside.

There was a scrabble of footsteps behind him and when he turned he saw an anxious-faced uniformed constable coming up the steps. He was in his early twenties and looked like a schoolboy caught in some misdemeanor.

"Where the hell have you been?" demanded Pascoe.

"Sorry, sir. I was on duty here when the lady next door asked me in to give her a hand with putting a new light bulb in the hallway. She's very old and afraid of steps."

"Miss Andover?"

"Yes, sir. And it's been very quiet for the past hour. And I kept an eye open from her window."

"While you were up a stepladder? Think yourself lucky it wasn't Mr. Dalziel who came around. Is Arany here?"

"My Arany? No, sir. He was earlier, but he went off about an hour ago."

"All right," said Pascoe. "Now plant your feet outside that door and don't move, not even if a river of lava comes rolling down Maltgate."

Shaking his head at the lowering of standards amongst the younger recruits to the force, and grinning at himself for shaking his head, Pascoe closed the front door and walked down the vestibule.

"Hello!" called Pascoe. He pushed open the door of the wrecked bar. Someone, Arany presumably, had done a good tidying up job. Just inside the door on a chair was a shopping bag and alongside it a gaudily wrapped packet. Pascoe picked it up. It looked as if it (whatever *it* was) had been gift-wrapped in the shop. A card was attached saying "Happy Birthday Sandra. From Uncle Maurice." The bag contained groceries—butter, tins of soup, frozen fish. Pascoe picked out a jar of pickled gherkins. He felt a sudden urge to eat one. I must be pregnant, he thought.

"Oh. Hello," said a voice behind him.

He turned. A girl in her early twenties wearing a denim suit and a flat cap had come into the room.

"Who're you?" asked Pascoe.

"I'm looking for Mr. Arany. I'm his secretary," said the girl.

"From the agency? How did you get in. Miss . . ."

"Metcalf. Doreen Metcalf. I just walked in. There was no one about. Who are you anyway?"

"Police," said Pascoe, thinking that the young constable was in for a nasty shock when the girl left.

"Oh, about the break-in, is it?" said the girl curiously. "Mr. Arany mentioned it when he looked in earlier."

But not the murder. Perhaps that was before he'd heard about Haggard's death. Once again Pascoe decided it wasn't up to him to enlighten anybody.

"What did you want him for?" he asked.

"Well, I get his shopping on a Friday night when I do

mine. He gives me time off. He was so quick in and out this morning that he forgot it. I finish at half-twelve, so I rang his flat, but he wasn't there. Then I tried to ring here, but the phone's not working. So I thought I'd call in."

"Very conscientious," said Pascoe.

"Well, he's a good boss. Normally I wouldn't bother, though, but with the present."

"Oh, yes. I noticed. His niece."

"Not really. She's just the daughter of one of the club secretaries. He's friendly with most of them."

"Good for business, I suppose."

"I suppose so," she said, slightly surprised, as though the notion had not previously occurred to her. "But it wouldn't matter. I mean, we're the main agency anyway. No, I think he's just naturally friendly."

It was Pascoe's turn for surprise. Nothing he'd seen of Arany to date had made him suspect the man of amiability.

"You always work on Saturday?" he asked.

"Oh yes. It's one of our busiest days. Everywhere's open on Saturday night, and there's always things to sort out during the day. Artistes going sick, that sort of thing. Look, are you hanging on here a bit?"

"Maybe," said Pascoe.

"I'll just leave this stuff, then. OK? I'll ring Mr. Arany later to see if he's got it. He can always pop up from his flat to pick it up, so you needn't hang about if you don't want to."

"That's kind of you," said Pascoe.

"Thanks," said the girl. "See you!"

Pascoe listened to her departure, smiling at his own ambiguous feelings. Much concerned with softening the prevailing hard image of the police, he nevertheless felt slightly piqued to be treated with such insouciance by one so young.

He found he had twisted the lid off the gherkin jar. One of the green fruit protruded temptingly above the level of the vinegar. He regarded it thoughtfully. The unity of the quality of life was a question he and Ellie had often debated. Were protests against motorways, contributions to Oxfam, demonstrations against apartheid and discussions of the merits of fresh over bottled mayonnaise part of the same grand whole? Similarly, would the eating of this gherkin put him in the same subclass as Dr. Crippen, the Great Train Robbers and people who cheated on their TV licenses? The gherkin's head was in the air; perhaps its roots lay in the eighth circle of hell.

Such a conceit deserved reward. He removed the gherkin and sank his teeth into it. And behind him something screamed like a mandrake torn from the earth.

Pascoe turned so sharply that the vinegar slopped over his fingers and he dropped the jar. In the doorway stood the devil sent to summon him to pay for his gluttonous theft. It took the shape of a small Siamese cat with dark brown head, tail and paws setting off its sleek ivory coat. Realizing it had caught his attention, it yelled angrily at him once more.

"Hello there," said Pascoe, recovering his self-possession. "Come here. Puss puss puss, pretty puss."

The cat ran forward, and he was congratulating himself on his subtle way with animals when, ignoring his downstretched hands, it picked up four or five of the spilled gherkins in its mouth and ran from the room.

He went in pursuit, following it up the stairs to the second floor, where it entered Haggard's living room and ran across to the kitchen door. Here it halted, swallowed what remained of the gherkins and addressed the slightly panting Pascoe once more.

He did what he was told and opened the door. The cat walked across the kitchen, sat down by the door in the far wall and repeated the instruction.

"Well well well," said Pascoe, understanding. He tried the door. It was locked. The cat rolled its eyes at his stupid inefficiency and began to wash itself.

Pascoe pounced. "You're under arrest," he said sternly. Then, softening instantly as the animal began licking his ear, the whiles purring like a circular saw, he added, "Let's go back to your place."

It was Miss Annabelle Andover who answered the door. She regarded him without surprise.

"I stumbled on this young fellow," said Pascoe.

"Girl. Where've you been, Acrasia? Step inside, Mr. Pascoe. Will you have a cup of coffee? I always have one after lunch. Ready-ground, I'm afraid, but the beans cost a fortune. It's a bastard this inflation when you're on a fixed annuity. In here. I won't be a tick."

She showed him into the Habitat-furnished living room and a few moments later reappeared with a tray bearing a steaming jug and two French coffee cups the size of small basins.

"I expect you've heard the sad news about Mr. Haggard," said Pascoe as she poured the coffee with steady hand.

"Yes. Devastating. Poor Alice was really knocked out. She's gone to bed with what she calls a fit of the vapors."

"I'm sorry to hear it."

"She'll recover. I'm a tougher old bird, but I must admit I was a bit shaken. What's the news? Are you hot on their trail? The killers, I mean."

"Killers?"

"Yes. Probably a gang, I'd say. Out for kicks. Gilbert wasn't all that old, but old enough to be fragile. Stupid kids. They all know how incredibly rich old folk must be but not how incredibly brittle old bones are."

"We're working very hard at it," said Pascoe. "Do you mind if we talk about Mr. Haggard?"

"I'll stop you if I do."

Pascoe stood up and wandered over to the window. "Did you consider yourself a friend of Mr. Haggard's?" he asked.

"I think so," said Miss Andover.

"You'd known him . . . how long?"

"Since he came here. Since he started his school."

"Let me see. Twelve years? Thirteen? What did you think when the school closed and the Calliope Club opened, Miss Andover?"

"No business of mine."

"Most people would consider such a major change next door their business. Sergeant Wield seemed to think a few tit-bits for your cats kept you sweet. You know—two dotty old women. I can't see it myself."

Miss Andover now rose also. "Young man," she said in ringing tones, "I am not accustomed to being insulted in my own home. The Lord Lieutenant of the county has been entertained in this house and his chief constable with him. We are not yet without influence and authority."

Pascoe grinned widely at her. "That sounds like something you picked up from Miss Alice," he said.

For a moment she tried to stare him down, then the old lady grinned too and picked up a packet of Park Drive from the mantelshelf.

"Smoke?" she said. "No? Very wise. They can't harm me, though. Not at my age. I'm seventy-six, Mr. Pascoe, and Alice is seventy-three.We bruise and break more easily than of old, but that apart, what can possibly harm people of our age? When Gilbert came and told us the school was closing down for financial reasons, we were distressed. Put me out of work for one thing! I had a few hundred to spare in the Funds and I went as far as offering to invest these with him, but he refused. I should have realized no one goes bust for want of a few hundred, but he spoke to me as if I had offered a fortune. Well, that's the sort of man he is. Was.

"For a while it looked as if he might have to sell the house. That did cause us some concern, not because of what it might become, for, as I say, how could offices or even bed-sitters bring any harm to us? No, we were concerned at the thought of losing a kind and considerate neighbor.

"So when Gilbert told us he was thinking of starting a club, what could we be but overjoyed?"

"You knew about the club before it was given the go-ahead?" interrupted Pascoe.

"Of course."

"And you didn't pass this information on to your neighbors in the Square?"

"Certainly not!" she said indignantly. "I do not break confidences so easily."

"Did Mr. Haggard tell you what kind of club it would be? I mean, the kind of entertainment that would be shown?"

She puffed out a jet of smoke and laughed. "I was brought up in a world deficient in many ways, Mr. Pascoe, but in this at least it got things right. It recognized that men must have their pleasures and, as long as scandal was avoided, it let them get on with them. Alas, it did not accord the same tolerance to women."

"I should have thought Mr. Haggard's club scandalized many people, Miss Andover."

"You do not know the meaning of the word!" she said scornfully. "How can you have scandal in an age which has abolished responsibility?"

"So, you had no objection to Mr. Haggard's proposals?"

"None. Men have always had their whores and these were only on celluloid. Indeed, as I have said, what harm could the real thing have caused to me and my sister? To tell you the truth, Mr. Pascoe, in some ways I preferred it to the school! During the day I could sit out in my garden and listen to such birds as have survived this polluted air, and never find them in competition with a gang of little brats singing hymns or chanting tables."

Pascoe finished his coffee and replaced the cup on the glass-topped table. "Thank you, Miss Andover," he said. "I won't keep you any longer. Thank you for speaking so frankly to me. I hope Miss Alice soon recovers."

"She will. I'm feeding her on raw eggs beaten up in a little sherry. That always gets her back on her feet."

"I should imagine it does," said Pascoe, smiling. "Oh, one thing more. I didn't tell you where I'd found Acrasia, did I? She was next door in Wilkinson House and she seemed to imagine she'd come through the communicating door which leads into Mr. Haggard's kitchen. Now that wouldn't be possible, would it?"

"Hardly. Damn thing's been locked up for years. But Acrasia is a bit of a mental defective, poor love. She was born on a Cumberland farm and reckons she's a trail hound."

"I see. Well, take care of her in case she strays again. Good-bye, Miss Andover."

It wasn't till Pascoe was walking back to the station that he remembered the cat had eaten Arany's gherkins. Not only the cat. He felt a momentary pang of guilt. Perhaps he should replace them. He slowed down as he crossed the road and a horn blared as a car swerved to avoid him. Pascoe turned, raised both hands and gave the angry driver the double figs, recalling that this had been the thief Fucci's gesture to God from the Eighth Circle.

It fitted. Fortitude was the only virtue, and submission the only sin. It was a reasonable thought to take into a conference with Dalziel.

Eight

In fact it wasn't until the following day that Pascoe saw Dalziel. On Saturday afternoon the fat man had been summoned by the Assistant Chief Constable to a top-level conference on matters too high for the likes of detective-inspectors. Whatever they had discussed, it hadn't put Dalziel in a good mood, and he listened with unconcealed scorn to the reports of those concerned in the Haggard case.

"That's a day's work, is it?" he demanded. "No wonder this country's in a mess!"

No one replied. There was nothing to say. Nothing that Forensic had produced was any help, no one in the Square had heard or seen anything suspicious. Pascoe had rung Blengdale's house again and this time spoken to his wife, who had told him Blengdale was not expected home till late that night, that he had a very heavily scheduled morning, but that he should be available for a while on Monday afternoon.

"Big of him," was Dalziel's laconic comment.

Fair enough, thought Pascoe. If he doesn't want to lean, why the hell should I, a mere ninety-eight-pound weakling, apply my weight?

"So no one's got any ideas?" said Dalziel. "Inspector Pascoe, we usually rely on you for the intellectual academic angle."

"Well, there's some interesting relationships," said Pascoe. "This man Arany—"

"The refugee? What's interesting about him? Did you ever hear him tell a joke? He didn't escape from Hungary, they paid him to leave!"

"Ha ha," said Pascoe. "You know the clubs then?"

"I know every bloody thing. But I don't know why I waste my time on you lot!"

The conference had broken up soon after. Pascoe had been left with a curious feeling that Dalziel, beneath his bluster, was more uncertain than any of them about how best to proceed with the inquiry.

Pascoe returned to his office and sat for a while wondering if he should ring Ellie again. It should have been his Sunday off, and he'd half planned to join Ellie in Orburn at her parents' house, but Haggard's death had put paid to that. In the end he decided against telephoning. It would be a sign of weakness and a man had at least to look strong if he were to survive.

Instead he picked up the file on Arany, carefully removed the sheets of newspaper and began to read.

The writer of the "Club and Pub" page in the *Mid-Yorkshire Courier* was called Johnny Hope. Subtitle of his article was "Where There's Hope, There's Life." Pascoe smiled and began to read.

The man had a bright and breezy style, in keeping with his job, which seemed to involve visiting at least six clubs and/or pubs most nights of the week. Perhaps he drank lemonade, or gins and tonic without the gins. Or perhaps he got down on his knees every morning and thanked God he'd survived to enjoy another splendid day.

So far as Pascoe could see, Hope made no special claim to critical powers but contented himself with reporting audience reaction with an occasional personal gloss. There were only two references to Arany's act, carefully ringed by Wield. They came from editions of the paper six years old.

Arrived at Littlefield WMC just in time to catch the end of Maurice Arany's act. Perhaps I missed the jokes, but there weren't many laughs in the last two minutes and when he went off, he didn't get much of a hand, just about two fingers, as the late, great Vic (shall-ah-tell-thee-a-poem?) Crawley used to say.

A few months later:

Maurice Arany got things off to a slow start at the Sledge and Reindeer last Thursday. I hate to see any artiste getting the bird, but the customers pay the money and are entitled to express an opinion. Fortunately better things were to come.

The next sheet was from an edition of January the following year. The ringed item read:

The frost made traveling slow, but I was glad I got to Westgate Social in time to see the Lulus, a trio of exotic dancers new to me. They've been got together by Maurice Arany, the onetime comedian who seems to be destined for more success with this side of the business. These girls were just the job for a cold night!

Alongside was a fuzzy picture of three women in scanty costumes and a lot of feathers.

So much for Arany's career as a performer, thought Pascoe. Obviously there'd been a lot more appearances, but gradually the word gets around—this one's a bummer, watch it or they'll start throwing glasses!

There were two more sheets—one about a year later in which Johnny Hope remarked in passing on the establishment of the Arany Agency, and another some nine months after this in which Wield had underlined all references to the Arany Agency in club advertisements. It was being used by a dozen at least. Pascoe was not very knowledgeable about the club circuit, but he assumed this meant good business. He reminded himself to check with Wield, who seemed to be the resident expert.

He wondered yet again how Arany and Haggard had come to be mixed up. It was a strange partnership, but most partnerships were, from marriage up, or down. There were many chains with queerer links than those joining the Misses Andover with, say, the Lulus. He looked again at the three feathery ladies and smiled at the thought of a confrontation. Not that Miss Annabelle, at least, wouldn't take it in her stride!

And then he looked yet again, taking out his Sherlock Holmes magnifying glass to bring the fixed provocative smiles nearer.

It was six years old. It was very blurred. But it was just possible that the Lulu on the left was Linda Abbott.

He got home at seven o'clock that evening after what felt like a completely wasted day. He ate some cold chicken, drank some cold beer and watched some cold television till Ellie got back shortly before midnight. Her committee meeting had ended with whisky in one of the resident staff rooms. She was in a very militant mood.

"We see Blengdale tomorrow afternoon," she proclaimed. "He's in for a shock."

"Don't make it too strong. I want him when you're finished," said Pascoe.

"What's he been doing? Cheating at the golf club?" asked Ellie; but she did not stay for an answer, being too taken up with enthusiasm for her own cause.

Pascoe, ever an opportunist, began to wonder if there was a chance of channeling her militancy into sexuality, but she greeted his subtle efforts with a plea of exhaustion.

"You were lively enough just now," complained Pascoe.

"That's different. That's work. It's like you getting up in the middle of the night when a case breaks. Doesn't matter how knackered you are, does it?"

"I suppose not," said Pascoe.

They didn't quarrel but there wasn't much loving-kindness between them when, back to back, they fell asleep.

But things looked up in the morning. "I'm sorry," said Ellie over the breakfast table.

"So am I, so am I," said Pascoe eagerly.

"What for?"

"I don't know, but you don't think I'm daft enough to let you get away with being sorry by yourself," said Pascoe.

They both laughed. Pascoe glanced at the kitchen clock.

"No," said Ellie.

"No what?"

"No, there isn't time. But tonight I'll get one of those little fat ducks from that farm shop. You get a bottle of something red and warm. How about it?"

"Oh yes," said Pascoe. "Yes, please."

He kissed her goodbye and she responded so enthusiastically that he began to wonder if there might not be time after all.

"No," she said, pulling away. "Just keep ticking over nicely through the day. Nothing too strenuous, mind."

"Oh Christ," he said. "I've got to go and have my teeth scraped this morning. By the liberated Lacewing."

"When she says rinse," breathed Ellie huskily, "tell her you want to keep the blood on your teeth."

Nine-thirty was chiming on a nearby church tower as he opened the front door of the dentist's surgery. Before he had time to announce himself to the receptionist, Alison, the dental nurse, came out of the waiting room and greeted him in some agitation. "There you are, Mr. Pascoe," she said.

"Yes, here I am," he admitted. "I'll just have a read, shall I? I'm up to the color supplements for 1969, you know."

But Alison prevented him from going into the waiting room. "Ms. Lacewing's waiting," she said. "She hates patients being late."

"I'm not late," he protested. "It's just half past now. Well, it was till you started talking to me."

The girl took his arm and drew him through into one of the surgeries. He had only glimpsed Ms. Lacewing distantly and fleetingly before and a strangely confused picture had developed in his mind, caused he had decided by the conflict between her gentle name and her violent activities. On first inspection, the name won, hands down. She was small and delicate, with large brown eyes which regarded him gravely from a young girl's unblemished and unmade-up face. "Mr. Pascoe?" she said in a soft, musical voice.

"Right," said Pascoe.

"Another minute and I should have crossed you from my list, Mr. Pascoe," she said. "Please try to be punctual in future. Lie down."

He lay down. The chair shuddered and descended. She hovered over him like a hummingbird seeking where best to pierce the gourd. Then she started.

Her slender wrists with their clearly accentuated bones seemed scarcely strong enough to lift the metal probes, but as she thrust and prodded, seemingly bent on re-arranging the whole relationship of his teeth and jawbone, he began to wonder if she had been practicing with a coal hammer.

When it was all over and he ran his tongue around a mouth which felt as smooth and as strange as the Elgin Marbles, he essayed conversation.

"How do you like it here Miss—Ms. Lacewing?"

"Hardly at all," she answered. "Would you please see the girl at the desk as you leave?"

Pascoe was reluctant to accept his dismissal so lightly, but he was still seeking a good exit line when outside he heard a crash, men's voices raised in anger and a woman shrieking.

"Seems you aren't the only one who doesn't like it," he said as he threw open the door.

The woman shrieking was Alison.

The cause of her distress was Jack Shorter, who was leaning drunkenly against the open doorway of his surgery clutching his stomach, with blood streaming from his nose and retching groans coming from his mouth.

The cause of *his* distress was three men in donkey jackets and overalls who were standing around him get-ting in each other's way as they threw punches wildly at his face and body.

Beyond the group in the surgery a patient was trying to raise himself from the chair, his eyes wide with fright and amazement, his mouth clanging and hissing with all the ugly appurtenances of a dental operation.

"Hold it!" cried Pascoe in his most authoritative tones.

They ignored him. It flashed through his mind that his best bet was to set Ms. Lacewing on them, but he also remembered the Home Office injunction against the use of excessive violence in effecting an arrest.

"Police!" he yelled, seizing the nearest of Shorter's assailants and pushing him against the other two.

One of them, a burly stubble-haired man with a dark round face, contorted now with a tremendous rage, swung a punch in Pascoe's direction.

"POLICE!" bellowed Pascoe again, determined that they wouldn't be able to deny knowing who they'd attacked.

The burly man's second punch was withheld. "Police?" he said.

"That's right," said Pascoe, flashing his warrant card to reinforce his claim.

"Just the man I want to see," said the burly man. It seemed an unlikely claim to Pascoe but he nodded encouragingly.

"I want you to arrest this bastard," he said, pointing down at Shorter, who had now slid to the floor.

"What for? Attacking you?" asked Pascoe satirically.

"It's no joke, mister. The bastard's been interfering with my daughter."

"What?"

Shorter looked up at him, eyes wide in what could have been appeal or fear or almost anything. He tried to speak but only the bubbly air sounds came.

"Men," said Ms. Lacewing in tones of icy contempt. Who specifically it was aimed at, Pascoe didn't know, but he spun around and addressed her angrily.

"You," he said, pointing to the distressed patient, "you go and see to that poor devil. And shut up. *You"*—to Alison, now sobbing instead of screaming—"shut up and ring for an ambulance and the police. Tell them I'm here. *You"*—to the faces which had appeared at the office and waiting-room doors—"sit down and wait till I come and talk to you, and *you"*—to the three men who had beaten up Shorter—"don't move a bloody inch, not a bloody inch, or I'll put it down as attacking a police officer."

"As long as you put me in a cell with *him*, it'll be worth it," said the burly man grimly.

But he said no more, and when Ms. Lacewing, having released the patient from his bonds, came across to administer first aid to Shorter, the three men accompanied Pascoe into the office without demur.

"Right," he said, helping himself to paper from the desk. "Let's start by mutual introductions, shall we?"

Nine

Shorter's principal assailant was called Brian Burkill. He was a man of about forty, his face ruddy from the open air and perhaps a bit of high blood pressure besides. His hair was close-cropped and his solid brawny frame just beginning to slide into fat. Pascoe would not have cared to be struck by the large rough fists which rested, still tight-clenched, on the table between them.

Burkill had confirmed his leadership by sitting down. The other two flanked him, one a tall rangy man of nearly fifty, the other a stocky youth aged about twenty, his hair long and lank, his demeanor a mixture of swagger and nervousness.

"These two, send them off," instructed Burkill. "They've nowt to do with it. Mates, came to help, that's all. OK?"

"Nay, we'll stick with you, Bri," said the taller man. "See fair play."

"Get off back to the yard, Charlie," instructed Burkill. "You too, Clint. Tell 'em I'll be along later."

"Hold it," said Pascoe as the two men began to move to the door. "What do you think this is? A union meeting?"

"You've no reason to keep them," protested Burkill. "I've told you, they just came along."

"And they can just bloody well stay," retorted Pascoe. "You—Charlie what?"

"Heppelwhite."

"And you?"

"Heppelwhite," said the youth. "He's my dad."

"Is your name really Clint?" asked Pascoe.

"Colin. I just get Clint."

"All right. Now, addresses."

He made careful notes of the information, partly to establish a strict official relationship in opposition to the freewheeling encounter of equals Burkill seemed to imagine was taking place and partly to give himself time to consider where to go from here. He had no facts yet, nothing but an assault and an accusation, but his own involvement with Shorter plus his knowledge of the damage that such an accusation could cause, even without evidence, made him more than usually circumspect.

There was a tap on the door and a uniformed constable stuck his head in. Pascoe knew him by sight. His name was Palmer.

"Hello, sir," he said. "We got a call."

"That's right," said Pascoe. "Is there an ambulance too?"

"Just arrived, but the injured man says he doesn't want to go. Says he's OK, just a bit bruised and winded."

"All right. Tell the ambulance we're sorry, but find out who we've got on call and ask him to get down here quick. I want Mr. Shorter looked at."

"Suppose he doesn't want that either, sir?" said Palmer.

"I'll see he does," said Pascoe. "Oh, and take these two somewhere quiet and do an identity check. Nothing more, understand?"

Palmer left with the Heppelwhites.

"All right, Mr. Burkill," said Pascoe. "Now, what's all this about?"

"What's your name?" said Burkill.

"Pascoe. Detective-Inspector Pascoe."

"You a patient here?"

"Yes," said Pascoe.

"You know Shorter, do you? Like a friend of his?"

"I know Mr. Shorter, yes," said Pascoe.

"I thought so, you being so handy on the spot. Right. I'm not talking to you."

Burkill emphasized his decision by folding his arms (with some difficulty; it was like folding two ham shanks) and sticking out his jaw.

"That's not a wise decision, Mr. Burkill," said Pascoe.

"Wise or not, what I've got to say isn't going to be said to no friend of bloody Shorter. You get someone else."

The door opened and Ms. Lacewing appeared. Glad of the interruption, Pascoe rose and went to her. "How's Jack?" he asked in a low voice.

"As well as can be expected."

"Can you sort out his patients without fuss?" asked Pascoe. "You realize how important it is to play things cool."

"Important for Jack Shorter, you mean?" she said.

Pascoe looked at her curiously. "What's wrong with that?" he said.

"I've no time for professional mystique and solidarity, Mr. Pascoe," she said. "But I'll see to the patients."

She left and Pascoe returned to the desk.

"What's that then?" demanded Burkill. "Stage one of the cover-up?"

"Look, if you're not going to talk to me, do it right, will you?" snapped Pascoe. "Keep your stupid mouth shut."

It was sheer irritation, but in the event it turned out to be a subtle psychological ploy.

"You can't talk to me like that!" said Burkill.

"Why not? I'm just *talking*. I'm not trying to knock your stupid head off."

"Listen," said Burkill, leaning across the desk and wagging a forefinger at Pascoe, who was relieved that at least one fist was now unclenched. "I'm having my breakfast, right? I'm just finishing when the wife tells me. This bastard's been at our Sandra, she tells me! At breakfast. At bloody breakfast!"

To Pascoe it seemed almost as if the timing of the news had upset Burkill as much as the news itself, but he kept the observation to himself.

"I thought there was something up. She'd been very restless that night. Turns out Sandra had come out with it on Sunday night when I was down at the club."

"Why didn't she tell you on your return?" inquired Pascoe.

"Said she didn't want to tell me when I'd been drinking. Five or six pints, you call that drinking? I suppose she were right, though. You never know, I might have done summat daft last night."

"Instead of which . . ." prompted Pascoe.

"I wanted to go right round to his house, there and then, and have it out. But the wife said no. She said I had to think about it, work something out. I were right upset, you can imagine. I went off to work—"

"Where's that?"

"Blengdale's," said Burkill. "I'm yard foreman there. I couldn't work for thinking about it. I told Charlie Heppelwhite. He lives next door and we drive to work together. I've known Charlie for years. I asked what he thought on it."

"And he advised you to come around here and assault Mr. Shorter."

Burkill considered. "No. Charlie said that buggers like that needed doctoring, but it was his boy, Clint, who got really mad. He's been like an elder brother to our Sandra. He was so angry he was going to set off by himself to see Shorter. Well, we didn't want that. It might have meant trouble. He's a wild un when he's roused, young Clint. So we decided we'd all come round and have it out."

"Why not go to the police?"

"Look!" said the man, "it was early days for the police. I wanted to hear what Shorter had to say for himself first."

"It's getting clearer," said Pascoe. "You came here partly to preserve the peace, and partly to protect Mr. Shorter's right to put his side of the matter. Well, in that case, I'm sorry I interrupted you. If I'd known what you were up to, I'd have stood there and watched the three of you kick him about a bit longer."

"I knew it was no good talking to you," grunted

Burkill. "What do you want me to do? I go in there and ask him to step outside for a chat. He tells me to bugger off. I don't want to talk in front of other people, but I see it's got to be that way, so I ask him straight out, what's he been doing to our Sandra. He goes bloody berserk, tries to push us out of the room. I don't like being pushed. It turns into a bit of a punch-up. What do you expect? Have you got any kids, mister? What'd you do?"

"Mr. Burkill, we'll have to talk with your daughter, you realize that? How old is she?"

"Thirteen. On Saturday she was thirteen. What a bloody birthday present, eh?"

"And what precisely did she tell you had happened here?"

"She told the wife that—"

"No," interrupted Pascoe. "What did she tell *you*. You spoke to your daughter, I presume?"

"Aye. I went up to her room."

"And what did you say?"

"I said something like 'Sandra, is it right what your mam tells me?' "

"And she answered?"

"She said '*Yes, Dad.*' "

"And you said?"

"I said nowt. That were enough for me," said Burkill.

Pascoe covered his face with his hands. "Oh God," he said. "And on that evidence you come around here and start knocking hell out of a stranger?"

Burkill stood up and both fists were balled again. "You've decided, haven't you? You've bloody decided. I knew you were one of his mates. So I'm wrong, I'm in trouble, and he's going to get off with it? Let me tell you, mister, it doesn't work like that any more, there'll be no cover-ups here. No, not if you were ten times the man I think you are!"

The door burst open as though hit by a sledgehammer. "There's a lot of noise in here," said Dalziel, entering the room. "Just calm it down a bit, Brian. They don't want to hear you in Newcastle."

"Oh hello, Mr. Dalziel," said Burkill. "Thank Christ you're here. This sod's trying to cover up for his mate and—"

"Brian," said Dalziel mildly, "you refer like that just one more time to Inspector Pascoe or any of my officers and there won't be enough left of you to cover up. Now sit down and shut up. Inspector."

He jerked his head at Pascoe, who followed out of the door.

"You're having a busy morning," said Dalziel. "This isn't one for you, you know that?"

"I was here," protested Pascoe.

"That's the trouble. As soon as I heard the name Shorter, I knew I'd best get down here myself. What's happened?"

Quickly Pascoe filled him in.

"And you've been doing what? Interrogating Burkill?"

"Just general stuff till someone turned up," said Pascoe.

"Oh aye. So general that he's crying police cover-up already!"

Pascoe didn't answer. He was all too aware of the messy inadequacies of his questioning of Burkill.

"You know Burkill, sir?" he asked.

"From way back."

"Officially?" said Pascoe, suddenly alert.

"You mean, has he been in trouble? No, there's no way out for your mate there. Burkill's not a good man to antagonize, but he's honest, industrious and well thought of. He runs the shop floor at Blengdale's like a Panzer division. No half-baked union disputes there about who turns what screw. No, you do what Burkill says or you sling your hook."

"Is that where you know him from?" asked Pascoe.

"Not me," said Dalziel. "I've nowt to do with Blengdale's. No, Bri's other great interest is Westgate Social Club. He's lived on the estate for years, helped build the club up from scratch and he's been concert secretary there as long as I can remember. I've done a bit of drinking there in my time, that's how I know him. No West End finesse, but by God, the buggers who perform there know they'd best put on a good turn, else they won't get paid! I'll have a word with him now. I speak the same language."

"I'll get out of your way then," said Pascoe rather sulkily.

"What the hell for?"

"Well, you said you didn't want me involved on the case."

"I don't want you talking to Burkill or Shorter, get that clear. But there's no reason why you should be sitting on your arse in the office while I'm stuck down here. No, you go and sort out that Heppelwhite pair, get their version of things."

"Burkill won't like me interrogating his mates."

Dalziel's face was as heavy and ugly as a slag heap.

"No one tells me who I can or can't use on a case, Inspector. No bloody one. Now jump to it and we'll see if we can't get round one over before closing time!"

Constable Palmer was in such earnest conversation with the Heppelwhites that he didn't hear Pascoe open the door. "There was a case up in Middlesbrough last month," he was saying. "Same thing. Only he were a teacher. Suspended sentence. No wonder someone thumps them!"

"You reckon we'll be OK then?" said Charlie Heppelwhite.

"Bound to be. He'll not want the publicity. Anyway, go for a jury if it comes to a case. You're entitled, and there's not a family man in this town but'd applaud you."

"Palmer!" said Pascoe.

"Sir."

"Step outside for a moment."

Pascoe heard himself reprimanding the constable with an ironic awareness of the parallels between this scene and his own recent interview with Dalziel.

Palmer was obviously unrepentant. "Sorry, sir," he said, "but I've got two little girls of my own."

"Proud of their dad?"

"I hope so, sir."

"Then you'd better learn to follow instructions, else they'll be wondering why daddy's spending so much time at home."

Palmer's face set with resentment, but he said nothing in reply, and Pascoe dismissed him, feeling full of guilt at uttering such a Dalzielesque authoritarian threat.

He spoke to the Heppelwhites separately. The father, though he expressed the feeling that scourging was too good for a man like Shorter, obviously had considerable reservations about the whole business.

"I didn't want to come here," he said. "But he were set on it, so I thought it best to come with him. Bri's a hard man when he wants. And our Clint's got a temper."

Pascoe regarded his thin earnest face and groaned inwardly. Here was someone else whose route to the punch-up was paved with good intentions.

"Who threw the first punch?" he asked.

Heppelwhite thought carefully. "I don't rightly know," he said in the end. "The dentist waved his arms about, you know, going shoo! shoo! like we were a lot of sheep. Clint grabbed one of his arms, just to restrain him a bit, and the fellow called Clint a smelly yobbo, some such thing. Then Clint pushed him in the chest."

"Punched or pushed."

Heppelwhite hesitated. "A bit of both," he admitted. "He swung at Clint and next thing Bri was banging away at him."

"And you?"

"I don't know. I just found myself going through the motions. Down our way, you don't hang around when your mate's in a fight."

"You could have tried to stop it."

"Last fellow I saw try to stop Bri in a fight got a busted nose," said Heppelwhite.

"Oh. Is Mr. Burkill a regular fighter then?"

"I never said that. It happens he's on the club committee and if there's ever any trouble down there, it's Bri they send for. It's usually visitors start it."

"Of course," agreed Pascoe. "Foreigners from Doncaster or Sheffield. I gather you've known Mr. Burkill a long time."

"Aye. Twenty years or more. I'm a couple of years older than him, but his missus and mine's of an age and they were best friends ever since school."

"Nice family?"

"Very nice."

"Close?"

"What?"

"I mean, they get on well together."

"Oh yes. Deirdre, that's Mrs. Burkill, she's always been dead proud of Bri and the way he's got on."

"And Sandra?"

"Lovely lass. I'm her godfather, like Brian's my Clint's."

"And she likes her father?"

"What a daft question!" said Heppelwhite. "Of course she likes her father. He's, well, he's her father!"

"Were you surprised when you heard what she said about Shorter?"

Heppelwhite hesitated before saying, "Of course I was surprised."

"You don't seem sure."

"Don't try to put words in my mouth, lad!"

"Nice-looking girl is she? For her age, I mean."

"Aye. Very bonnie. For her age."

"They grow quick these days, don't they? Suppose I suggested to you, Mr. Heppelwhite, that if Sandra had been caught up to some hanky-panky with a young lad, you'd not have been in the least surprised. Would that be nearer the mark? It was Mr. Shorter's alleged interference which surprised and shocked you."

"Perhaps," said Heppelwhite cautiously. "There's mebbe summat of that in it."

He was clearly unwilling to go further, and without having seen the girl himself, Pascoe didn't feel able to pursue the line.

Clint began defiantly, asserting a Wild West notion of chivalry and vengeance. "She's only a kid, isn't she? She needs protection."

"All girls need protection, do they?"

"Decent girls do," said Clint boldly.

"How old are you, Clint?"

"Nineteen."

"Been around a bit?"

"What?"

"*You* know. Had your share? Know what I mean?"

"I do all right," said Clint.

"Do you really? That's interesting. Mostly slag, though?"

"What?"

"You know. Scrubbers. Old bits that you pay."

"Not bloody likely," said Clint hotly.

"No? Well, stuff that's there for everyone, then. There's always one or two like that around. You know, snap your fingers and it's yours."

"Get stuffed!" exploded Clint.

"You mean, it's not just the easy stuff? You don't mean to tell me you've been making it with . . . decent girls?"

It was a petty triumph and Pascoe felt disgusted with himself for seeking it. Besides it was bad technique. Burkill might be provoked into talking by such an attack, but all it served to do with this youngster was drive him into a surly silence.

Finally Pascoe sent both the Heppelwhites off with the warning that they would probably need to be seen again before the day was through and the threat that charges of assault were more than likely. Not that Pascoe believed this last himself. The girl's allegations would have to be closely investigated, but he couldn't see Jack Shorter doing anything which was likely to bring them into the public eye.

He caught the police surgeon just as he was leaving. Shorter had evidently been happy to be examined and treated and the doctor was able to tell Pascoe that apart from the possibility of a cracked rib, the damage was superficial. He also told him that Dalziel had just joined the dentist. Pascoe felt relieved. It removed from him the temptation to see Shorter, which, perversely, Dalziel's interdict had only served to make the stronger by dint of corresponding with Pascoe's own reluctance, of which he was ashamed.

Ms. Lacewing appeared in the hallway. "I've sorted out Shorter's patients," she said.

"I bet they hardly felt a thing," said Pascoe.

She suddenly grinned. Her own teeth were small and white and looked very sharp. They changed the whole character of her face, giving it a kind of sly sexuality which was not unexciting.

"I'm going to have some coffee. Join me," she said. She

led him into her surgery, where an electric kettle was jetting
steam onto a pile of dental records. She made their instant
coffee swiftly and lay in the patient's chair with Pascoe
perched gingerly alongside her on the dentist's stool.

"Are you related to Ellie Pascoe?" she asked.

"In a way," he said. "She's my wife. Do you know
her?"

"Of her. She sounds interesting. I think we may be
friends."

It was an alliance Pascoe did not much care for the
sound of.

"Who's been saying nice things about her?" he wondered.

"My uncle. He says she's an arrogant, loud-mouthed
troublemaker."

"What?"

"Yes. That's what attracted me."

"Who is this uncle?" demanded Pascoe hotly.

"Why? Are you going to do the knight-errant bit and
thump him? I doubt it. He's Godfrey Blengdale."

"Oh," said Pascoe.

"Didn't you know?" she said, smiling up at him
sweetly. "In fact it's Gwen, his wife, that I'm related to.
She's my mother's sister. Poor cow. I like her a lot, but
she's too stupid to tell Uncle God to go jump. I was there
last week when he came home from a meeting that your
wife had attended also. That's when he gave her the testimonial. Do you think she'd be interested in WRAG?"

"I doubt if she needs it," said Pascoe.

"I see," said Ms. Lacewing. "You make up her mind
for her, do you?"

"No," said Pascoe, suddenly tired of being the second

fiddle in someone else's orchestration. "On the contrary, it's me who lets other people make up my mind. Take this business of Jack Shorter, for instance. You say you're not interested in professional solidarity, so tell me, do you think he did it?"

"What," she replied, "is he alleged to have done? Precisely."

Pascoe was obliged to say he didn't know.

"Then your question's meaningless."

"Whatever the specifics," he protested, "surely the notion of interference is narrow enough in itself to permit an answer."

"A typically naif masculine point of view," she said. " 'Was she touched? Was he provoked?' That's the extent of your thinking, I bet."

"I'd like more notice of that question," said Pascoe cautiously. "But yes, they *are* important questions."

"Reverse them. Was *he* touched? Was *she* provoked. Have you ever had a case where *those* questions suggested themselves to you? Suppose a strange woman pinched your bottom in a train, would you feel that a crime had been committed?"

"No. But then the sexual element's not present."

"How do you know?"

"Well, I don't," admitted Pascoe. "But I wouldn't feel sexually assaulted."

"Suppose she grabbed your privates?"

"It would depend whether the motive was to give me pain or herself pleasure."

Ms. Lacewing laughed. "For a policeperson," she said, "you are not too idiotic."

"We have mental hygienists. But let's get this straight. You seem to be saying that men are hard done to, that what for a man is a crime, for a woman is nothing at all."

"Perhaps you *are* too idiotic," she said. "What I'm saying is that whether this poor girl *has* been interfered with, or *imagines* she's been interfered with, or *wishes* she'd been interfered with, or is merely *pretending* she's been interfered with, a crime's been perpetrated on her mind far graver than any you'll charge Jack Shorter with."

"Bloody hell," said Pascoe. "You know, for a while there I thought we were speaking the same language!"

Before she could answer, Pascoe heard his name bellowed outside.

"It'll have to wait till my next appointment," he said.

Dalziel was standing by the office door looking as if he'd been waiting for hours. Behind him Pascoe could see Shorter, who looked rather pale and had a couple of pieces of tape on his forehead.

"There you are," said Dalziel. "I'm done here. The doctor's advised Mr. Shorter to take things easy for the rest of the day, and I've said the same. I've also advised him in his own interest not to discuss this business with anyone."

"Except a solicitor," said Pascoe clearly.

"That's up to him. I don't think Burkill will go running to the press just yet, but there'll be talk at Blengdale's and it can easily get about. We'll want to see you again, Mr. Shorter, after the girl's made a statement. If you are not going to be at home, make sure we know where to find you. Are you fit, Inspector? Let's get a move on then. There's work to be done."

He set off purposefully toward the exit. Pascoe hesitated, looking into the room at Shorter, who met his gaze with a kind of frustrated resentment.

"Take it easy, Jack," urged Pascoe. "It'll be OK."

"Inspector!"

With a final helpless shrug, Pascoe turned and went after Dalziel.

Behind him Shorter stood up and kicked the door shut with a resounding crash.

"If I were you," said Dalziel, "I shouldn't let him at my fillings for a couple of weeks."

Ten

"Sure you won't have one?" asked Dalziel.

Pascoe shook his head and the fat man replaced the bottle of Glen Grant in his filing cabinet.

"It's medicinal," he said, lifting his tumbler in salutation to God knew what God and taking a substantial draft. "Wash the taste of that place out of my mouth."

"You've made your mind up then? You haven't even heard the girl!"

"There's a WPC there now taking a statement. I'll have a go when I've seen it. But I'd be surprised if it didn't stand up."

"Why, for God's sake?"

"*One*—Brian Burkill's not daft. He wouldn't do what he didn't see cause to. *Two*—this dentist of yours started putting himself in your way last week, coming the old pals act. Right?"

"Hang on!" protested Pascoe. "He drew my attention to a possible breach of the law, that's all."

"He told you some cock-and-bull story about a girl being beaten up, that's what. It *was* a cock-and-bull story, wasn't it?"

"Yes," admitted Pascoe. "He was mistaken. But he could have found an easier way of putting himself in my way, as you put it. Why link himself with the Calli at all?"

"Suppose he knows the girl's going to talk? They all do eventually. We investigate him, find out his favorite hobby's watching skin flicks. It doesn't look good, does it? So he clears the decks. It's in the open. I bet his wife knows all about it."

"Yes, she does," said Pascoe. "I met her."

"Did you? I wonder how long she's known. Did she look the type who'd like a bit of way-out thrill?"

"Not really. But you never can tell."

"I'll be able to tell by the time I'm done," said Dalziel grimly.

"I'm sorry," said Pascoe. "Frankly, I think this is all half-baked. It's too tortuous by half."

"To you, aye. It's not your problem. But think on, when you're in dead lumber and things start looking black, *any* idea that seems to offer a chance of getting out comes on you like a flash of light. It doesn't matter how daft it is. How many poor sods have we put away who hit on the brilliant notion of solving their money troubles by borrowing a few hundred from the till, putting it on a horse and then replacing the borrowed money from their winnings? Now, *that's* daft, but it still gets done."

"I'm not convinced," said Pascoe. "Anyway, that was *two*. Is there a *three*?"

"Oh aye. *Three*. When I talked to him just now, I got a feeling he'd been up to something."

"A *feeling*!" mocked Pascoe.

"That's it," said Dalziel. "A feeling. There's something there. Last time I had this feeling . . ."

"Yes?" prompted Pascoe as Dalziel finished his Scotch.

"I lost fifteen quid on the Leger. But there's more important things than dirty dentists. There's this Haggard business. What are you on today?"

"I'm seeing Blengdale this afternoon. Three o'clock."

"And what are you hoping from that?"

"Well, he's possibly the last person to see Haggard before the attack—"

"So what? I mean, that's usually a lot of bloody use, isn't it?"

"I won't know till I see the man!" snapped Pascoe in exasperation.

"No. Of course you won't," said Dalziel pacifyingly. "But you watch him, Peter. He's a hard bugger, and if he thinks his public image is being tarnished. . . . Any road, you'll see for yourself."

"Yes," said Pascoe, rising. "About Shorter . . ."

"I'll keep you posted," said Dalziel. "Don't worry. It'll be done proper. Like I said, I'll see the girl myself. If it looks straightforward, I'll pass it on to some nice safe Puritan like Inspector Trumper. You keep clear unless I say otherwise. It wouldn't surprise me if Shorter didn't try to get to you somehow, so be ready. Choke him off."

"Policemen mustn't have friends," said Pascoe bitterly.

"Oh no, lad. Nowt to do with that," said Dalziel. "Be as friendly as you like. It's just that I want to save you up till he's sweated a bit and might be ready to cough. That's when a friendly shoulder comes in really useful!"

The business at the dentist's had taken a large slice out of the morning and it was one o'clock before Pascoe knew it. He didn't feel particularly hungry but he had learned early that in detective work only a fool voluntarily passed up a meal break.

At least he wouldn't be seeing Shorter today, he thought as he entered the Black Bull.

Sergeant Wield was there, sitting alone, and Pascoe joined him. They sat in silence for a while.

"Well, I'll finally see Blengdale this afternoon," he said to break the ice.

"Want me along, sir?" said Wield.

"Not this time. Informality's the thing. Merge with the background till I see what's going on. If anything."

"Oh aye. I doubt if Priory Farm's a background I'd merge easily with," said Wield. "Not *inside* anyway." He looked hard at Pascoe.

Oh Christ, he thought. Is it a joke or a social comment?

Pascoe took the plunge and grinned broadly. To his relief Wield's craggy face landslipped into a wide smile.

"Any ideas yet what's behind all this?" asked Wield. "If it's not just tearaways, I mean."

"Not a clue. I don't really understand Haggard, that's the thing. Diplomat, schoolteacher; old ladies love him.

Runs a dirty film club and gets his kicks from having his bum beaten. How's that for complex? And how did he and Arany come into partnership? It's a curious relationship."

"I've known curiouser," said Wield. "Tell you who might know something. Johnny Hope."

"Who?"

"Pub and Club man for the *Courier*. What *he* doesn't know about the club people we're not going to be able to find out."

"Fine," said Pascoe. "I'd like to meet him. Straight after lunch we'll call around."

"Oh no," said Wield. "He'll be in bed. You'll make an enemy for life of Johnny Hope if you disturb his sleep. Best thing is to meet up with him on his rounds. How're you fixed tonight, sir?"

Pascoe began to nod, then recalled Ellie and her promise of duck and more besides. "Make it tomorrow night," he said. "Here. Something else since we're on about the clubs. Do you know a man called Burkill? Concert secretary at the Westgate Social."

"Bri. Works at Blengdale's. Aye, I know him."

"What sort of fellow is he?"

"Hard but honest. He really puts himself heart and soul into that club. You don't get bad turns there, not more than once."

"Yes. The super said that," he said, adding as a memory popped up toastlike into his mind, "Would he know Arany?"

"Oh aye. He'll book acts through him. Not only that, though," said Wield, chuckling like a subterranean stream.

"The one time Arany appeared at the Westgate when he was still trying to peddle his act, Burkill switched off the mike after five minutes and pulled him off. Literally."

"Ah," said Pascoe. "So there'd be no love lost?"

"Well," said Wield, "Burkill's a fair man. If he thinks someone's not trying, he'd refuse to pay and like as not thump 'em. But if he reckons someone's just got no talent, he'd slip 'em a quid and advise them to get out of the business. That's just as bad for some fellows, I know, but Arany's sharp. He'd begun to get the message anyway. That's more or less when he turned to agenting. And he's been pretty pally with Burkill since."

"Has he now? And his family?" said Pascoe, remembering the gift-wrapped packet he'd seen at the Calli. "Friendly enough to buy the girl a birthday present?"

"Wouldn't surprise me," said Wield.

"You know the family?"

"I've seen Mrs. Burkill at the Social Club. And I saw the girl once in the club office waiting for her dad. Come to think of it, Arany was there too."

"What's she like, this girl?"

"Just a girl. Can't tell the difference between 'em nowadays. Her mam's a fine-looking woman though. Are we interested?"

He sounded reproving. Oh God, thought Pascoe, I'm doing it again, keeping the poor sod in the dark. Quickly he explained about Shorter and Sandra Burkill's allegations; also about Dalziel's theory that Shorter had somehow been paving the way for this revelation by inventing the *Droit de Seigneur* story.

"Bit farfetched that," said Wield, to Pascoe's delight. "Mind you, Shorter, the Calli, Arany, Burkill, Shorter. It's a bit of a coincidence, don't you think, sir?"

"You're not suggesting some kind of frame, are you?" said Pascoe incredulously. "You're worse than Mr. Dalziel!"

"When it comes to catching villains, most of us are, sir," said Sergeant Wield.

Priory Farm was a long low whitewashed building, tastefully extended and beautifully maintained, and it gave Pascoe great pain. He was not an overly envious man, but this house felt so right for him that it was as if Blengdale had tricked him out of it.

Blengdale was not there, and his wife invited Pascoe to wait in a room furnished with quiet (and expensive) good taste.

None of this stuff had been knocked together from Blengdale's do-it-yourself furniture kits, thought Pascoe.

Blengdale's wife, who seemed somehow familiar though he had not met her before, also had much of the same patina of value and breeding. Pascoe knew nothing of her provenance, but he would have classified her as genuine English county, probably with a good seat but not erring on the side of tweediness, equally able to be unobtrusively elegant (as now) in simple twin set and sensible shoes, or discreetly radiant at a hunt ball. If she was a trifle more faded than high—or indeed low—society expects its womenfolk to be in their late thirties, then this merely confirmed that she was "right." The English Rose fades early, but she fades exceeding slow.

"I'm sorry my husband's not here, Inspector," said

Gwen Blengdale. "He had a meeting at one-thirty and did not anticipate it would go on very long."

"That's all right," said Pascoe, peering enviously out the window. "What a lovely setting this is. We're looking toward the golf course, aren't we?"

"That's right. And to the right we abut on the grounds of the college. Your wife works there, I believe."

"Yes. Have you met her?"

"We spoke on the phone once. Some committee of Godfrey's—"

She was interrupted by the violent passage before the window of a little fat man on a big black horse. Pascoe wondered how far he was ahead of the posse.

"Excuse me," said Mrs. Blengdale.

She left the room. Pascoe heard voices distantly, or rather one voice which came rapidly closer till the door burst open and the speaker appeared.

He was an ugly little man, round and red, with a foxy stubble of hair broadening out below the jug-handle ears into luxuriant sideburns. He wore a hacking jacket and jodhpurs, clearly specially tailored to accommodate such shortness of leg with such breadth of buttock. It was also clear that his naturally rubicund complexion was enhanced by deep emotion.

"What a fucking day!" he said. "What a fucking day. You wouldn't believe it. My time's not my own. You're Pascoe, are you? Well you ought to try keeping your sodding wife in order, that's all I can say."

He sat heavily on a chair which, being a non-Blengdale product, merely groaned slightly.

"Mr. Blengdale, I presume," said Pascoe.

"Presume, is it? I've had enough presumption from Pascoes for one day. Is she like that at home? You deserve police protection. Is that why you joined?"

Pascoe felt a protest was called for, though, knowing his Yorkshiremen, he suspected it would be useless.

"Mr. Blengdale, what my wife does in her own professional capacity is her business. But I don't feel you're entitled to be abusive—"

"*Me* abusive? A fascist pig she called me! Feathering my own sty! *That's* abusive, *that's* what I call abusive!"

"It's certainly an abuse of the language," said Pascoe. "But I dare say Mrs. Pascoe was carried away in the heat of argument and in truth meant to offend you as little as you meant to offend me."

The reproof took a little time to sink in but finally it penetrated the carapace of indignation Blengdale was carrying around, and while he wasn't equipped to look shamefaced, he lumbered into an explanation which might or might not have been second cousin to an apology.

"Bad day. Looked so nice too. There was a meeting at the college. Liaison committee. *Liaison!* There was better liaison with the SS in 1939. Anyway, the weather was so good, I saddled up Trigger and rode over to the college after lunch."

"You went to the college on your horse?" asked Pascoe.

"Yes. Why not?"

"No reason. Not the slightest in the world," said Pascoe, picturing this rotund cavalier crashing into the senior common room during the post-luncheon period, which Ellie had once described as bedpan time in the geriatric ward.

"That's where I've been ever since. It's ring-a-bloody-roses, ring-a-bloody-roses! Round and round. Reason? Argument? Some of them wouldn't recognize an argument if it had a British Standard label. I neglect my business, I neglect my recreation, I get no thanks, all I get's a lot of fucking abuse. Do you wonder I'm a bit short?"

"I'm amused at your good humor," said Pascoe. "What I wanted to talk about was Friday night at the Calliope Kinema Club. You've heard what happened, of course."

"Aye. Roughly. I was bowled over when I learned old Gil was dead. Bloody yobbos! Why don't you lot sort the buggers out?"

"Yes," said Pascoe. "Why don't we? Now, I believe you're not actually a member of the club, Mr. Blengdale?"

"No, but I've been along a few times as a guest."

"I see. Whose?"

"Eh?"

"Whose guest?"

"Gil's of course. Gilbert Haggard. I was lunching in the Con Club on Friday and he was there too. Said if I fancied a good laugh to come round to the Calli that night."

"You find these films amusing?"

"Some of them. You sound a bit disapproving, Inspector. I'm not ashamed of me appetites, you know. It's natural for a man to like to look at female flesh, wouldn't you say?"

"It depends what's happening to it," said Pascoe. "When it's being beaten and maltreated—"

"I notice you've seen the picture then," said Blengdale with heavy irony. "Didn't corrupt you, did it? Then why're you so worried about me? It's a laugh, that's all. You can't take that kind of thing seriously."

"Of course not. What happened afterwards, Mr. Bleng-dale?" said Pascoe.

"After the film, you mean? Well, I had a beer in the bar, then Gil said it was a bit crowded there, did I fancy a drop of the real stuff upstairs? I never say no to Gil's cognac. He knows—knew—what he was about in that line. So we sat and had a couple of glasses and a yarn."

"Where?"

"Where? In his study, it was."

"And what did you talk about?"

"This and that," said Blengdale. "Cricket prospects for the summer. He was quite an enthusiast, Gilbert. The state of the nation. Just general stuff like that."

"You didn't talk about the show you had just seen?"

"It might have been mentioned, but I think we'd said most of what there was to say about that downstairs."

"And what time did you leave?"

"About eleven-thirty, I'd say. In fact, I'm pretty sure. I got back here just before midnight, which would be about right for the roads at that time of night. Gwen can confirm that, if you like."

"I see," said Pascoe. "Did he say or do anything to give the impression of expecting company after your departure?"

"No, there was nothing of that," said Blengdale. "It was pretty late and I'd have noticed if he'd said anything like that. He looked like I felt, ready for bed. Is there anything to show he *was* expecting another visitor?"

"I can't say," said Pascoe, thinking of the six weals on Haggard's buttocks.

"Well, there's nowt more I can tell you," said Bleng-

dale, rising. "I'm a busy man and I'm right behind now.
What a bloody day this has been! I'll see you to the door.
Sorry I can't be more help. I'd offer you a drink, but I've
heard that you're a bugger for duty."

I'm getting the push, thought Pascoe as he found himself swiftly transformed to the front door. But he could
think of no way of—or reason for—resisting the process.

But Blengdale wasn't quite finished with him. He
seized his elbow tight and brought his face close to Pascoe's shoulder. "What's going to happen to that dentist?"
he asked.

"I'm sorry?"

"Burkill's my yard foreman. When he took off this
morning, I made it my job to find out why."

"Is he a good worker, Mr. Blengdale?"

"Very fair. A bit bolshie, but show me a workingman
who isn't these days. And he's as tough with the men as he
is with the management."

"Do you know his family?"

"I've met his wife at a works dinner."

"But you don't know Sandra, his daughter?"

"Never laid eyes on her. Why do you ask? Is there any
doubt? The way Burkill talks, it's an open-and-shut case."

"It's being investigated," said Pascoe cautiously. "We've
got to move carefully."

"I suppose so," said Blengdale. "Bloody women can
say owt and get away with it. Look, I'm sorry if I said anything out of place about your missus just now. I'm old-
fashioned, you see. Not used to fighting with women, so I
look around for their menfolk to have a go at. That used to
be the way of it. Gwen, my love, the Inspector's just going."

"Goodbye, Mr. Pascoe," said Gwen Blengdale, who had appeared from the garden bearing a bunch of narcissi. "Would your wife like these, do you think? I'm thinning them out and it's such a shame to waste them."

"That's most kind of you," said Pascoe. "She'll be delighted, I know."

He took the flowers and laid them beside him on the passenger seat of the car.

Blengdale spoke through the window. "You have much to do with Andy Dalziel?"

"Well, yes. He's my boss, in fact," said Pascoe.

"Is he? Well, you've got my sympathy. He's a right hard bastard, that one. Cheerio, Inspector."

"Cheerio," said Pascoe.

"And take it easy down the drive," said Blengdale, adding, as Pascoe wondered how to respond to this solicitude, "That bloody Z-car stuff knocks hell out of the gravel."

Eleven

Dinner went well that night.

He arrived home at six-thirty to smell his favorite roast duck just beginning to spit in the oven and to find between the front door and the bedroom a trail of garments which even a chief constable could have followed without difficulty.

"What," he said to Ellie as they lay on the patchwork counterpane, "would you have done if I'd been late?"

"Eaten cold duck," she answered. "Now tell me, what kind of day have you had?"

"The last fifty minutes have been great."

"A nothing," she said. "An appetizer. A mere prolegomenon. Let's start eating. I mean literally."

"Anything new on the political front?" he inquired as they scraped the green flesh from their avocados.

"We had a meeting this afternoon," said Ellie. "God, that man Blengdale!"

"The fascist pig who feathers his own sty," said Pascoe.

"I couldn't get the words out properly," said Ellie, shamefaced. "Hey, how do you know I said that?"

"We have sources. What brought on that particular bit of abuse?"

"Well, I had a phone call at lunchtime. It was your dentist friend—"

"Shorter?" said Pascoe, amazed.

"No. Thelma Lacewing. Did you know she was related to Blengdale?"

"Yes."

"That's the trouble with being married to a policeman."

"What did she want?"

"Well, first of all she wondered if I'd care to lunch with her one day this week. She thinks I may be interested in WRAG. But then, just before she rang off, she asked me what the college staff thought about the place becoming a country club. I thought she was joking, of course, but no, she insisted, very cool, that that's what she'd heard. Close the college, bring the survivors into town and lease the site and buildings to a private consortium for development into a combined country club and sports complex!"

Pascoe whistled. "Sounds a bit farfetched!" he said.

"That's what I thought till I saw Blengdale's face when I mentioned it," said Ellie grimly. "I've no doubt about it. I've been on to the local papers, the lot. We'll soon ferret out the truth. But you haven't told me how you know what I said to God."

Pascoe hesitated. Usually he was very careful not to discuss his cases too closely with Ellie. It wasn't a matter of trust, merely of professionality. Like a priest or a doctor, he mocked himself. But such olive branches as had been waved in his direction tonight deserved more than self-righteous reticence.

"Typical," said Ellie after he'd finished. "If the bastard was mixed up with Haggard, he's even rottener than I thought. I'm sure Ms. Lacewing would disapprove, but would you like to assert your masculinity and carve the duck. How was she, by the way? As a dentist, I mean?"

She'd done it with cherries, his favorite. Might as well be hung for a duck as a lamb, thought Pascoe.

Ellie listened fascinated. "My God!" she said. "You can't get away from it, can you, Peter? What exactly is the girl alleging?"

"I've no idea. Dalziel was seeing her this afternoon, I think."

"Poor sod," said Ellie.

"The girl? Or Dalziel?" said Pascoe.

"Shorter. Innocent or guilty, the poor sod's in for a rough time. What do you think, Peter?"

"I don't know. I can't really believe it, but I haven't had a chance to talk to him."

"But you were there," said Ellie.

"Jack was being patched up. And when Dalziel arrived he kept us well apart. Also he suggested we should stay well apart."

"Did he?" said Ellie. "Afraid of friendship, is he?"

"He just doesn't want either of us to run the risk of this man Burkill stirring up hints of collusion, that's all. In any case, I'm not sure I am a friend of Shorter's in any real sense."

"You confide your fantasies to him."

"*One* of my fantasies," said Pascoe. "I've never had any of his in return."

"Perhaps you have now," said Ellie.

They ate their duck in silence for a while. The skin cracked between the teeth and was sharply flavored. The rich meat slid and crumbled and dissolved against the tongue.

"What does fat Andy think?" asked Ellie.

"Thumbs down. I think he's building up to claiming foresight. Last week when I told him what Shorter said about that film, his only reaction was that people like dentists and doctors shouldn't react to erotic stimuli. Since then Shorter's been accused of assaulting a minor and his film theory's turned out to be a load of cock. Dalziel reckons he was just trying to pave the way for the revelation he knew must come."

"That's a bit farfetched."

"So I said. Dalziel says that under stress everyone can behave in an extraordinary fashion. The courts seem to support him."

"Still . . . More wine?"

"I'll leave a mouthful to wash down the cheese. There *is* some cheese?"

"Stilton. After my green fig flan."

"Oh Jesus."

The figs were rich and sticky and sweet as decay; the Stilton pungent and creamy.

"Now, a large brandy and fifteen minutes' rest."

"Fifteen minutes? I'll need a day."

He held out for ten.

"Peter," said Ellie sometime between ten P.M. and six A.M.

"Yes?"

"How'd you find out that Shorter's theory was a load of cock?"

"On Friday. I told you."

"We haven't exchanged more than ten polite words since last Thursday, remember?"

"We've exchanged more than that tonight."

"I know it. So, what happened on Friday?"

"I saw the girl," said Pascoe. "The woman in the film. Linda Abbott. Nice woman. Unmarked face. All her own teeth."

"Lucky old thing. You saw the woman who played the kidnapped wife?"

"That's what I said."

"And you just saw one woman?"

"Yes. Why? There only was one."

"Oh Peter," said Ellie, laughing. "God, you men! One tit's just like another!"

"What," said Pascoe, growing more and more awake, "are you talking about?"

"I saw that film on Friday night, remember?" said Ellie. "Believe me, the actress who got banged on the chin and the actress who played the blushing bride at the beginning and end of the film were two completely different people!"

* * *

Dalziel was offensively unimpressed. "Suppose she's right, so what?"

"So I haven't proved that Shorter was wrong."

"So what, again?"

"So there's still a chance that he was right, and if that's so, your notion that he made it all up as part of a subtle ingratiation plan falls a bit flat."

"Why?" said Dalziel, scratching the folds of skin on his neck. "Let's imagine, because it's only public money we're wasting by sitting here imagining things, let's imagine your Ellie is right. Further, let's imagine that Shorter is genuinely convinced something nasty really did happen in that scene. What's it all amount to? When he wanted an excuse to get chatting to you, he didn't have to make anything up, that's all. Except perhaps his deep concern. Am I right?"

Distasteful though it was to have to bow to ratiocinative powers wielded like a shillelagh, Pascoe had to admit he was right.

"Now, listen to this," said Dalziel. "I saw Sandra Burkill yesterday afternoon. She'd already made a statement to a WPC, so she was quite happy to talk. She'd got the difficult bit over, actually giving the details."

"And what were the details?"

"Well, a couple of months ago the girl started a course of treatment. Her teeth were in a bad way and she needed a lot of fillings plus a bit of straightening-out work. She said she didn't mind too much as it got her out of school. First time there, her mother went with her, but after that she went alone, except sometimes she was accompanied by a friend, Marilyn Brewer.

"The assaults started on her third visit. While drilling a tooth, Shorter pressed very close against her and she realized that his penis was erect."

"She said that?" asked Pascoe.

"Of course not. She said she could feel something hard."

"But she didn't know what?"

Dalziel glared at him in exasperation. "Of course she bloody well knew what. She's thirteen, living in the 1970s, where they draw diagrams and show films about it in the junior schools. For God's sake, there was none of that when I was thirteen, but I tell you, the lassies around then would have known what, too!"

"I'm convinced," said Pascoe. "Go on."

Dalziel unfolded the rest of the story succinctly. The girl hadn't been too distressed. Shorter was fairly "dishy" and she'd boasted about it as a conquest to her friend Marilyn. Each successive visit had seen an advancement of the intimacy, and eventually the pretense of the accidental touch had been discarded.

"So the girl is saying she was a willing partner?" said Pascoe.

"At twelve? With a dentist? In law there's no such thing and you bloody know it," answered Dalziel. "Any road, that's not the end of it."

The end of it had been full sexual intercourse, in the surgery, with the girl (according to her version) now feeling too involved and too frightened to resist.

Now Pascoe was incredulous. "In the surgery?" he demanded. "You must be joking. What the hell was Alison—the nurse—doing all this time?"

"According to Sandra, she had been sent off early to lunch so that she could pick up some X-ray prints Shorter said he must have for afternoon surgery."

"And according to Alison?"

"According to Alison, dear Mr. Shorter couldn't possibly do anybody any wrong and at the first hint of close questioning she burst into tears."

"Who was asking the questions?"

"Inspector Trumper. Last night I went round to see Shorter."

"And?"

"He's suffered a relapse since getting home, his wife told me. Their doctor had been and the poor chap was in bed, heavily sedated, unable to talk to anyone."

"I don't blame him. Look, sir, you saw him yesterday after the attack. Can you really imagine Shorter laying the girl in his dentist's chair in the middle of the day, even if the nurse was out of the way? Anybody could walk in— MacCrystal, Ms. Lacewing, the receptionist, even a lost patient!"

"Perhaps. Last of the morning, though. Everyone going off to lunch. MacCrystal's in the Conservative Club bar at twelve sharp most days. It all adds up."

"There's little enough to add," said Pascoe skeptically. "I hate these cases. You get an unsupported allegation and it all comes down to guesswork and prejudice in the end."

"Not quite unsupported," said Dalziel in his diffident tone, which Pascoe knew usually heralded a triumph.

"What?"

"The girl Marilyn. She was Sandra's confidante—is that right? There's no fun in anything for a woman unless she can tell someone else about it. Well, Marilyn's had a blow-by-blow account. Just hearsay, but it is supportive. Also, when I talked with her last night, she said that on one of the early visits she was actually in the surgery when Shorter was working on Sandra and noticed him pressing his crutch up against her. After that, she says, Shorter asked her to stay in the waiting room."

He paused. Pascoe knew he wasn't finished but refused to prompt.

"The quack took a look at Sandra last night. She's not a virgin."

"It can easily happen," said Pascoe. "All kinds of ways. Any doctor'll tell you."

"Mebbe," said Dalziel triumphantly. "But there's not many will say that cycling over cobbles can get you pregnant too!"

He looked at Pascoe challengingly. When there was no reply, he continued. "Her last period should have started a fortnight ago on Monday, that is yesterday. She saw Shorter at the beginning of last week. Tuesday morning I think it was, and told him she was late. He told her not to worry, it often happened. She was to come back this week and tell him how things were. But things didn't work out."

"What happened?"

"Sandra's mum began to get worried. Sandra was an early developer. Her periods have been coming for nearly two years now, regular as clockwork. Mrs. Burkill has the usual job of keeping her daughter's room tidy. She noticed that she wasn't using any towels. Said nowt at first—it's pointless worrying the kid if it was just going to come late. But when it got to nearly a fortnight, she had a chat with her. One thing led to another. Finally it all came out. That was Sunday evening. Mrs. B. had a sleepless night, I imagine, but decided she had to tell Brian in the morning. But she just told him about Shorter interfering with the girl, didn't mention the possibility of her being pregnant. It's just as well. When he heard last night, he nearly blew a gasket. I think he'd have really put the boot into Shorter if he'd known yesterday!

"Any road, there it is, lad. Starts to amount to something, doesn't it?"

"I suppose so. Thanks for putting me in the picture, anyway," said Pascoe, rising and heading for the door.

"A pleasure," said Dalziel. "I know how you'd like to help Shorter. In fact—"

"Yes?"

"There is something, if you've a spare half-hour from this Haggard business."

"Yes?" said Pascoe again, very suspiciously.

"The nurse, Alison. She's not being very cooperative. I think Inspector Trumper was probably the wrong man for the job. He's got a touch like a steam hammer. And as you know her already, and she knows you're by way of being a mate of Shorter's, I wonder whether you could get a statement from her."

"You mean you want me to use my personal connection to get Alison to incriminate her boss?"

Dalziel produced his wire-rimmed reading glasses, polished them with a huge khaki handkerchief, put them on and started reading.

" 'It's quite impossible. Mr. Shorter couldn't have, not

a thing like that, not Mr. Shorter. I won't believe it, she's a liar whatever she says and I know that he wouldn't, not even away from the surgery.' "

He removed the glasses and looked up from the file. "That's the gist of what Trumper got out of her. It seems to coincide pretty well with your opinion, Inspector. That's a fair enough starting point for the accused, isn't it? Interrogator and witness both reckoning he's innocent? Hop to it, lad, and let's not have too many tear stains on the statement. It makes the ink run."

Working with Dalziel made you expert at accepting the inevitable. Occasionally you could grab something useful as you fell over the edge.

"This film business," said Pascoe. "I'd like to check it out again."

Dalziel looked at him thoughtfully. "You've a lot on your plate," he said. "But if you can square it with your conscience that it's tied in with the Calli affair, well, you know I try never to interfere with the man on the job."

"And I'm to be Queen of the May, Mother," said Pascoe. But only after he'd left the building and was on his way to the dentist's.

Even detectives are susceptible to familiar blindness, realized Pascoe now that he was taking a close look at Alison Parfitt. Always before she had been a mere white-coated presence, leading him into the surgery, passing Shorter the bricks and mortar of his trade, always comforting and efficient, but as anonymous as a servant in a big house.

Such anonymity implied a relationship he did not like, on either personal or professional grounds, and he wondered how many more people he had it with.

She was twenty-four years old, unmarried, pretty in a fresh-faced milkmaidish kind of way, and had been working for Shorter for over two years.

They were drinking tea in Shorter's office. With the dentist off work, she had plenty of time to spare.

"Look," said Pascoe. "Would you mind taking that white coat off? I keep on thinking you're about to ask me to spit my tea out."

She laughed and wriggled out of the overall. She had a pleasant rounded figure; as a milk maid she might well have caught the village squire's eye.

"Do you come from these parts?" asked Pascoe.

"Yes. Born and bred. I still live at home with my parents."

"Never fancy a place of your own?"

"You mean marriage?" she asked.

"Not really. I meant a flat. You know, independence, home when you want, do what you want."

"But I do," she said. "I may be conditioned in what I want, but I want it, and generally I do it."

"You sound as if you've been talking to Ms. Lacewing."

"We have chatted a bit," she said. "But I don't need to have all my ideas spoon-fed, Mr. Pascoe."

She spoke firmly rather than acidly, but Pascoe took the hint. She wasn't about to be condescended to. He was glad. He had little stomach for wheedling information out of an emotionally immature girl. The village squire might be in for a surprise.

"I'm sure you don't," he said. "Let's be frank. You made a bit of a fool of yourself when you talked to Inspector Trumper."

"I know I did. It was silly. But it just happened. Everything he said just made me want to cry."

"You're all right now?"

"Oh yes. It was just the shock. A night's rest has put me right."

And you've had a night to think about it, thought Pascoe.

"Let me put things straight to you, Alison," he said. "I'm one of Jack Shorter's patients and also I know him a bit socially. I hope there's nothing in these charges, but I've got to keep an open mind. Now, all you did by your performance yesterday was make it look as though there was something you didn't want to tell us. I dare say that wasn't the case, but that's how it came over. I've been asked to talk to you because you know me. They thought a familiar face might be reassuring. I can see now it wasn't necessary, so if you'd rather talk to someone else, say so. And remember, I might know Jack Shorter, but whatever I find out, good or bad for him, it goes back to the officer in charge."

He looked at her squarely, wishing he could feel as honest as he hoped he looked. Like most so-called free choices, this one contained an offer she could hardly refuse, and he was guiltily conscious that he'd not really risked the horror of explaining to Dalziel that he'd let the girl opt for someone else!

But she was taking a long time to make up her mind.

"All right," she said in the end. "I'll stick with you."

"Good. Now, Alison . . ." He hesitated. "All right if I call you Alison?"

"You always have done. You mean, does it make me feel inferior? No, I don't think so. Would it bother you if I called you Peter?"

Pascoe grinned uncomfortably. "It might do," he said. "I think perhaps—"

"You call me what you like," she said. "And I'll try not to call you anything."

"Fine. To start with, can I just verify when this girl Sandra Burkill had appointments with Mr. Shorter?"

She produced the appointment book and Pascoe made a note of the dates and times.

"Now I see that the first two appointments were on Wednesday afternoon. That's your normal children's afternoon, isn't it? Crazy afternoon."

"Yes," said Alison.

"But after that she started coming in the morning, a variety of mornings. Why was that?"

"Oh, it's not unusual," said Alison. "The children's afternoon is usually concerned with diagnosis and small jobs. And it's always full of hysterics and delays! You never know what's going to happen and in the end the appointment system usually falls to bits. It just becomes a queue. It really *is* crazy! So when Mr. Shorter worked out a long course of treatment for any particular child, he often transferred it out of that afternoon to some other time. Look, there are one or two others I can show you."

She proceeded to indicate three other cases where a

child shifted from Wednesday afternoon to some other time in the week.

Pascoe made careful notes, thinking as he did so that Trumper's questions may have caused hysterics but they hadn't caused amnesia. The girl had done her homework.

"Another thing I notice is that the girl's appointments are invariably the last of the morning. Twelve-fifteen."

"The girl's school is only five minutes away," answered Alison promptly. "That meant she would only miss a few minutes' schooling at the end of the morning."

"Very considerate," observed Pascoe, turning the pages of the appointment book. "He doesn't seem to have been quite so considerate with regard to the others."

"Oh no. You've got it wrong," insisted Alison. "It's not Mr. Shorter's idea. *I* make the appointments, I've done the same with you. You know, gone to the desk and had a look at the book."

"So it was your idea to have her come at the end of the morning?"

"That's right."

Pascoe made a careful note. "But it was Mr. Shorter's idea to transfer her appointments from Wednesday afternoon?"

"Yes."

"Fine. Now, I've never seen Sandra Burkill. What kind of girl is she? Can you remember much about her?"

"Appearance, you mean? Well, she's got long brown hair, hangs all over the place, you know how they wear it these days. Quite tall, a bit podgy, puppy fat, I think. That's about all, really. Curiously, though, I remember her friend much better, even though she only came with her two or three times."

"Oh yes?"

"She was a much more striking girl. She had bright red hair like a freak-out wig, and one of those sharp little faces. A bit common but full of life. She never stopped talking. And her clothes, all the latest gear. Cheap stuff, most of it, but she knew how to wear it. She could have been nineteen rather than thirteen. I reckon *she* knew what it was all about. Now if it had been her—"

"If it had been her accusing Mr. Shorter, you'd have thought there might be something in it?" said Pascoe gently.

Alison put her hand to her mouth in the classic repertory theater gesture of one who has said too much. "No. I didn't mean that! All I meant was I could see her as the type that might make such accusations. Though it does make you wonder . . ."

"Yes?"

"Well, couldn't it be that the other girl, Sandra, is just trying to impress her friend? Girls are like that. And once you start boasting, you can get carried away. I can remember!"

Not only her homework, but she's worked out theories too, thought Pascoe. She's not quite clever or experienced enough to let us think we've dug them up for ourselves, but that apart, she's really doing very well. Now, why? I wonder. Loyalty?

"How did Sandra dress? Very with it, like her friend?"

"Oh no. Much sloppier. T-shirt, jeans, sometimes. Big flares and platform soles, but she didn't have the style."

"So she didn't look the type to turn anybody on."

"No. Honestly, I just couldn't see it. I'm sure it's all just in her mind, put there by her mate."

"Not quite," said Pascoe. "She must have turned somebody on. She's pregnant."

Now Alison's hand flew to her mouth again, but this time the gesture was completely involuntarily. "Oh! And she says . . ."

"She says it's Mr. Shorter's."

The girl reached blindly for her handbag, took out a handkerchief and pressed it to her filling eyes.

The door opened and Ms. Lacewing entered. "What's going on?" she demanded as she took in the scene. "What are you doing to this child?"

Before Pascoe could answer, Alison looked up and shouted angrily, "Oh, go to hell!"

Amazed, Ms. Lacewing looked from the girl to Pascoe, who gave her his best imitation of an Arany shrug. She responded by turning and leaving.

"Child!" said Alison after blowing her nose. "You'd think she was my grandmother!"

"Don't worry," said Pascoe. "Another couple of years, unless she avoids all feminine patterns, she'll be claiming to be your sister. You OK now?"

"Yes. I'm sorry. It was a shock. Tell me, when's Mr. Shorter supposed to have . . . done this?"

"In the surgery, during an appointment."

Alison laughed with relief. "Well, that proves it! Good lord, it would be impossible! I must have noticed something!"

"You were in the surgery all the time?"

"Of course not. But I'm in and out pretty regularly. Honestly, there wouldn't be time."

"Mr. Shorter never got you out of the way?"

"What do you mean?"

"Sent you off on errands, little tasks which would keep you out of the surgery for some time?"

"Never," she affirmed.

"The lunch hour was coming up," Pascoe reminded her. "He never sent you away early?"

"Not that I recall."

"You mean you've always been here till twelve-thirty. You never left for lunch while a patient was still in the surgery? Any patient."

She looked speculatively at him. "Is this a trap, Mr. Pascoe?" she asked. "Last time Mr. Shorter saw you, last Wednesday, wasn't it? he told me to go and get my lunch while you were still here."

"No trap," said Pascoe. "An *aide-mémoire*, that's all. The girl says that on the occasion of the intercourse Mr. Shorter had sent you away very early, asking you to collect some X-ray photographs which he needed. Do you recollect that?"

"I have collected X rays, yes. But I can't remember every occasion."

"Presumably you have to sign for them?"

She nodded.

"Then it will be easy to check," he said.

"You don't sign against a time, just a date," she protested.

"Even so. Is there anything else you'd like to tell me, Alison?"

"I don't think so."

"Good. Well, I've noted down the main points of what you say insofar as they're relevant to the case. Would you mind if we put them together in the form of a statement?"

"I'd have to sign it?"

"Yes."

She shook her head. "No, I don't mind."

"OK. Would you do it now while its all fresh in your mind? And let me see it before you sign it, please. Just a matter of procedure."

"Of course."

"Right," said Pascoe, standing up with the appointment book in his hand. "I'll leave you to it for a few minutes. Just two last things, though. You mentioned traps before. Don't set yourself any. Everything gets checked. Second, it's a statement, not a character testimonial. Emotional declarations of absolute truth can be easily misconstrued. Give me a shout if you want me."

He left and went to the reception counter to talk to the blond receptionist, whose wide blue eyes pleaded with him to gossip. He resisted, just as a few minutes later he resisted the invitation in Ms. Lacewing's expression to consider himself a worm.

"I read in the paper about Dr. Haggard's death," she said abruptly. "Tell me, does that mean *that* place will close down?"

"I've no idea," said Pascoe in surprise. "Possibly."

"Well, there could be some good of it," she said. "Strange what it takes to end what any true civilization would consider an affront to its dignity."

She went back to her surgery and Pascoe returned to

the office, his head full of speculations. "Finished?" he said to Alison.

"Just."

He read what the girl had written. Her handwriting was bold and well formed, only a few words to the line, so that, though short, the statement occupied a side and a half of foolscap.

"I see you repeat that you booked the girl's morning appointments."

"Yes."

"Are you sure of that, Alison."

"Certain."

"I've been talking to the receptionist, Miss White. Normally she'd make the entries in the book wouldn't she?"

"Not if she was busy, answering the phone or something."

"No. True. I showed her the book. She identified her own hand twice. She says the rest of the entries relating to Sandra Burkill's appointments are in Mr. Shorter's writing."

She flushed bright red. "You said you didn't set traps!" she said accusingly.

"I warned *you* not to," said Pascoe gently. "The trap would be really set if I let you sign that and try to support it in court. Let's start again, shall we?"

Twelve

Dalziel was out when Pascoe returned to the office, so he left the nurse's revised statement on the fat man's otherwise perfectly clear desk and went to Sergeant Wield's more modest and more cluttered cubbyhole.

"I'm off down to the Calli. Fancy a walk?"

"Why not?" said Wield. "I've only got five or six years' paperwork here."

Because he was beginning to value the man's judgment and also because he wanted someone to talk at, Pascoe gave him a full account of the latest developments in both cases.

"You'll want another look at that film," said Wield. "If it exists."

The young constable had been removed from duty at the Calli and the door was locked. Sergeant Wield produced a bunch of keys and opened it at the third attempt.

"Anyone here?" called Pascoe.

There was no answer, but Wield went wandering away just to make sure that the place was empty while Pascoe went up to the storeroom where the fire had been.

The walls were still smoke-blackened but the debris had been cleared away. There was no sign of any film, damaged or not.

Wield came into the room. "No Arany," he confirmed. "Only this."

He was holding the gift-wrapped package that Arany's secretary had left on Saturday afternoon. At least it looked like the same package, but now there was no greetings card with it.

"There wasn't a bag of groceries as well? Or some spilled gherkins?" asked Pascoe. Wield didn't bother to answer but just somehow managed to make a minute but significant change in the atmosphere.

"Sorry," said Pascoe. "Let's go and see Arany."

The agency was at the top of a three-story Edwardian building, apparently untouched by human hand since its erection. On their way up the progressively narrower stairs they passed an italic insurance broker, two peeling-gilt solicitors, a copperplate-on-card ship's chandler and a very fine gothic correspondence college. The Arany Agency was a bold roman typeface on a pane of clear glass, through which he could see Arany's secretary typing. Her technique was Lisztlike. It must cost them a fortune in typewriters, thought Pascoe as he pushed open the door.

She looked up, then smiled as she recognized him. Usually it was the other way around, he thought.

"Hello, Doreen," he said. "Mr. Arany in?"

"He's on the phone at the moment," she said, glancing toward a door behind her which presumably led into an inner office. "He shouldn't be long."

Pascoe put the package on top of the typewriter.

"He didn't forget it?" said the girl. "I left him a note in the office too!"

"Must have done, I'm afraid," said Pascoe, adding casually, "How long have you been buying things for Sandra Burkill?" Beside him Wield stiffened.

"Three, four years now. Since I came here. She's done well out of her Uncle Maurice. He thinks a lot of her."

Pascoe thought he detected something in her tone. "More than you do, eh?" he coaxed.

"She's all right. She's reached the sort of surly age. It's just a phase. I remember what I used to be like!"

"I can't imagine it," said Pascoe gallantly.

The inner door opened and Arany emerged. He expressed no surprise when he saw his visitors. "Come in," he said.

Pascoe followed him into the inner office but Wield lagged behind.

"Just thought I'd drop in, Mr. Arany, to see if by any chance you'd remembered anything else. Also you forgot your parcel. I brought it around with me. Sandra must have been disappointed."

He really was a difficult man to get to, thought Pascoe as he regarded the unsurprised and unsurprisable face.

"I'll give it another time," said Arany. "Thank you. And no, I have remembered nothing more. Was there anything else?"

"Just one more thing," said Pascoe. "The damaged film. What became of it?"

"It was useless," said Arany. "I put it in the dustbin."

"Ah yes. And the bins are collected in Wilkinson Square on . . . ?"

"Mondays."

"Of course. Well, I suppose if I wanted to take another look at *Droit de Seigneur* I could get hold of another print from the distributor?"

Arany shook his head. "I was on the phone to them yesterday. Told them what had happened. They weren't pleased. That was their only print of *Droit*."

"Really," said Pascoe. "Isn't that unusual?"

He got the Arany shrug again.

"Perhaps another distributor? Or the makers. Homeric Films, wasn't it? You don't happen to have their number?"

"No," said Arany. "We don't need to contact film companies direct."

"Not even as an agent? Don't ring us and we won't ring you? Well, thanks a lot, Mr. Arany. See you later, perhaps."

When he opened the door to the secretary's office, he was met with a great deal of laughter and the remarkable sight of Doreen perched on Sergeant Wield's knee.

"I told her I used to be a ventriloquist, asked for an audition," said Wield.

"And?"

"I've no dummy, have I? So she sits on my knee in front of the mirror. I pinch her bum. She yells. My mouth doesn't move."

"Jesus wept," said Pascoe. "It's nearly lunchtime. You can buy me a pint for that."

"What about you, sir?" asked Wield.

"Well, he didn't sit on my knee, I'll tell you that! He says the film was ruined. It's been chucked away, what remained of it. Also he reckons it was the only print."

"Ah," said Wield. "Can I get it straight, sir? You've half a mind to think that destroying that film might have had something to do with the Calli break-in. I mean, that was the purpose. Because you'd shown an interest."

"Possibly."

"A bit drastic thought, wasn't it?" said Wield, dubious. "Why smash the place up like that and start a fire? All they had to do was lose it in the post, or let the projector go wrong and chew it up. And why kill Haggard? Just to make it look for real?"

"Yes, yes, all right," said Pascoe testily.

In the Black Bull, he let Wield go to the bar while he went into the telephone booth outside in the passage between the bar and the small dining room.

First of all he got Homeric's number from the directory inquiries, but when he rang it there was no reply. After a moment's thought he dialed again and a moment later was speaking to Ray Crabtree.

"Hello, Peter," said Crabtree. "Don't tell me. You want a transfer."

"It might come to that. No, it's a favor. I've been trying to ring that film company, Homeric, but no joy."

"Probably all out on location. Up on the moors shooting *Wuthering Heights* in the nuddy. How can I help?"

"They made a film I'm interested in. *Droit de Seigneur.*"

"Yes. I remember."

"I'd like to find out how many prints there were, who's got them, and whether they've retained a copy themselves. I'm too busy to make the trip myself and it's probably not all that important anyway. So if you've got a car out their way any time . . ."

"Glad to help. If the office is shut up I'm pretty certain where I can find Penny at opening time tonight, if that's not too late."

"No, that'll be fine."

"Good. Wife all right? Dalziel had his heart attack yet? Well, we've got to take the rough with the smooth. I'll ring you later."

Smiling, Pascoe left the booth and re-entered the bar. As he did, someone came up behind him and grasped his arm.

He turned around and his heart sank. It was Emma Shorter.

"Mr. Pascoe, I must talk to you," she said urgently. Her voice still had that right-to-rule note in it, but other things had changed. She was by no means so cool, nor so contained and perfectly ordered, as last time they had met. Her hair had some loose strands drifting out from the neck and her make-up was sparse and uneven. She wore no gloves.

"Hello, Mrs. Shorter," he said. "Listen, if it's about Jack . . ."

"Of course it's about Jack," she snapped. "I hoped I'd find you here. You're a friend of his, aren't you? Well, tell me what's going on. I've rung and rung the station. I managed to get a few words with that awful fat man who called last night, but he was no help. And when I asked for you, all that I got was you were out. That's no way for a friend to act, Mr. Pascoe."

"I'd no idea you'd phoned, believe me," said Pascoe. "On the other hand, I think it might be a perfectly reasonable way for a friend to act in the circumstances."

"What does that mean?"

"There's nothing I can do, really. And any suggestion that I *was* trying to do anything could just work against Jack."

"Why?" she demanded angrily. "Can't you just tell this slut's family that she'd better pick on someone of her own kind to slander?"

"And stop bothering decent folk? I'm sorry, Mrs. Shorter. The allegation must be investigated, I'm sure you see that. Then it'll be decided whether there's enough supporting evidence to merit a charge. Really, that's all I can tell you."

"Thank you," she said nodding vigorously. "I see how things are."

"I didn't mean that," said Pascoe. "Only—"

"I must go now. I see your friends are arriving."

"How is Jack?" asked Pascoe, but already she was moving off, forcing a passage between his "friends" who were coming from the bar.

"Good day, Mrs. Shorter," cried Dalziel genially. "Hello, Inspector Pascoe, surprise, surprise. The sergeant said you were close behind. Thirsty morning?"

"You fat bastard," said Emma Shorter venomously.

"Cheerio, Mrs. Shorter," said Dalziel, his geniality undiminished. He led the two men to an empty table and sat down. After swallowing a gill of beer and belching contentedly, he sank his teeth into the best half of a pork pie and washed it down with the second gill.

"What's she want?" he asked through the resultant sludge. "Offering you her lily-white body to save her husband's reputation? Don't be tempted. Not if she had tits like the Taj Mahal, she couldn't do it. I guessed she'd be after you when she started on me this morning, so I told the switchboard you were permanently out to her."

"How kind," said Pascoe. "Is there something new?"

"Nothing dramatic. That nurse's statement, I just had a quick glance. Sounds vague with a faint smell of cover-up. How did she strike you?"

"A bit like that," admitted Pascoe. "But it's just loyalty, I reckon."

"Perhaps. You didn't get any hint that she'd been having a whirl on Shorter's high-speed drill too, did you?"

"Christ, what do you think he is? Some kind of satyr?"

"That's one of them hairy buggers that lurk in bushes, isn't it? Like at the Art School. No, I'm not saying he's indiscriminate, but being married to that cactus must leave a lot of water in his well. Do you think the EEC know about these pies?"

He was in high spirits, thought Pascoe, which boded ill for Shorter or anyone else whose case he'd been investigating that morning.

"Even if he has been at Alison, what's it signify?" asked Pascoe.

"The more some men get, the more they want. It's well known," said Dalziel. "The jury would lap it up. Makes the women feel threatened, the men feel proud."

"So you think there's definitely a case?"

"Well, fair do's. I haven't seen Shorter yet. He may come up with some startling new evidence like he was castrated when he got engaged to Emma. I'm going round there this afternoon. Want to come?"

"I thought you'd warned me off."

"Peter, lad, I don't think it matters a toss now. It's my bet it'll go to court. It could be better for him if it did. Burkill might go berserk else."

Pascoe shook his head. "I'll see him sometime then. But by myself. Maybe I'll drop in this evening."

"You haven't forgotten we're seeing Johnny Hope, sir?" said Wield.

"No. But there'd be time."

"Hope?" said Dalziel. "The club man?"

"Yes, sir. I thought he might be able to give us something on Haggard and Arany."

"Oh, you're still chasing that hare, are you?" said Dalziel. "Well, you may be right. Interesting fellow, that Arany. Do you reckon he thinks in English or Hungarian? Never mind. Let's have another pint and you can tell me everything you've been up to and why none of it's been any fucking use so far! Barman!"

Pascoe hated beery lunchtimes. He hated the feeling of vague benevolence with which he returned to his office, he hated the visits to the loo, and he hated the mid-afternoon drowsiness with its sour aftermath.

Above all he hated the thought that he might come to be as unaffected by them as Dalziel, who for the moment seemed to be taking a breather from his diet.

He excused himself after the third pint and set off at a brisk walk heading away from the station. His intention was to exercise the beer out of his system, but he was distressed to find himself beginning to puff slightly after only a couple of minutes. It was time to dig out his old track suit and amuse Ellie by taking some regular exercise. He recalled how a couple of years ago he'd been entertained by Dalziel's commencement of a course of Canadian Air Force exercises. The fat man had given up at the bottom level of the first chart, remarking that if God had wanted Canadians to fly, he'd have fitted rockets to Rose Marie's arse. Perhaps he still had the book.

Suddenly Pascoe saw his future ahead as clearly as the pavement along which he was walking. A steady rise in the police force till he reached his level of incompetence. Investigation after investigation, with more failures than successes unless he managed miraculously to beat the statistics. Streets like these in towns like this. Intermittent worries about his physical condition, but a gradual acceptance of decline. Intermittent worries about his intellectual and spiritual condition . . .

He almost bumped into someone and they did a little mirror dance in their efforts to pass each other. "Sorry," said Pascoe.

She was a girl of twenty, probably heading back to work. She smiled widely at him. She had a round, pretty face.

A steel-clad fist would drive bone and teeth through the ruin of that soft-fleshed cheek.

There was an equation here somewhere.

But three-pint solutions were just the froth on barroom philosophy. What he needed now was a pee and a coffee and a flash of creative intuition. He had the first two, rang Ellie to announce he would not be home for dinner, and was still awaiting the third when at half past five after an afternoon of solid paperwork he closed his eyes for a well-earned forty winks and dreamt most sentimentally of his wedding day.

Thirteen

The bells that awoke him were not the church bells of his dream but the more strident peals of the telephone.

"Hello, hello," he croaked, half asleep.

It was Ray Crabtree with a background of Muzak. "Peter? You sound half doped! Well, at least you're not one of those cops who head for lounge bars in posh hotels on the stroke of opening time."

"There's a lot of them about," said Pascoe.

"Indeed. Well, duty's dragged me here, of course. Penny Latimer and some of her mates are here. I had a word. I was right, they've been out on the job—sorry, on location—all day."

"You asked about the film?"

"I did. They looked at each other a bit blankly. No one seemed to know if there was another print of *Droit de Seigneur*, but Penny says she'll check in the morning."

"Who else is with her?"

"Gerry Toms, for one. He got back at the weekend."

Pascoe thought hard. This still felt and smelled like a red herring. He had neither the time nor perhaps the right to go shooting off at a tangent when there was so much else to do. It was arrogant, self-indulgent, all caused by an undigested image irritating the lining of his imagination.

But perhaps it was its very indigestibility which made it so important. A policeman must treasure and preserve what is most sensitive and vulnerable in him against the day when someone tries to find his price.

"Ray," he said, "I'd like to talk with her again."

"Oh. Shall I bring her to the phone?"

"No. I mean personally. Her and Toms. Could you ask if they'll be available first thing in the morning."

"OK," said Crabtree. The Muzak came through louder as he left the phone dangling, then faded again when he returned.

"She says she'd love to see you any time. Only thing is, they'll be filming again tomorrow—and they start bright and early. She says to remind you she invited you to spend a working day with them, something about it doing you good."

"I remember," said Pascoe. "Where will they be?"

"You're in luck there. It's not *Wuthering Heights* they're doing after all, so you won't have to go to Haworth. No, they're using an old mansion the other side of Wetherby. So that'll cut a few miles off your driving. Here's the address. Hay Hall, near Scrope village. Got it? Right. Enjoy yourself, Peter. And keep off that producer's couch!"

"You too," said Pascoe. "You too."

* * *

After egg and chips in the canteen, he set out for the Shorter household. He felt more uncertain now than he had previously, recognizing that his visit was more an act of defiance than an act of friendship. But there was the element of loyalty in it, he reassured himself. And also he felt genuinely uneasy about the way Dalziel seemed to have made up his mind about the case.

The Shorters lived on Acornboar Mount. The houses there were big enough and desirable enough to have earned the area the envious sobriquet of "Debtor's Retreat," and an extra element of poshness was implicit in the "Private Road" sign which marked the beginning of the Mount.

Pascoe parked his car by it and proceeded on foot, not out of any sense of what was socially fitting but because he knew that like most private roads, Acornboar Mount had more craters in it than the far side of the moon. Someone else seemed to have had the same idea, for there was a large motorbike parked in the lee of the thick blackthorn hedge which shut out the proles from the lush greensward of number one.

Shorter lived at twenty-seven. Pascoe enjoyed the short walk in the growing dusk with the smells of spring staining the air.

If I'd been a dentist, I could have lived up here too, he thought. Days spent peering into other people's mouths. How vile a thing was human interdependence! No way for a constabulary sociologist to be thinking. No, he should be contemplating the degree of conscious elitism inherent in building houses like these on a hill like this—or wondering what that shiny fellow there was up to.

The shiny fellow in question he had glimpsed momentarily through a gap in a beech hedge moving with furtive speed from a holly bush to a magnolia tree. The gap may have been caused by the recent passage of a body. The shininess was certainly caused by the last glimmers of daylight sliding off the man's polished black tunic.

Pascoe remembered the motorcycle.

He also saw as he reached the gate of the house that his fit of abstraction had brought him unawares to number twenty-seven.

The shiny man was on the move again and now Pascoe realized that his erratic motions had a purpose other than merely making the best use of cover.

He was carrying two small cylinders, aerosol cans of some kind, Pascoe guessed, for from the one in his left hand he was directing a fine spray onto the lawn.

Whatever it was, Pascoe did not care to risk getting a faceful of it. Carefully he slipped off his shoes, removed the laces and tied them together. Next he returned along the pavement to the gap in the hedge and fastened the length of lace from one side to the other at just below knee height.

Finally he returned to the gate, stole through it bent double, tiptoed up the drive till he was behind a hydrangea bush directly opposite the intruder, and suddenly leapt three feet into the air, flinging his arms wide and screaming, "You're under arrest!"

It was nice to have got it out of his system. The man in the leather jerkin was impressed too.

With a startled yelp he turned and fled. Pascoe followed at his leisure till the man hit the gap in the hedge at speed. Then as his quarry went sprawling forward and the aerosol cans bounced clangingly on the pavement, Pascoe accelerated into the kill. But his ingenuity proved his downfall and the laces which had brought the pursued to earth, now by their absence upended the pursuer. One of his shoes slipped flaccidly from his foot and his first stride onto the herbaceous border drove what felt like a six-inch nail through his nylon sock.

"What the hell's going on?" demanded Shorter, not sounding much like a man recently prostrated by physical assault and nervous shock.

With a groan Pascoe pushed himself upright. He had discovered that the six-inch nail was in fact a very small thorn from a recently pruned rosebush, so instead of proudly displaying the wound he hastily pulled on his shoe to cover it.

Distantly he could hear the fugitive's fast-receding footsteps. Pascoe knew his limitations. The race was to the swift and at the moment that didn't include him.

Briefly he explained what had happened and Shorter went out and collected the cans while Pascoe replaced his shoelaces.

"John! John! What's going on?" called a panicky female voice from the open front door.

"Nothing, dear. It's all right. Better come up to the house," invited Shorter.

In the light of the hall, the impression of their voices was confirmed—Shorter looking fit and (adhesive tape apart) well, his wife pale and strained.

Pascoe explained again what had taken place and

Shorter banged the cans down on the telephone table. One was weed killer, the other red paint.

"The bastard!" he said.

"I don't think he had time to use the paint, but I'm afraid you might have something nasty written on the lawn in a couple of days," said Pascoe.

"The lousy bastard. And you've let him get away!"

There's something wrong with this picture, thought Pascoe as he met Shorter's accusing glare.

"Only temporarily," he said. "I saw his bike and I reckon I can remember most of the number. We'll have him in half an hour."

He picked up the phone, but Shorter's hand went over the dial. "No," he said.

"What?"

"I'd rather you didn't."

"Why on earth not?"

"It's obviously linked with this other business," said Shorter. "You catch him, he'll be charged and up in front of the magistrate in a couple of days. I don't want that. I'm going to beat this thing, Peter, but it may take a bit longer than that, and I don't want some stupid moron shooting his mouth off in court."

"A minute ago you were cursing me for letting him get away," observed Pascoe.

"Yes, I was. I'm sorry. It was a stroke of luck I see now. OK? You'll forget it?"

"No," said Pascoe. "I won't forget it. But I'll postpone action for a while."

"Thanks," said Shorter. "Emma, give Peter a drink,

will you? I'll just see if I can dilute that bloody stuff with the hose pipe."

"You'll probably just spread it," warned Pascoe.

"At least I'll blur the letters a bit," said Shorter as he went out.

"He seems to be in reasonable spirits now," said Pascoe, following the woman into the lounge. It was a cold white clinical room that made Shorter's surgery seem the epitome of Edwardian fussiness by contrast. He settled gingerly into an aluminum cage dangling from the ceiling and Emma Shorter poured him a Scotch from a pyramidal decanter into a hexagonal glass.

"He's been better since he talked to his solicitor this morning," she said, adding as she gave him his drink, "Inspector—may I call you Peter?—Peter, I'm sorry about the pub at lunchtime. I was overwrought."

She remained close to him, staring fixedly into his face. She didn't exactly seem underwrought now, he thought. The silence finally became too intense for him.

"Mrs. Shorter," he said.

"Please call me Emma. I don't feel up to formalities at the moment. I'm so grateful to you for coming."

She gave him a grateful smile and he disliked himself for seeking calculation in it. But there was no denying the reality of the strain she must be under.

"I can only stay a couple of minutes," said Pascoe. "I just wanted to say hello. I was a bit worried, you know."

And not without cause, he thought. Suddenly he saw himself in the witness box being led on to make broader and broader claims about Shorter's probity and basic decency, while Dalziel glowered at him from behind the prosecutor.

"We have a good life together, you know," said the woman, turning away abruptly as if he'd somehow disappointed her.

"Yes, yes, I'm sure you do," agreed Pascoe, looking around the room, which, notwithstanding its lack of appeal, had obviously cost a few gold fillings.

"No. I don't just mean money," she said acidly. "I mean every way. Physically we have a good life."

Pascoe sipped his whisky. He lacked Dalziel's discriminatory nose, but it tasted expensive. "Yes," he said, seeing that a response was expected and thinking a bare affirmative, ludicrous though it might be, was the least he could offer.

"There would be no need for John to . . . I'd say so in court if I had to." She spoke defiantly.

"Good, good," said Pascoe. "Let's hope it doesn't come to that."

He observed Emma over his glass and wondered cynically if their solicitor had planted these seeds. Dalziel had met her last night and his first impression had been like Pascoe's—a cold, self-contained woman. By lunchtime today she had begun to crack, and now here she was in the evening offering to reveal details of her sex life in her husband's defense.

Shorter re-entered. "I've left the sprinkler on," he said. "It might do some good. Let's stiffen that for you, Peter. What's new from the Inquisition?"

"Just a social call, Jack," said Pascoe evenly.

"Your man Dalziel was around again this afternoon," said Shorter. "I saw him this time. Not a social call."

"I didn't know," lied Pascoe. "I mean, I knew someone would be around to talk to you, but I didn't know Mr. Dalziel had been again."

"Oh, I thought you might have cooked something up over your lunchtime beer," said Shorter.

So Emma had told him about her approach earlier that day. Or perhaps it had all been done by collusion. There were situations where it became important to react as normal ordinary people would react—or rather, would *expect* you to react.

Whatever the truth, it didn't make Shorter any more or less suspect.

"There are other crimes to investigate, Jack," said Pascoe.

"No doubt. Glad you could drag yourself away."

"John!" protested his wife. "We're very grateful to you for coming, Inspector . . . Peter. We need friends at a time like this."

"Yes," said Pascoe, using the noncommittal affirmative again. "How've things been today? No other trouble?"

"Other?" said Shorter.

"I'd call that mess on your lawn trouble," said Pascoe. "You haven't had any phone calls? Either nasty or the press?"

"Same thing," said Shorter.

"Not so," said Pascoe. "If Burkill's been on to the papers, they'll just be doing some preliminary sniffing. You can't blame them, but they won't—*daren't*—print mere speculation. I'd be friendly, but say as little as you can, and tell your solicitor. He'll know how to make sure they keep the top screwed on if it's necessary. As for the other kind of approach, well, you've found out already how this kind of case soon works up a fine head of indignation."

"Are you trying to frighten us?" said Shorter.

"Somebody else might, that's all I'm saying. A phone call, a letter. It's best to be prepared."

"People are vile!" exclaimed Emma Shorter.

"But not all the time, fortunately," said Pascoe.

He fell silent now and sipped his drink. He would have liked to be talking to Shorter alone, but was uncertain how to suggest it.

Shorter, however, seemed to have reached the same conclusion. "Would you make us a pot of coffee, love?" he suggested. "I don't want this business to drive me too deep into drink."

She rose and left instantly. Whatever their usual relationship, this explosion in their lives had temporarily at least turned them into a team.

"Are you going back to work?" asked Pascoe.

"Do you think I should?"

"If you can manage it."

"My solicitor said the same," said Shorter. "I can't dispute two expert opinions. I thought I'd go in tomorrow." He added, with a bitter laugh, "I'll keep Alison chained to my drill."

"Do that. I spoke to her this morning."

"She told me. On the phone. She rang specially."

"She's a loyal girl," said Pascoe.

Shorter who all this time had been standing restlessly by the fireplace now sat down in the seat vacated by his wife and peered closely into Pascoe's face. "It's a funny side effect," he said, "but since this started, I keep reading significance and double meanings into everything anyone says."

"That's called paranoia," said Pascoe, "and is not recommended. I said Alison was loyal. That's what I meant. Simple statement."

" 'My country right or wrong,' that's loyal," said Shorter, smiling. "Are you suggesting Alison's loyal like that?"

He looked and sounded perfectly relaxed and Pascoe felt an urge to give him a jolt.

"I certainly think she fancies you," he said. "Has it gone further than that?"

Shorter ran his fingers through his thick black hair and looked boyishly embarrassed. "A bit of tight hugging at Christmas, birthdays and public holidays, but I haven't been to bed with her, no. I think she's ripe for it, but I don't want to complicate my life. Or hers, for that matter."

"Big of you," said Pascoe. "What did you tell Mr. Dalziel?"

"Aren't copies of statements pinned on the canteen wall?" asked Shorter. "I told him I'd been treating Sandra Burkill for several weeks; to the best of my knowledge I'd never been alone with her for any period longer than two minutes; at no time did I touch her in any way other than that required by the performance of my profession; at no time did she touch any part of me with her hands, nor did I invite her to do so; at no time did I have intercourse with her. That's about it."

"Succinctly put," said Pascoe. "Can you think of any reason why this girl might want to get at you, Jack?"

"Dalziel asked me that too. I suggested that he didn't

have to look far to discover that young girls in a professional relationship with older men—pupils and patients in particular—were very prone to sexual fantasizing. Not too infrequently this overflowed into reality in the form of either a declaration or an accusation." He sounded as if he were quoting a *Reader's Digest* article.

"The girl is *pregnant*," said Pascoe. "Some overflow!"

"Dalziel made just the same point. It doesn't negate my point. Someone's put her up the stick. She points the finger at me. It fits in with her adolescent sex fantasies and it takes some of the pressure off her."

"I don't quite see what you mean," said Pascoe.

"Well, for God's sake, what's your traditional working-class moron's attitude to the news that his daughter's got one in the oven? He cuffs her around the ear and chucks her out into the street! But not in this case. She gets the whole class thing going for her. Wealthy, educated professional man takes advantage of naïve innocent girl. So in this case, instead of thumping his daughter, Burkill comes around and starts thumping me!"

Emma Shorter came in with a tray. Pascoe stood up. "I'm sorry," he said. "It's very good of you, but I really can't stay."

"Other crimes, Peter?" said Shorter.

"That's it."

"Well, thanks for coming. I won't forget it."

"I'll see Peter out," said his wife putting the tray down on a stainless steel table.

Pascoe left the room thinking that he too was now suffering from a double-entendre neurosis. "I won't forget it." What did that mean?

Emma put her hand on his arm at the front door. "We really *are* grateful," she said.

"That's all right," said Pascoe, disengaging himself from her grip.

"What do you think now? After talking to John, I mean." She looked at him appealingly, lips apart, small even teeth glistening damply, as white and as perfect as a dentist's wife's teeth ought to be.

Was there an invitation there? wondered Pascoe. Or had he just been watching too many toothpaste ads?

"Don't worry too much," he said. "Things will take their course. I'm sure it'll be OK."

He walked swiftly down the tarmacked drive, the words he had wanted to say so loud in his mind that he wasn't absolutely sure that he hadn't in fact said them.

"After talking to him, I think he's probably innocent," he had wanted to say. "But, after talking to him, I like him a bloody sight less than I thought I did."

On the other hand, he found he liked Emma Shorter a little more. Loyalty is the better part of love. He wondered if *her* loyalty was the "my country right or wrong" type.

Fourteen

They caught up with Johnny Hope at the Branderdyke Variety and Social Club. This was a bit larger than most of the local clubs and somewhat different in character. It had a real stage with a proscenium arch, and though in origin it was, like the rest, a meeting and drinking place for locals, it had taken a larger step than most toward the status and dimensions of Wakefield or Batley.

Top of the bill that night was a singer who was either on his way up to, or down from, the Top Thirty. But it was in the communal changing room shared by the lesser artistes that they found Johnny Hope.

He was talking to a young sullen-faced girl, so slim and slight that it was difficult to gauge her age. She wasn't answering, however. Every time Hope asked a question, a suspicious-eyed matron with a mouth like a saber cut replied, draping one arm protectively over the girl, who was wearing a cream and lavender Bo-Peep costume.

"How old are you, Estelle?" Hope asked as if sensing Pascoe's problem.

"Seventeen," said the matron.

"When did you first get interested in the trampoline, Estelle?" asked Hope.

"She saw Olga Korbutt on the telly at the Olympics in 1972 and she thought she'd like to start doing the gymnastics," said the matron. "One thing led to another."

"One more thing," said Hope, but he was interrupted by the entry of an elderly man eating a frankfurter with onions.

"Your girl's got two minutes, missus," he said splodgily.

"Come on, luv," said the matron. She led her daughter out, glaring ferociously at Pascoe as if he had indecent thoughts written in a balloon above his head.

"Isn't she," inquired Pascoe, "a trifle overdressed for trampolining?"

"Johnny," said Wield.

"Hello, Edgar!" said Hope.

Edgar, thought Pascoe.

"This is my inspector, Peter Pascoe."

"Glad to meet you, Peter," said Hope, shaking his hand vigorously. "Any mate of Edgar's a mate of mine."

Now the women had disappeared, Pascoe took a closer look at the man. He was small, ruddy-faced, his bright blue eyes ringed with crow's-feet from (perhaps) too much time in too many dimly lit rooms, his cheeks crazed with broken blood vessels from the same cause. He was about

fifty, wore a bright green and yellow checked jacket, and
gave off what seemed a totally spontaneous affability.

"We wanted to chat about Maurice Arany," said Wield.

"Maurice, eh? Well, not now, not now. I missed Estelle
last night, got mixed up in a barney at the Turtle. Can't afford that again. Come on, we'll just get a pint afore she
starts."

They did but only because Hope's waved hand won
them instant attention at the crowded bar at the back of
the hall.

On stage was a trampoline. Music started, loud enough
and poured from amplifiers enough to drown the chatter
and clinking and other noises attendant on the drinking of
pints and devouring of scampi and chips.

It was a nice bouncy tune, and when Estelle strolled on
and clambered onto the trampoline, Pascoe settled back
for a pleasant athletic balletic routine, thinking how easily
pleased these Yorkshiremen were. The girl looked quite
good, though her full skirt and frilly blouse obviously
hampered her.

"I wonder," said Pascoe, then said no more.

The girl was taking them off. To cries of encouragement which penetrated even the ten-decibel music, she
jumped right out of her skirt, shed her blouse sleeves like
duck down, took four somersaults to get out of her lacy
stockings, and with a mid-air spin twisted out of what was
left of her blouse. Now in panties and bra, she did a series
of maneuvers which to Pascoe's untutored eye looked first
class. Higher and higher she leapt and it was hard to spot
the moment when she took off her bra.

She was so slender that as a conventional stripper she would probably have been mocked off the stage, but her grace and strength of movement filled the act with erotic promise.

"You don't get this in the Olympics," bellowed Hope in his ear.

"No," agreed Pascoe. One thing had certainly led to another.

But how was she going to get off? he wondered. Movement was of the essence. Once let her stand still and she would be but a seventeen-year-old looking like twelve.

The answer was simple. The highest bounce yet; she reached up her arms, caught at a bar or rope behind the drop curtain and swung her legs up and out of sight. A moment later a pair of panties fluttered gently down to land on the trampoline.

When she appeared to take her bow she wore an old woolen dressing gown and it was a measure of her act's success that even the loudest of club wits were applauding too hard to invite her to take it off.

Pascoe felt ashamed when he realized he'd clapped till his hands were sore. Ms. Lacewing would elevate him several places on her death list if she could see him now, which, thank God, was not likely.

"Good evening, Inspector," said Ms. Lacewing.

It was she, looking ravishing in a long white gown. Her appearance had been changed by the wearing of a Grecian-style hairpiece pulled around over her bare left shoulder, but he would have recognized those sharp little teeth anywhere.

"Don't look so amazed," she said. "I'm on a reconnaissance tonight. You've got to spy out the land before you attack, haven't you? Policemen know that, surely?"

Pascoe realized she was rather tipsy. "Drunk" seemed too coarse a word.

"Are you by yourself?" he asked.

"What do you think I am?" she asked in mock indignation. "Uncle Godfrey! Come here!"

Pascoe turned. Sure enough, it was Blengdale who approached, leaving behind a bunch of smiling cronies.

"He doesn't like me calling him Uncle," said Ms. Lacewing. "But Gwen is Mummy's sister, so you really are my uncle, aren't you, Uncle? Though," she added, stretching up to whisper none too quietly in Pascoe's ear, "it doesn't stop him wanting to screw me."

"Ha, ha," said Pascoe. "Nice to see you again, Mr. Blengdale."

"You here on business or pleasure, Pascoe?" said Blengdale.

"Bit of both," said Pascoe vaguely.

Blengdale nodded as though he knew what that meant.

"Uncle Godfrey, I think our steaks have arrived," said Ms. Lacewing. "Shall I help you back to the table, Uncle?"

For a moment Pascoe felt sympathy for Blengdale. Then the girl turned to him and he decided to reserve all his sympathy for his own defense.

"You look as if you might be quite a ram, Inspector," she said. "I must ask your wife when I meet her. She sounds as if she might be sympathetic to my plans."

"What are your plans?" he asked.

"See you in court," she giggled. "Perhaps they'll put me up on the same day as Jack Shorter."

Pascoe turned away to meet another pint being thrust his way by Wield.

"Drink up," said the sergeant. "Then we're off to the Westgate Social. There's a singer there that Johnny wants to catch. I said we'd go in his car and make our own way back here later."

The night was slipping out of his control, thought Pascoe a couple of minutes later as he and Wield clung together in the back of an old Morris Minor which smelled as if it had lately been used for transporting sheep. The passenger seat had been removed entirely and replaced by a crate of brown ale, and Hope's hand, through instinct or inaccuracy, frequently rattled among the bottles as he groped for the gear lever.

"Now, about Maurice Arany," yelled Wield.

"Well, I don't know," replied Hope dubiously.

"It'll be all right, Johnny," said Wield.

Pascoe had a sense of a bargain being struck, or a promise made.

"What do you want to know?" asked Hope.

"Nothing much," said Wield. "Just anything you wouldn't expect us to find out any other way."

This seemed a pretty broad demand, thought Pascoe modestly, and when Hope relied, "He's a Hungarian," he thought at first he was taking the piss.

Wield seemed prepared to accept this as a serious contribution, however. "Yes?" he urged.

"And there was some bother there in 1956," Hope went on slowly as though divulging state secrets.

"So there was," said Pascoe.

Hope heaved a sigh, which might have been relief at this acceptance of his assertion, or exasperation that he had to say any more.

"This fellow Haggard, now, that got killed, he was something or other in the British Embassy in Vienna. That's in Austria."

Suddenly Pascoe was no longer amused by this parade of the obvious. "Hang on," he said. "You're not saying that—"

"I'm saying nothing," said Hope heavily. "I'm just saying what I've heard others say. Arany either knew or knew of Haggard before he came here."

"But he'd just be a boy in 1956," said Wield.

"Quite fond of boys, so they say," said Hope. "Me, I hate owt like that. Anything a bit perverted, I won't touch. You'll never see me mention a drag act in my column, Pete. Edgar'll back me up there."

Pascoe was now so interested that he was able to forget the erratic progress of the Morris, exacerbated by Hope's habit of turning around to face his auditors every time he spoke.

"So the theory is that Arany had got something on Haggard?" he said.

"It's a strange mix else," said Hope. "I mean, it stands out a mile if you look at the facts. You don't have to be a detective!"

"You do if you want to be sure," said Pascoe reprovingly.

What after all did they have? Arany's family come out of Hungary in 1956 and are transported, very probably via Vienna, to England. Haggard is in Vienna as a British

Embassy official in 1956. The following year he leaves the service, possibly under a cloud, and comes home with a bit of money to invest. The inference in the Rugby Club think tank was that the cloud was sexual, but Rugby Club philosophers see everything in physical terms. Suppose there'd been a bit of graft, queue jumping, buy yourself a trip to sunny Britain? Arany, or his family, is involved. In 1962, Haggard's northward progress brings him to Yorkshire and their paths cross again. But when?

"When did they start to associate, Johnny?" he asked.

"Six, seven years ago. I don't know. One or two reckons. Haggard was a sleeping partner in Maurice's agency. You know, put the money up. It'd take a bit of financing and one thing's for sure, he didn't make it doing his turn round the clubs."

Johnny Hope laughed so violently at the thought that the car came near to making a dramatic entry through the side wall of the Westgate Social Club. When it finally came to rest mostly inside the car park and with hardly more than two wheels overspilling onto the pavement, a fast-approaching constable sheered off in some confusion as Wield and Pascoe staggered gratefully into the cold night air.

They were inside and drinking another pint before Pascoe had time to think better of it. An acned youth was just finishing a spirited version of "Young at Heart" which a benevolently drunk Sinatra might have accepted as a tribute. Johnny Hope applauded with more enthusiasm than the rest of the fairly sparse audience put together.

"He's the wife's cousin's lad," he explained.

"Does your wife ever come with you?" asked Pascoe.

"No. She can't stand the clubs. Doesn't drink either. She's not religious, mind, just prefers the telly and a cup of tea. But she likes the family to stick together. Hello, Bri! Not a bad turn, young Sammy, is he?"

"He'll get paid," said Brian Burkill ungraciously. "Friends of yours, Johnny?" He looked without much favor on Pascoe and Wield.

"Evening, Bri," said the sergeant. "Don't crack your face, will you? You know Mr. Pascoe."

"I know him."

"Evening, Mr. Burkill," said Pascoe. "You haven't got a motorbike by any chance?"

"No. Why?"

"No reason. What time does your show start?"

"Eight o'clock, after the bingo."

"Who runs that?"

"Whoever's handy."

"And tonight?"

"I did the calling tonight. What's up, Inspector? Someone robbed a train?"

"I'm just interested in how these places run, that's all."

"Ah. Slumming, is it?" said Burkill.

Pascoe ignored him, though he recognized a trace of truth in the sneer. Like all detectives he had a pool of more or less useful informants, but the small-club circuit was very much the prerogative of Dalziel himself, and, of course, the indispensable Wield. "You're a saloon bar man," Dalziel had told him early in their association. "It's them trendy shirts and the way you turn your head away when you pick your nose. Stick to your last, lad. The low life's not for you."

It had been a joke, another Dalziel story to tell old friends, but Pascoe had since realized what he recognized once more now as he looked around this smoke-filled room with its gaudy vinyl wallpaper, its formica tables and stackable chairs, its shouted conversations and screeched amusement, its pints of bitter and port and lemons—that some catch of self-awareness in him could never be released sufficiently to let him plunge without restraint into these less than Byzantine pleasures. It wasn't just the natural watchfulness which becomes second nature to most detectives. It was a need to assess before experiencing. It was a distrust of the commonality of pleasure. It was a sense of the cry of bewilderment in human laughter. Above all, it was a longing for joy and a fear of being duped and debased by some shoddy substitute.

Such were Pascoe's extrapolations in his more self-analytical moments. He sometimes thought he was going quietly mad.

On the other hand, he had been totally immersed in the delight offered him by Estelle, the teenage trampolinist. Perhaps there would be something else tonight which would engage his whole attention, though the standard of the group presently offering harmonic near misses in a nasal falsetto did not bode well. The audience seemed indifferent, too, drinking and talking as though they weren't being told by four epicene young men that angel face with wings of lace had taken off to another place. At a table quite close Pascoe recognized the Heppelwhites, Burkill's associates in the great assault. With them was a portly woman, in cast of feature not dissimilar from Estelle's mother. Presumably this was Mrs. Heppelwhite joining

her men for a jolly family outing. Clint caught his eye and
nudged his father, who looked up and then looked quickly
away. The youth picked up his pint and took a long draft.
There was a fresh white bandage around his palm.

"Back in a minute," said Pascoe to Wield. "An old
friend. Look, before William Hickey here gets totally in-
sensible, see if he can give us anything more. Ask him
about Haggard in particular."

As he approached the Heppelwhites' table, the older
man developed an intense interest in the group, while his
son spoke animatedly to his mother.

"Evening, Mr. Heppelwhite, Clint," said Pascoe. "Enjoying the show."

"We were," said Charlie.

"Shut up," said the woman. "Our Colin says you're a
copper, mister. Well, sit down then before you have the
whole room looking."

Pascoe sat.

"I suppose it's about what these two silly buggers got
up to with that Brian Burkill? He's a menace, that one. It's
always been Brian-this, Brian-that. You'd think he'd built
this place brick by brick with no help! Concert secretary,
that's what he is, and bedlam like this, that's what we've
got to suffer. I've got a cat sounds better on the prowl!"

"Oh, Mother," protested Charlie.

"Shut up," she said. "They're easy led, these two, Mister Whatever-your-name-is. I wouldn't get to see their
wage packets if Bri Burkill wanted first dip."

"That's daft talk, Betsy, love," said Charlie.

"I thought I told you to shut up. And my glass is empty.
I'll have a lager and lime this time. And don't forget to

bring one for the sergeant. Keep in with the fuzz, my dad taught me."

"I'm an inspector," corrected Pascoe.

"You're still only getting the one," said Betsy Heppelwhite. Pascoe found himself warming to this formidable lady.

He waited till her husband had reluctantly gathered their glasses together and set off to the bar, then asked, "You agree that it was a daft thing to do, then?"

"You've enough to do to fight your own battles, mister," she said. "That Brian Burkill always goes on like Cassius Clay, he's big enough to fight his own fights. Always has been."

"You've known him a long time?"

"Longer than I care to remember. I was at school with Deirdre, that's Mrs. Burkill. A nice lass, but soft, always soft. Well, she paid for it."

"What do you mean?"

"Him, that's what I mean. They've been married best part of twenty years and I doubt if he's spent more than two evenings in that house."

"Mam, you shouldn't be talking like this," said Clint suddenly.

"Don't you tell me how I should or shouldn't talk or I'll take the back of my hand to you, big as you are!" snapped his mother. "I'm not saying owt I haven't said a thousand times before."

"That's the trouble," muttered Clint almost inaudibly, then gave a sharp cry of pain, from which Pascoe surmised that Mrs. Heppelwhite had substituted the point of her shoe for the back of her hand. Angrily the boy stood up, shoving his chair back into a neighboring table, and shambled out of the room.

His mother watched him go indifferently. "I've told him, while he lives in my house, he behaves like I want him. He's got the choice."

"He seems to have hurt his hand," said Pascoe.

"Aye. Came off his bike tonight. That's another thing I don't like, that bike. He'll kill himself one of these days. I don't know what these lads are coming to these days. It's the police I blame."

With difficulty Pascoe resisted the lure of this fascinating by-road and brought her back to the main track. "Burkill mistreats his wife, you say?"

"He doesn't thump her, if that's what you're getting at. Not enough to bother her, any road. It's just that he spends every night here. Always has."

"You're here," observed Pascoe.

"Couple of nights a week maybe. And we arrive together at a decent time, have a couple of drinks, then off. Bri's first in, last out. Even if Deirdre comes, she never sees him, he's so bloody important."

"Is she here tonight?"

"No. She usually sits with us if she does."

"I suppose Sandra's too young to come?"

Mrs. Heppelwhite's formidable lips tightened significantly. "Aye. By her birth certificate."

"What's that mean?"

"Haven't you seen her? She could pass for five and twenty, that lass. And does. I've seen her. I hardly recognized her once a few months back. She had more paint on her than our front door."

"Does Mrs. Burkill permit this?"

"Of course she doesn't, but kids these days! She'll have it in her handbag or hidden somewhere outside. Once she's away from the house, out it comes and on it goes. I'd have flayed her back for her if she'd been mine."

"And Mrs. Burkill?"

"*Spoke* to her. Didn't dare tell Bri. That's one thing he's some use for. He'd have knocked seven bells out of her."

"He doesn't seem to have touched her after this recent business," observed Pascoe.

"No. He had someone else to thump there, didn't he? And he got my two men mixed up in it too. All for that little madman. I'll tell you what," she added emphatically. "Mebbe I shouldn't say it, but if that poor sod of a dentist did touch her, it wouldn't be without encouragement."

"I'm afraid that won't help him much in court, Mrs. Heppelwhite," said Pascoe.

"No. No doubt she'll turn up in her old school clothes looking the picture of innocence. Well, them's the risks these rich buggers have got to take for their money. Not that I care. But I feel sorry for his wife, that's all. It's always the woman who suffers!"

Storing this in his collection of unanswerable assertions somewhere between "God Is Good" and "There's No Place Like Home," Pascoe waited just long enough to say "Cheers" to Heppelwhite on his lager-laden return, then retreated to the bar. Wield and Hope were in close conversation with Burkill nearby.

"Collecting evidence, are you?" said Burkill. "What about Shorter? Has that bastard been arrested yet?"

"I'm not in charge of the case, Mr. Burkill. Remember, you were rather insistent that I shouldn't be."

"Mr. Dalziel will see me right, Inspector," averred Burkill. "He doesn't much care for this kind of thing."

"I think we may all trust Mr. Dalziel. What about your lass?"

"What the hell do you mean?"

Pascoe realized that his sentence juxtaposition had led him into trouble. He made haste to pour oil, knowing it would do no one any good if he had to arrest Burkill for assault.

"I meant, What happens to her now? Is she going to have the baby or—"

"Abortion, you mean," said Burkill, subsiding. "I don't know. We haven't really talked about it. You can get that done, can you? I mean, officially?"

"Oh yes. In a case like this, young girl and everything, there's no problem. Look, would you like someone to come around to talk it over with you and your wife, and Sandra too, of course."

"Police, you mean."

"No, I don't mean police. Someone from the social services. I know the man in charge there. Of course, you could ring him yourself. I just thought it might be easier if I put you in contact."

"Another of your mates." Burkill sneered. "Official snouts."

"Oh go and get fucked," said Pascoe wearily and turned away. Wield was at his elbow.

"You ready for off, Sergeant?"

"Yes, sir. You haven't forgotten our car's back at the Branderdyke?"

"Oh Christ. Well, I'm certainly not asking Johnny Hope for a lift back!" said Pascoe. "I'll treat us to a taxi."

As they made for the door, Burkill grasped his arm. "Look, I'm sorry," he said. "We need to talk to someone about Sandra. Could you get in touch with this chap for us?"

"All right," said Pascoe. "I'll ring him tomorrow."

Outside as they walked through driving rain not even Wield's news that according to Johnny Hope Haggard had been promised the running of Godfrey Blengdale's new country club at Holm Coultram College could dislodge from Pascoe's mind the hopeless longing to be in a job, and in a part of the world, where kindness was not met with suspicion, and love and taxis filled the sunlit streets.

Fifteen

"**W**hat," said Ellie, looking incredibly fetching propped up against the kitchen door with uncombed hair and face still puffy with sleep, "the hell are you doing at this hour in the morning?"

Pascoe paused in mid-cornflake to look at his watch. It was five forty-five. "I'm sorry. Did I wake you?"

"Yes. I just thought you'd gone off for your fifteenth pee. Why don't you drink Scotch?"

"I don't know. I don't really want anything and in these places when you don't really want anything, they give you beer. I thought I told you last night I'd be up at the crack."

"Maybe you did. I was tired, you were incoherent. God, it's cold."

"It's not surprising. I saw a stripper last night who ended up with more on than you."

"If it bothers you," said Ellie, retreating into the hall

and reappearing wearing his oldest raincoat. It changed her from Titian Venus to Central European refugee.

"I'll have some of that coffee. Where are you going? View a corpse? Torture a suspect?"

"I'm going to see a dirty film being made," said Pascoe with some satisfaction.

"God, Peter, you're becoming an obsessive! What are you trying to prove?"

"I can't understand," said Pascoe, "why no one else but me thinks it's important. And Shorter."

"Your Danish dentist? You make a fine pair."

"A girl may have been badly injured. Even killed."

"*May* have been. Shorter *may* have had a motive for starting all this. And you checked out the actress."

"*You* said there were two of them," protested Pascoe.

"I *may* have been wrong. But even if I'm not, even if all that was for real and not just a ketchup job, you're still getting obsessed by a single symptom when there's a whole disease to cure."

"I deal in symptoms," said Pascoe.

"Wrong," said Ellie. "There's nothing clinical about you, my love. Wrong profession, medicine. The Church, that's more your style. Priestlike task of pure ablution round earth's human shores. Bloody Shelley."

"Bloody Keats."

"Same thing," she said. "You're a pure ablutionist. And like most priests, you're obsessed with sex, when it's *sexism* you should be after. *That's* the disease."

He pushed back his chair and stood up. "You should have a word with Ms. Lacewing," he said. "She's got plans."

"I intend to," she said. "Didn't I tell you she rang? We're meeting for lunch today?"

"Oh God. Liberated gossip!" he said. "My raincoat, please."

"But you hardly ever wear this raincoat," grumbled Ellie as she removed it.

"Nor," he said, looking at her appreciatively, "do you."

As he backed out of the gate, she was standing naked on the doorstep, waving everything at him. He beeped his horn and drove away.

Hay Hall would have been totally unfindable without the help of what he took to be a plowman workward plodding his weary way, and even then it was only because he had the wit to follow the man's gestures rather than his words (right arm shooting out as he said, "Sharp left at Five Lanes End") that Pascoe found himself turning through an unmarked and uninviting gateway in a crumbling lichen-pocked wall. The drive was potholed worse than Acornboar Mount, the vegetation consisted mainly of dark and dripping conifers and yew, and the whole atmosphere seemed more conducive to the chilly thrills of horror than the slippery blisses of pornography. This supernatural ambiance was reinforced when the house itself came into view, for now he got a tremendous sense of *déjà vu*. It was a two-storied building which not even time and neglect could make beautiful. The ground floor looked as if it had been designed by someone who had a distant acquaintance with Georgian proportion and style, but the first floor, with its lancent windows and Gothic cornices, seemed to have been sliced off some romantic folly and dropped, not very accurately, onto its ill-matched base. Even the unkempt festoons of ivy couldn't hide the join.

Parked in front of the house were two cars and a large van. Pascoe slid his Riley alongside them, still wrestling with this sense of having been here before. It was something he had heard of, but never experienced, and he was surprised at the uneasiness with which it filled him.

"Oh, it's you," said Penelope Latimer from the portico. She came toward him, huge in a white silk trouser suit, and added apologetically. "Sorry to sound so unwelcoming but I thought it might be the generator truck."

"I need my exhaust fixed," said Pascoe.

"Don't we all. Come inside, Peter isn't it? We can't start anything till the power arrives, so you may detect away, darling, detect away. Anything wrong?"

"It's just this house," said Pascoe slowly, peering up at the facade.

"Hideous, ain't it? But very useful. No one else will look at it, so we rent it for a song."

"I've a peculiar notion that I've seen it before," said Pascoe.

Penelope Latimer laughed beautifully, the kind of spontaneous silvery gurgle that film stars paid thousands to voice coaches for, and her soft frame shook like a snow-filled col touched by the warmth of spring.

"Of course you have, darling. Everyone who's seen a Homeric film has seen Hay Hall. Do step in out of the raw."

Pascoe felt as relieved and disappointed as most people feel when the apparently supernatural is explained. *Droit*

de Seigneur was the answer. This was the manor to which
the lecherous lord had abducted the blushing bride.
Which also made it the manor in which the blushing bride
had been, perhaps, assaulted.

They passed through an entrance hall with no furniture, tattered wall hangings, a rather elegant curved stair-
way and creaking floorboards, into an equally dilapidated
drawing room which was occupied by half a dozen people
standing around a gas heater drinking coffee from flasks.

"Relax, folks," said Penny. "It's only the fuzz. Gerry,
my dear, come and be fingerprinted."

A tall thin man with a scholarly stoop detached himself from the coffee drinkers and joined Pascoe and the
woman. It wasn't just the stoop that was scholarly. He had
a thin-featured face, at once vague and ascetic, that would
have looked at home at an Oxbridge high table; wire-
rimmed spectacles pinched his long nose, and he even
wore the baggy gray flannels and ancient sports coat with
leather elbows which are the academic's uniform in the
popular imagination. His age was about thirty.

"Gerry Toms, Peter Pascoe. Coffee, Peter?"

"No, thanks. Is there anywhere we could talk privately,
Mr. Toms?"

"We could step into the shooting room, if you don't
mind the cold," said Toms. He spoke hesitantly with a
touch of East Anglia in his voice.

"It shouldn't take long," said Pascoe.

The director led him via the hall into another, larger
room. This one was furnished after a fashion. Drapes had
been hung over the windows, a square of carpet laid on

the floor in front of the almost Adam fireplace, and on this stood a chaise longue and a small table set for tea. The final touch was a huge tigerskin rug.

The other end of the room was full of equipment—cameras, some sound recorders and a variety of lights.

"There's no power here, of course," said Toms. "That's why we need the generator. It isn't really enough, but a bit of gloom suits most of our scenes and hides the cracks in the plaster."

"Why do you use the place if it's so inconvenient?" asked Pascoe.

"I didn't say it was inconvenient," said Toms. "On balance, it's great. First, we've got the whole house for interiors. Give us an hour and we can have any room looking habitable—on film anyway. And any period. Second, we've got nice private grounds for exteriors. You can't shoot our kind of footage in a public park. Third, it's cheap. Fourth, it's bloody cold, so we get things done quickly. What is it you want to talk to me about, Inspector?"

"A film you made, *Droit de Seigneur*."

"Ah yes. A masterpiece of my social commentary period," said Toms blandly.

"Your what?"

"I was trying to say something about the repression of woman."

"She didn't look very repressed to me," said Pascoe, 99 percent sure that he was being set up.

"Of course not. The whole thing is a male fantasy. You noticed that surely? The young husband and the wicked lord are, in fact, the same person. The husband in the end does not rescue the girl; he merely offers her a different form of victimization."

"That's a fairly cynical view of human relationships," said Pascoe.

"Then it's one that should recommend itself to you," answered Toms. "Cynicism is the basis of law, otherwise why should compassion need to be the better part of justice?"

Gobbledygook," said Pascoe with some force.

"Come now. Let us restrict ourselves to matters sexual. A woman comes to your station saying she has been attacked by a man. How do you and your colleagues react? You investigate the man because you believe any man capable of sexually assaulting a women. You investigate the woman because you believe any woman capable of sexually provoking a man. At the conclusion of your investigations you apportion blame, you don't establish innocence. Am I right? Or am I right?"

Pascoe found himself taking a hearty dislike to Gerry Toms, not so much because of his undergraduate debating manner as because of the impression he gave of intellectual condescension. He quite clearly believed that it needed very little effort on his part to leave a poor policeman floundering in his wake.

"All that's as it may be, sir," he said heavily. "I can't say I agree with what you say, though I'm not sure I've picked you up right. Any road, what I want to ask you now is about that scene in the film where the young lady gets beaten up."

"Yes?"

"It's been suggested that at one point in that scene, the young lady really *is* being beaten up. What do you say to that?"

"I say, how incredible! At which point?"

"When the gent with the metal boxing gloves clips her jaw, sir." Pascoe watched Toms closely. Having opted to play out the role of dull policemen, he hoped that Toms might be tempted to overact in his desire to impress his stolid audience, but the man merely shook his head.

"And at that point only?" he said. "But why? Our actresses may not be Royal Shakespeare stuff, but they bleed and bruise just as easily and like it just as little. It's all done with tomato ketchup, Inspector, didn't you know?"

"The suggestion was made, sir, and by someone with claims to expertise," said Pascoe steadfastly.

"A wife beater, perhaps? Have you not seen the actress concerned? Linda Abbott, I think it was. Did she have any complaints? Or bruises?"

"None."

"So what is this all about?" cried Toms, moving now across the thin line which divides the academic from the histrionic.

"It's also been suggested that for this scene there was another actress in the role," said Pascoe.

"What? By *another* expert?"

"In a manner of speaking," said Pascoe, thinking of Ellie standing on the doorstep that morning.

"You'd better change your experts, Inspector," said Toms, pushing his spectacles up the bridge of his nose with a nicotine-stained forefinger. "There was only one woman in that part. Ask anyone who worked on the film."

"I notice you don't suggest looking at the film itself," said Pascoe.

"Why not? Look away!" said Toms. "I'll sit and look with you."

"You have a print of the film, sir?" asked Pascoe.

"I think not. They'll be all out, I expect."

"All?"

"We usually made a couple of prints, sometimes three. It depends on the kind of demand we envisage."

"And in this case?"

For the first time the shadow of a smile appeared on Gerry Toms's face. "Two only, I think. You see, I'm realistic. This kind of social allegory isn't altogether what the modern cinéaste is looking for. Yes, there were two, I now recall. But only one survives. I remember there was some trouble, a consignment went astray at our distributors. It sank without a trace. It's the kind of people one has to employ these days. So the only surviving print is the one you must have seen. Presumably it's moved on elsewhere now. Never fear. It will be easy to catch it up."

"Not too easy, sir," said Pascoe. "I'm afraid that's gone too. There was a fire at the Calliope Kinema Club where it was showing. Perhaps you heard about it?"

"No, I didn't. Good lord, that means, unless the last copy surfaces, it's goodbye *Droit de Seigneur*. Or perhaps I should say *Adieu*."

"You don't seem worried," said Pascoe.

"Why should I be? A film director writes on water, Inspector. And besides, that period of my life is dead. Now I'm into escapism. Symbolic romance."

"Elinor Glyn?" inquired Pascoe.

"What? Oh, I see," said Toms glancing at the tigerskin rug and nodding approvingly, as at a sharp pupil. "No, but nearly right. We're doing a little squib loosely based on the tales of Baroness Orczy. It's about a group of noble ladies who are smuggled out of the shadow of the guillotine disguised as *filles de joie* in a traveling brothel. We're calling it *The Scarlet Pimp*."

"Oh God," said Pascoe.

"Oh Montreal," said Toms. "Is that all, Inspector?"

"Just a couple of other points. What time did you get back on Friday?"

"Oh, I don't know. Ten, eleven P.M."

Pascoe did a couple of quick calculations. "Did anyone see you when you arrived, sir?"

"What? Of course they did. I'm not invisible, you know. Customs men, taxi driver, hotel receptionist. Am I establishing some kind of alibi?"

"I meant, did anyone see you when you got back to Harrogate?"

Toms began to smile. "I'm with you, I think. You've misunderstood me, Inspector. It's true I should have been back in Harrogate early Friday evening. But we got held up. Barcelona was absolutely fogbound. It was *London* I reached on Friday night. I didn't get back to Harrogate till Saturday lunchtime."

The door opened and Penelope Latimer came in. "Generator's arrived, darling."

"Great," said Toms. "Any way I can help, Inspector, you're just got to ask. Will you excuse me."

He left. Pascoe smiled to the woman and said casually, "Mr. Toms was telling me he got held up in Spain."

"Yes. Bloody nuisance. We lost a day. Should have started this lot on Saturday, you know."

"Where is it he stays in London? I meant to ask."

"The Candida," she said. "I think he'd be there. Yes, he definitely was. Their switchboard girl put him through to me when he rang."

"He rang? Why?"

"To say he was delayed, of course. What's all this about, Peter?"

"Nothing. Nothing," said Pascoe. "Interesting ideas your partner has, though."

"You think so? He sees himself as the poor man's Warhol. Or do I mean the rich man's Warhol? But he's certainly got what it takes for this business."

"Talent, you mean?" said Pascoe.

Penelope laughed her joyous laugh. "Talent! Gerry could stick his talent between the cheeks of his tight little ass and it would fall out when he stood up. No. He knows which way to point a camera, and up from down, but his real asset is face. Sheer bloody effrontery. He got this place for us from old Lady Campsall. There was a bit of bother when her agent latched onto what kind of outfit we were, so Gerry went along and saw her. 'Ma'am,' he said, 'what we are making are vulgar films for vulgar people. It's a new form of peasant taxation, and as such, you owe it your keenest support.' She bought it. That's Gerry's real talent. Not filmmaking, but getting out of jams when they occur, which in this business is every two minutes. I know a dozen guys could make a better film than Gerry with one eye closed, but they couldn't get it put together within a time limit if the leading actor had a hernia, the banks foreclosed and a drunken assistant peed in the hypo tank. Gerry could, would, and has done."

"I begin to see his value," said Pascoe. "You said he owned a third of the company."

"Did I?"

"On the phone. You own another third, I presume. Who's the other lucky shareholder?"

"No one really," said the woman. "It was just a manner of speaking. Gerry and me do the work. We have to twist a few arms to finance any new project, that's all I meant."

The room suddenly began to fill up with bodies and a tangle of cables.

"Time to work," said Penelope. "Stay and enjoy the view."

"Some other time," said Pascoe despondently. "I've other bodies to see."

Penelope regarded him curiously. "Look," she said. "I'm not sure I know what this is all about, but don't let it get to you, darling. It's a crummy planet. Crummy things happen. We can all suffer without looking it up in the Yellow Pages. So be happy and come up and see me again sometime—without those official eyes. 'Bye now."

As he sent the Riley down the dark tunnel of conifers and yew, Pascoe was not certain whether he had been comforted or warned. Either way it didn't matter. Or, to be less precise, they were equally irrelevant. To take warning, to take comfort: these were the prerogatives of the people. It was the duty of the priest class to give them, not to take them, especially not from fat women in the pornographic film business.

Still, he thought, it was a terrible thing this pure abluting. Duty meant sacrifice. It might have been quite interesting to see what the Scarlet Pimp did with that tiger rug.

On the other hand, though she did not yet know it, he had a date with a movie star.

Sixteen

"**O**ne thing I'll give you lot," said Linda Abbott. "You start early."

"But they let us finish late," said Pascoe, glancing at his watch. It was only nine o'clock in the morning and already he'd contrived to do— He totted it up. Very little.

Linda Abbott did not seem likely to change things. No, there definitely hadn't been another girl on the set. What would have been the point? The shooting had taken about a week, four or five days, that was. This was a lot longer than the back-street boys, three hours of an afternoon would do them, but the thing about Mr. Toms was that he made *real* films. Some of them even had certificates and made it to Screen Three at the local Gaumont. She'd appeared in one of these, a small part. But hadn't she had to join Equity?

Pascoe sat in the bright neat kitchen and talked softly over a mug of coffee for fear of disturbing the sleeping Bert.

"How'd you get into this film business?" he asked.

"It wasn't that hard," she said. "None of your struggling to stardom stuff. I used to be an exotic dancer. I still am when the kitty's low. I was asked if I'd like to make a bob or two doing a film. I was a bit dubious at first."

"Why?"

"I knew right off what kind of film he meant."

"He?"

"Chap who managed us. I was a Lulu then, part of a team, the Three Lulus. Maurice, that was the chap who ran the agency, said he could get us into films. Like I said, we knew what he meant, or thought we did. Getting humped on some flea-ridden bed of home movies. We told him to take a jump, but he ran us out to meet Mr. Toms, showed us a film he'd made. Well, it wasn't *Gone With the Wind*, but it was a cut or two above the do-it-yourself kind. Most of the sex, he said, was put on. Them as felt like going the whole hog for a few quid more were very welcome, but there was plenty of work for well-built girls who just wanted to go through the motions. I talked it over with Bert and said all right."

"This Maurice," said Pascoe, casually, "does he still manage you?"

"Not really *manage*. When we were the Three Lulus, he was more our manager then. But you don't have proper managers in this game. If he knows of anything that might suit me, he gets in touch. If I'm a bit short, I might ring his agency just to see what's going."

"Arany, that's a funny name," mused Pascoe. "Doesn't sound English. Just a business name, perhaps."

She put her cup on the table and stared at him with blank unblinking eyes. "What's the game, love?" she asked.

"Eh?"

"I never said Maurice's second name was Arany."

"Didn't you. Surely you did!" said Pascoe brightly. "Otherwise how would I know?"

"That's the question, right enough. So what's the game?"

Pascoe was acutely embarrassed. It had been a stupid slip. Dalziel would probably not have made it—he rarely underestimated people. But if he had, he wouldn't have been in the least embarrassed.

"Association of ideas," he said. "Maurice Arany's name came up when I was talking with Penny Latimer of Homeric. I just put two and two together when you mentioned a Maurice."

She laughed disbelievingly. "Look," she said. "I had Lorraine the year after that first film job. Times were hard. Bert and me had a lot of financial commitments. Well, Maurice subbed me while I couldn't work. He got it all back, mind you. I didn't want charity. But there's not many as would have bothered in our game. Afterwards he helped me get back in as quickly as possible. I used to take Lorraine with me in her carry-cot. I felt right daft at first, but Maurice said it'd be all right. Everyone'd love the kid. Having a baby around made them feel sort of respectable. He was right. Any road, what I'm saying is, I'm not about to say owt that could harm Maurice Arany. So you can bugger off somewhere else with your sneaky questions!"

She had raised her voice, and before Pascoe could reply, there was a series of bangs on the floor above.

"Now you've woken Bert up!" said Linda Abbott.

"I'm sorry, I'm sorry," said Pascoe. "You've got it all wrong—"

"Just shove off," said the woman wearily. "No wonder they call you pigs! You revel in muck."

Pascoe rose. At the door he said in a quiet, reasonable voice. "Lady, you get annoyed because people think that running around without your clothes on makes you a dirty, immoral woman. Well, policemen get annoyed too when people assume that running around trying to solve or prevent crimes makes them some kind of nasty animal. The only difference is, you can tell me to bugger off and all I can say in reply is thank you very much and good morning."

It was feeble and plaintive, thought Pascoe. And also only partly true. Under Dalziel's patient tuition, he'd learned when to tell people to bugger off and when to keep his mouth shut. Now he felt almost as guilty as before when Linda Abbott caught up with him in the hall and said, "I'm sorry I said that. It's your job, I shouldn't blame a man for his job. Women especially shouldn't."

"Yes," said Pascoe. "A man's gotta do what a man's gotta do."

"That film," she said. "Really, there wasn't another girl. Just me. And it was put on."

"I believe you," he said. But he didn't move; he sensed there was the possibility of something else.

"Mr. Toms was very economical," she said finally. "He'd always want to get it right first time."

"Just the one take, you mean," said Pascoe.

"That's right. I think he was quite proud that all he had to do was more or less stick his shots together to make the film."

"No editing?"

"Oh aye. I suppose he had to do a bit, but what I'm getting at is, if owt went wrong, he didn't have a lot of other takes to fall back on. I don't know much about it, mind. Just what I heard some of the others say when we were chatting during dinner break or whatever. One of the girls reckoned she'd gone to see one of the films she was in and there was a bit from another film in it, if you follow me. She wondered if she could get an extra payment."

"And did she?"

Linda Abbott laughed. "Some bloody hope!" she said. "They're as careful with cash as with film. Oh God, there's Bert banging again. I'd best take him a pot of tea, see if that'll quieten him."

"Goodbye then, Mrs. Abbott," said Pascoe. "And good luck."

She wished him goodbye in return but nothing was said about luck.

About two hundred yards from the house there was a telephone box. He stopped the car, entered the box and dialed Linda Abbott's number, which he had noted as they stood talking in the hallway. He got the engaged signal. Replacing the receiver, he next dialed the number of Maurice Arany's agency. That was engaged too.

Finally he dialed Ray Crabtree.

"All those naked bodies too much for you," asked Crabtree cheerfully.

"I didn't stay long enough to see, Ray. Just a couple of points you might be able to help with. You don't happen to know how Homeric got their films processed, do you?"

"Not offhand," said Crabtree. "Is it important?"

"I don't know. I just wondered if there was a gap in a film, you know, something went wrong in the processing, could you slot in a bit from another film fairly easily?"

"Hang on," said Crabtree. "There's a lad in our lab who's pretty hot on camera stuff, I'll give him a buzz."

There was a lengthy pause during which Pascoe had to feed another couple of ten-pence pieces into the slot.

"Hello? Still there? Good. Yes, dead easy. And also he reckons Toms does most of his own stuff. He's evidently pretty hot on the technical side. I suppose he doesn't care to let the stuff he's working on get far out of his sight."

"Thanks a lot, Ray."

"Anything else?"

"I don't think so."

"Just one thing from this end, Peter," said Crabtree apologetically. "You will keep us posted about what you're up to? I mean, in case of any overlap."

It was a reproof and a justified one, Pascoe had to admit.

"Of course. And I'm sorry, Ray. You know how it is. Any trespass on other people's land will be signaled in advance. OK."

"Great. Watch how you go. My love to the Great Buggernaut. Cheers!"

Before leaving the box, Pascoe dialed Linda Abbott's number again. It was still engaged.

The road was full of long slow lorries and it was mid-morning before he got back to the station. He was guiltily aware that he was still a long way from being able to justify the time he had spent on the *Droit de Seigneur* business and it was with a sigh of relief that he gained his office without bumping into Dalziel.

Now he turned his thoughts to Haggard and what had emerged the previous night. Haggard and Arany. Haggard and Blengdale. Why should Haggard go into partnership with the Hungarian? Why should the rotund councilor want to set Haggard up as the manager of the proposed Holm Coultram Country Club?

It would be interesting to know the story behind Haggard's resignation from the Diplomatic Service, but he guessed that official channels would be locked by all manner of protocol, closing of ranks, pleas of confidentiality, etc.

On the other hand, there was almost certainly someone in the Met who would know someone in Whitehall who could look in a filing cabinet during his lunch hour.

He picked up the phone and a few moments later was speaking to Detective–Chief Inspector Colbridge, whom the previous summer at a police college course he had saved from being caught drunk and half naked in the ornamental fish pond of a local lady magistrate.

"Willie," he said. "Peter Pascoe. How are you?"

"Relieved," said the voice on the other end. "I've been

waiting for this call for nine months. What do you want, you blackmailing sod?"

Pascoe told him. Colbridge said airily that he saw no difficulty there, leave it with him, always ready to help the provinces.

"If it's so damned easy," said Pascoe, "there's something else."

"Oh God! Why don't I keep my big mouth shut. Go on."

"A man called Toms—would you believe Gerry Toms?— claims he was staying at the Candida Hotel last Friday night. Could you check for me without treading on anyone's toes? Great. Fine. I'll buy you a pint of real beer next time you're up this way. Oh, and listen, while you're at it, if there was any way of getting a look at his bill . . . It's a phone call I'd be interested in. To Harrogate. Could you? Many thanks."

As he himself had said earlier that day, it was always worth checking the obvious. Toms said he was in London and that he'd phoned Penelope Latimer in Harrogate. She confirmed that he was at the Candida. It was almost certainly true. But all the same it would do no harm to check.

It was after one when he made his way to the Black Bull and he expected to find either Dalziel or Wield there already, probably both. But there was no sign of either. On the off chance they might have opted for something a cut or two above their usual pie and peas, he glanced into the little dining room where business executives could sit at tables with nearly white cloths and eat their pie, peas, and chips like real gentlefolk.

The first people he saw were Ellie and Ms. Lacewing, drinking coffee and brandy.

"Hello!" he said. "I didn't think they served unescorted ladies in here."

Ellie rolled her eyes and groaned. "I'm beginning to believe what Thelma tells me."

"And what does Thelma tell you?" asked Pascoe, regarding the beautiful dentist distrustfully.

"That peaceful compromise isn't possible. Nothing but all-out revolution will do."

"And the Black Bull dining room was the nearest thing to a bastion of male chauvinism you could find!" mocked Pascoe.

"The nearest thing that sells the nearest thing to food," corrected Ms. Lacewing.

"Are you eating in here, Peter?" asked Ellie.

"No. Just looking for Andy Dalziel. I'll sit in the bar as usual and pick at a bag of crisps," he said plaintively.

"I shouldn't wait too long for your colleague," said Ms. Lacewing. "Not if he's that gross man with fleas."

"That sounds like him," said Pascoe. "Why?"

"He turned up at the surgery just as I was leaving and arrested Jack Shorter."

Pascoe sat by himself and ate some salted peanuts. Ms. Lacewing's news had taken him aback. She had been unable to give him any details beyond the bare facts that Shorter, having turned up in mid-morning and occupied himself with paperwork (his appointments having been canceled), had been on the point of going out to lunch when Dalziel arrived and took him away. Emma Shorter had appeared soon after, evidently expecting to eat with her husband.

"I was on my way out to meet Ellie then, so I left her in the hands of Alison. They have a lot in common, those two. Well, something."

"What's that?"

"Usability," said Ms. Lacewing. Upon which Pascoe had left.

He no longer felt hungry. The peanuts were merely something to ease the burning the beer caused in his guts. Perhaps he had joined the club and was getting his first ulcer. He thought of Burkill and Shorter, Arany and Haggard, Toms and Penny Latimer. Everything had the smell of disaster.

"For a man who's avoided both Dalziel and this place's food, you look strangely down in the mouth."

Ellie sat beside him. She had brought her brandy glass with her, newly replenished, and her eyes sparkled with the afterfire of a boozy lunch.

"You'll fall asleep during your lectures," said Pascoe.

"If you can't beat 'em," said Ellie.

"Where's Mary Wollstonecraft?" asked Pascoe.

"Gone to scour a few more mouths. I told her to let the bastards rot, but she's very conscientious. And pretty, don't you think?"

"Yeah. She'll fill a nice cavity in some lucky man's life," said Pascoe cynically, adding thoughtfully, "Or woman's. She's not a high flier, is she?"

Ellie looked blank.

"I mean, what do you think she was after? Your sharp mind or your shapely body—or just your fat purse?"

"My energies, I think. She wants me to join, well, not join, because she doesn't believe in the concept of joining. She wants me to discover that I'm one of her lot, these Women's Rights Action Group people."

"WRAG," said Pascoe. "And are you?"

"I think I may be," said Ellie solemnly.

"Yes? You try Lysistrating around me, I'll fetch you one round the ear," said Pascoe in a heavy Yorkshire accent.

"You've been watching those films again. How *was* your morning, by the way?"

But Pascoe wasn't listening. Over Ellie's shoulder among the ruddy puffy cheeks of the double-gin-and-tonic boys he had spotted a pale set face with dark and desperately questing eyes.

It was Emma Shorter and he had no doubt who she was questing after. Last night he had seen the strain in that face, but there had been action to take, motions to go through. Jack was up and about and full of aggression. But now Dalziel had laid hands on him, taken him in for all the world to see. Now the strain was all on her.

"Oh shit," he muttered to himself. He felt desperately sorry for the woman, but there was nothing he could do, nothing he could tell her. He just didn't feel equipped at this moment to take any more pressure himself.

"Look, love," he said. "Someone I don't want to see. Must dash anyway. See you later."

He got up and went out via the dining room, keeping his head bowed low and resisting the temptation to glance back. Outside in the car park he took a deep breath and for a moment felt the exhilaration of escape. He set off toward his car, then stopped so suddenly that a man behind him cannoned into his back.

What the hell am I doing! wondered Pascoe.

In his mind he saw again the woman's face. She was seeing her life collapse and desperately looking for whatever slender comforts anyone could offer. A face falling apart on celluloid had haunted his thoughts for days now and sent him back and forward across the county looking for something to scour away the image. But a real face, a life falling apart before his eyes, a few feet away, a few seconds away, had put him to flight.

He turned around and walked back to the pub. But when he re-entered the bar, there was no sign of Emma Shorter, and Ellie was just going out the main door.

Full of shame, he resumed his walk to the car.

Seventeen

Back in the office he tried to see Dalziel, but the fat man was still busy with Shorter. Pascoe knew his technique well—periods of intensive questioning building up to a climax, then a break, then a recommencement of the questioning as though the previous bout had not taken place, then another break, then the questioning again.

Pascoe did not doubt that Shorter could stand up to all this, or rather that the man would imagine he had stood up to it all. But Dalziel would know this too. He would merely be probing for weaknesses at this stage, not expecting a quick breach.

Why the Superintendent was interesting himself so closely in this relatively minor case when there were more important matters, including a murder, on hand, Pascoe did not know. Perhaps he owed Burkill a favor. He seemed to think highly of the man. One thing was certain—he'd have a good reason.

At three o'clock, Colbridge rang back.

Pascoe had not expected a reply till the following morning at the earliest, but Colbridge obviously saw this as a chance to keep his provincial friends in due awe of metropolitan efficiency.

"Haggard was dead easy. The pubs around Whitehall are full of gossipy old disappointed civil servants who'd tell you anything for a sympathetic ear and a gin and tonic."

"I'm sure," said Pascoe.

"According to my source, Haggard was bent in every sense. Little black boys were his downfall in the West Indies, so they shipped him out. They don't object to that kind of thing in the Diplomatic as long as you don't do it on the Queen's Birthday. But Austria was different. When the Hungarians started coming across the border in 1956, Haggard seems to have set himself up as a private travel agency. It's pretty clear he'd been in a lot of fiddles before this—Vienna was still a pretty hairy place in those days—but he went too far this time. Again, no drama. They know how to look after their own! Just the invitation to resign. That any good to you."

"Thank you," said Pascoe. "It's confirmation. What about the other business?"

"Hang on. I got one of my lads to check that. Here we are. Yes, a fellow called Toms was a guest at the Candida that Friday night. Yes, he rang Harrogate. You want details?"

"If you've got them."

Evidently the number called plus time and duration of the call were all on the bill. Pascoe noted them down, listened to a short digression on the extortionate charges these hotels made for phone calls and was about to give his thanks and ring off when Colbridge said, "Are you interested in his other calls?"

"Other?"

"Yes. You just asked about the one to Harrogate, but after that he made three other calls, all to your part of the world."

"Might as well have them," said Pascoe with affected indifference.

They were all local numbers. None of them meant anything to Pascoe, but he suspected they were going to. And with the second of these there came an extra bit of information, coaxed from the hotel switchboard girl. (Besides being efficient, the bastards want us to know they're sexy too, thought Pascoe!) The call had been put through, the telephone lifted at the other end, then everything had gone dead and subsequent inquiries through the exchange had merely produced the reply that the line was out of order.

"Toms made a lot of fuss, that's why they remembered. Probably that's why they charged the poor sod for it too. One second, no conversation, you know what they charged? Go on. Guess."

Pascoe guessed and finally, full of excitement, got the phone down. Quickly he checked the numbers with the local exchange.

The Harrogate one was Penelope Latimer's. The other three in order of phoning belonged to Godfrey Blengdale, Gilbert Haggard and Maurice Arany.

"Well, well, well," said Pascoe.

When Dalziel walked into his office ten minutes later, he was still examining the implications of what he'd got.

"Nice of you to drop in," said Dalziel. "Thought you might spend the day wandering round on other people's patches."

So there'd been something in Crabtree's warning.

"I've been back since the middle of the morning," protested Pascoe.

"Have you now? If I'd known, you could have helped me with this mate of yours. God, he's a hard nut."

"Have you charged him?" asked Pascoe.

"Not yet. I just thought the time was ripe to have him in."

"Ripe?"

"Well, first the bugger went back to work, so he couldn't play sick any more. And I didn't have that wife of his on my back when I picked him up at the surgery. Though she found out quick enough."

"Has Mrs. Shorter been here?" asked Pascoe.

"Too bloody true," said Dalziel. "I can't abide hysterical women. Wanted to know what right I had to arrest her man. I told her I had more than a right, I had a duty. That shut her up."

"Duty?" said Pascoe.

"Like any right-thinking man," said Dalziel ponderously. "These buggers need sorting out."

"But you said you hadn't charged him."

"Not yet, but I will. I reckon we've got enough now, though," he added wistfully, "an admission's always nice for tying things up."

"Enough?"

"Oh aye. There's the girl. She'll not be budged. Then there's her friend Marilyn. Detailed observation there, and when it comes to sex, she knows what she's talking about. Then there's that lot at the surgery."

"Who do you mean?"

Dalziel laughed meaningfully. "His friends and colleagues, people he'd expect to rely on as character witnesses. Some help they'll give! Old MacCrystal doesn't want to know. Washes his hands of the fellow. La Lacewing reckons he's capable of anything. I think he probably tried his charms on her when she arrived. Well, she's a good-looking lass, that's what's behind these half-baked ideas of hers. What she wants is a month with a squint and buckteeth; that'd soon put her right. Any road, put either of these in the box, and he'd be lucky to escape lynching."

"But his nurse. Alison Parfitt."

"Oh yes. I read that statement carefully. Then when I went to the surgery this morning, I had a chat with her myself. That's what made me decide I was right to bring him in."

"But surely her testimony will favor Shorter. A bit biased, perhaps—"

"Biased! Bloody right it's biased! All the weight on one side and that's her backside. He's been screwing the arse off her this twelvemonth, you knew that?"

"You're sure?" said Pascoe, knowing full well Dalziel must be sure. Bitterly he recalled Shorter's man-to-man totally convincing denial. "I did wonder; but—"

"I did more than wonder, I found out. You know what it's like round here. If you do it in ditches wearing a hood,

you might just about keep it quiet for a week. But once
you start having the cocktails before or the little dinner
afterwards, you soon get spotted. She didn't deny it long,
they never do if you press 'em. That's what they all want,
these fancy women. To be found out. Get it in the open. It's
their only hope if you look at it right. So no one'll pay
much heed to any testimonial she gives."

"But her evidence about time?"

"Vague," said Dalziel. "Only significant date is the day
Sandra says the deed took place. Remember, Alison went
off to pick up some X-ray plates? Well, she had to sign for
them, with a note of the time. Twelve-fifteen she got 'em,
and it's a good quarter of an hour from the surgery. Sandra
had a double appointment that day. Tricky job, said Shorter.
No doubt, said I. So tricky you send your nurse off. That
shut him up. Well, I suppose I'd best go and finish him off.
I've wasted too much time on this as it is. What about
you? What have you been wasting your time on?"

Quickly Pascoe gave an outline of his own investigations.

"If I take you right, lad, you're now thinking there's a
link between Homeric and this affair at the Calli?"

"There's certainly a link," said Pascoe. "The phone
calls did take place. It's whether it's a significant or coin-
cidental link that needs to be decided."

Dalziel looked at him in mock surprise at this bold
affirmation. "All right. Let's take it step by step. Toms
rings Latimer to explain why he's not back in Yorkshire
as promised. You reckon she mentioned your interest in
that film, right? He rings off, then gets on to Blengdale.
Why?"

"No idea," said Pascoe, who knew just how far you dared go when presenting hypotheses to Dalziel.

"Then he rings Haggard. Why?"

"To say get rid of the film."

"But he can't get through because the phone goes dead. So presumably whoever was doing up the house, picked up the receiver and then cut the wire? That what you think?"

"Possibly."

"OK. So why does Toms ring Arany?"

"To say he can't get hold of Haggard and it's urgent that they get rid of that film."

"So what would Arany do?"

Pascoe knew exactly where he was being led to. He had explored the winding track too thoroughly already not to know each curve along the way. But he knew also that there are times to resist and times to go quietly.

"He would slip out of his flat, walk the quarter-mile to the Calli and let himself in."

"Then he and Haggard would burn the film and mess the place up to make it look like vandals?"

Pascoe said nothing.

"Then Arany would beat Haggard up to add to the verisimilitude? Jesus, I mean, how far does anyone go in pursuit of realism! And what about whoever it was that cut off the phone? Where were they? What were they doing while all this was going on? Just how many people were wandering around the Calli that night? Perhaps Ms. Lacewing and her gang of demonstrators were there too? And the Wilkinson Square Protection Society?"

Against his judgment, Pascoe was stung to speech. "Look, sir, all I'm doing is trying to fit a theory around the evidence—"

"Evidence!" bellowed Dalziel. "Evidence's what I've given you to show that your mate Shorter assaulted one of his patients. Not that you believe it. Oh no, *that* evidence is nowt to you! Then, next breath, you expect me to believe some fairy story which has got less hard evidence in it than meat in a poorhouse stew. Come on, lad, don't choke on it, spit it out. What do you really think's behind all this? I've been amazed, now astound me."

"All right," said Pascoe, roused to defiance, which was probably Dalziel's intention anyway. "This is what I think. I think there's a film, at least one, perhaps more, a snuff film, a film in which some poor bloody whore who thought she was going to be screwed a couple of times found out too late that the real climax was her being killed. Toms might have made it, or just have got hold of it, I don't know which. Either way, it's not unlike *Droit de Seigneur* in some of its sequences. Perhaps Toms plagiarized. Perhaps he merely had to tone down his own idea for our nice middle-class audiences. So when an important sequence went wrong in the processing, he kept his reputation for speed and economy by merely editing in a print of the same sequence in the snuff film. It's essential for continuity and thrills, but it's so brief and the girl's face is so badly beaten that it doesn't seem possible anyone'll notice. He reckons without my dentist on the one hand and my wife on the other."

He paused for breath and also for thought. Now he had

spoken, he could see all the huge flaws in his theory and the even huger areas of sheer vagueness. But he was glad he had spoken.

Dalziel had begun a facial scratch as he talked, taking the right-ear-to-Adam's-apple route. "Evidence?" he said.

"You've heard it all," said Pascoe defiantly.

"I have? I'll listen more carefully next time. So. Presumably to make it worthwhile risking either making or even possessing such a thing, you'd need an audience that was not only bloody bent but bloody rich?"

Pascoe agreed.

"Any suggestions who'd fit the bill round here?"

Pascoe hesitated. "I don't know. The only possibility seems to be . . . Godfrey Blengdale."

"Ah," said Dalziel. "I thought you were heading in that direction. Well, he's rich certainly. Not bloody rich, mind you. Not a millionaire, but he's worth a bob or two. But bent? Perverted? Twisted?"

"I don't know," said Pascoe. "Who can say?"

"What about his missus? You've met her, have you? Do you reckon she's the type to put up with that kind of thing? I'd say not. Any road, what's your next move?"

Pascoe was amazed by the gentleness of the response so far. And emboldened by it. Dalziel, he knew, would never be kind out of mere sentiment. Something had rung a bell with him, distantly perhaps but clear enough to make him hesitate the blasting, blaspheming, coruscating scorn that was his favorite response to the vague and the absurd.

"I'm not sure. See Toms again. Ask him about the

phone calls. Get to Arany and Blengdale at the same time."

Dalziel considered, then nodded. "That makes sense if anything in all this lemon curd makes sense. But leave it till tomorrow, eh? No one's going anywhere."

Pascoe was surprised. Dalziel was not a man to waste a moment, particularly of his underling's time.

His surprise must have shown, for Dalziel added, almost apologetically, "I'm tied up myself today and I'd like to have a go at God Blengdale myself, if you don't mind."

If I don't mind! thought Pascoe convinced now there were things going on he knew nothing about. Well, Dalziel was entitled to his secrets, but he'd be stupid not to take advantage of this rare conciliatory mood.

"Of course, sir," he said. "There was something I'd like to do this afternoon, though, if you wouldn't mind. I'd like permission to have a go at this girl Sandra Burkill before you charge Shorter. I've never seen her. I'd like to get a personal impression."

"Likely that's what Shorter said," grunted Dalziel. "All right. If you can get past her dad, that is. Be it on your own head."

Pascoe glanced at his watch. She'd be home from school shortly and Burkill would be still at work.

"I'll go around now," he said.

"Aye. Get a move on. I want this bugger charged before I go off for my tea," said Dalziel. "I'll give you to five."

It was hardly a vote of confidence, thought Pascoe. It looked as if nothing on earth was going to stop Dalziel going ahead.

But even Dalziel was not completely master of the universe.

On impulse Pascoe did not drive straight to the Westgate Estate but diverted to the lusher pastures of Acornboar Mount. It was a humanitarian move, he told himself. Emma Shorter might need someone to give her a bit of reassurance, tell her her husband was still only being questioned, not charged. That was what he told himself, but he knew that in fact he was just attempting to assuage his guilt feelings at ducking out of the Black Bull when the woman had appeared there at lunchtime.

This time he did not leave the car at the foot of the road, but sent it bumping up over the potholes and cracks. To live up here you really need to be able to afford something with superefficient suspension. A Range Rover, perhaps.

Or an ambulance.

There was one up ahead of him. He knew as soon as he saw it which house it was parked outside.

He arrived just as the stretcher men appeared and for the second time that day he saw Emma Shorter's pale, pale face.

Eighteen

"An overdose," he told Dalziel on the phone.

"Oh aye. Usual thing, was it? Half a dozen tablets and ring a neighbor?"

"A bit more serious than that, sir," said Pascoe evenly. "She's very ill indeed. And it was just chance she was spotted. The window cleaner."

"I dare say she knows when her window cleaner's due," said Dalziel cynically. "Well, I suppose I'd better send Shorter round there, hadn't I? Stroke of luck for him."

"Luck?"

"Aye. Can't you just see him standing up in court with a black armband and bags beneath his eyes? They'll be mopping out the jury box."

Pascoe took a deep breath. "You haven't charged him then?"

"No. I'll leave it now till we see which way his missus

decides to fall. Any road, I said I'd let you see Sandra first. Which reminds me, Acornboar Mount's a funny road to the Westgate Estate."

"I'll go there tonight instead," parried Pascoe.

"Good. But tread careful, Peter. Remember, they're nice people too. You're apt to be a bit heavy-handed on occasion. Hello! You still there?"

"Yes," said Pascoe.

"You should breathe a bit louder. Take care now. Cheerio!"

The Westgate Estate was a living history of local-authority domestic architecture of the twentieth century.

The first group of houses belonged to the 'twenties. The windows were small, but the brick was good and had weathered well, and they all had quite substantial gardens separated by privet hedges of considerable maturity. Built in blocks of three and four, they had a closer relationship with the agricultural cottage than the urban back-to-back.

Next came the 'thirties, and now the suburban villa was the model. The roofing had changed from black slate to red tiles, the upper storys were pebble-dashed and there had been some attempt at stylistic variation. This part of the estate had won a prize at the time, Pascoe recalled reading, and when you compared it with the immediately postwar development, you could see why; lines of barrack-like houses faced with the kind of roughcast on which new paint only looked new for a couple of months till the rain beneath the narrow eaves stained and darkened it once more.

More recent development, still continuing, was trying hard to balance speed and economy with environmental concern. It wasn't Acornboar Mount but it was good housing.

Burkill lived in the oldest part of the estate. The house was in darkness and after banging at the door for a couple of minutes, Pascoe decided he was out of luck. The Burkills were probably down at the club and Sandra had gone out with friends.

He recollected that the Heppelwhites lived next door and recollected also that some of the pressure under which Emma Shorter had so horrifyingly cracked had come from Clint. At least he had assumed it was Clint last night, though at Shorter's insistence he had let the matter slide. Now suddenly he wanted to be certain. He wanted to be able to tell this pair, father and son, to their faces that their vicarious rage and retributive action had probably killed a woman.

No, that was too strong, far too strong. Women like Emma didn't crack overnight or even in a couple of days. There must have been longer, steadier pressures. Such as? God! He laughed grimly. You didn't have to look far. Not if Shorter *was* screwing his nurse and Emma knew about it. Knew the marriage was on the rocks. Money too, perhaps. OK, he lived on Acornboar Mount and everyone knows that all dentists have Swiss accounts packed with gold fillings. But Pascoe had learned by hard experience that there's no art to read a man's bank balance in his public face.

So, dilute the anger a bit. But they'd helped to put Emma Shorter in hospital or worse, no doubt about it. And with Dalziel poised to charge the man, the publicity threat no longer applied.

He went up the path.

Burkill's front garden had been neat enough, a square of rough lawn with narrow, empty borders. It was the garden of a man who had little time to care about gardens, but sufficient community pride to reject a wilderness. Heppelwhite's small rectangle was a different matter altogether. The few square yards of lawn were as lushly green and as precisely swathed as Shorter's half-acre or Blengdale's half-dozen, and the scalloped borders were full of the flowers of spring—crocuses and daffodils, narcissi and tulips—in regimented profusion.

Burkill's front door had retained the original cast-iron knocker, but here there was a bell push which filled the air with a melodious three-tone chime. A pause, then the door opened.

"Good evening, Mr. Heppelwhite," said Pascoe.

Charlie Heppelwhite didn't look as if he agreed. He also gave no sign that he was contemplating letting Pascoe into his house.

"Who's there, Charlie?" demanded his wife from an inner room, her voice easily drowning the manic chatter of some television compère.

Heppelwhite called back, "It's all right, Mother," and now motioned Pascoe to enter, having decided that this was the lesser of two evils. He didn't quite put his finger to his lips and make shushing noises, but Pascoe found himself almost tiptoeing as he followed the long gangling figure into the cold front room. Here again was all the evidence needed to indicate a proud do-it-yourselfer. The paint and paper looked as though they had been put on yesterday and the light which revealed all this splendor came from a pseudo-crystal chandelier suspended on a gleaming brass chain. Pascoe knew the crystals were pseudo because they did not tinkle when he walked into them.

"Sorry," said Heppelwhite. "The ceiling's not high enough."

"That's one way of looking at it," agreed Pascoe. "I wonder if your son's in, Mr. Heppelwhite."

"Oh, Clint, You want to see *him*?" Heppelwhite sounded amazed.

"If he's at home," answered Pascoe.

"Yes, sure. Well, he's down the garden," amended Heppelwhite. "He's doing something with his bike. He keeps it in the shed down the garden. Shall I give him a call?"

"No, that's all right," said Pascoe, thinking it would be useful both to see the bike close up and also to interview the youth away from his parents. "I'll just chat to him in the shed."

"Right," said Heppelwhite. "I'll show you." He led the way out and as they passed the open door of the rear living room, he stuck his head in and said, "Betsy, it's Mr. Pascoe come to see our Clint."

Pascoe tried to keep going. He suspected that Heppelwhite's apparent indifference to his reason for wanting to interview the boy would be more than compensated for by his wife. Ahead was a door which opened to reveal a kitchen and, beyond, the back door of the house. But he was not to escape.

"Pascoe? That Inspector? What's he want? Fetch him

in here, Charlie," commanded the voice. And to reinforce the seriousness of the order, the television sound was turned down.

Down, but not off. "Off" was for deaths in the family, recalled Pascoe from memories of his own family on his father's side (not much referred to by his own family on his mother's side). There was a range of permitted sound level for other events and visitors ranging from almost inaudible for the vicar, non-family deaths and juicy scandal, to full blast for the insurance man, the rent man and anything political.

"Police" obviously came almost alongside non-family deaths, and on the twenty-six-inch color screen a man with the face of a dissipated gnome whispered in manic glee as an old woman tried to jump through a hoop.

Mrs. Heppelwhite was not alone. Seated alongside her on the calf-hide sofa was another woman, of an age but not yet thickened into monolith. Pascoe had often remarked the strange process by which northern women of a certain age became their own statues—solid, monumental, larger than life-size. This one had missed it and, though far from slim, was well proportioned, had shining black, elegantly styled hair and a round, attractive, vaguely Oriental face.

"What's our Colin done?" demanded Betsy Heppelwhite, rising menancingly as the reluctant Pascoe was ushered in.

"I just want to talk to him, that's all," said Pascoe. "A few questions."

"What about?" demanded the woman. "Is it still this business with Sandra?"

The other woman started and Pascoe guessed who she was before Heppelwhite intervened to say, "Inspector, have you met Mrs. Burkill, Sandra's mam?"

"No, I haven't," said Pascoe. "How do you do? I just called at your house, Mrs. Burkill. I thought I might have a chat with Sandra, if that's all right. But she wasn't in."

The woman looked surprised. "She was in when I came round here," she said.

"Oh, she'll have gone down to the chippie," said Mrs. Heppelwhite. "You still haven't said what you want with our Colin, Inspector."

"Just to talk," said Pascoe blandly, though he knew that more than blandness was going to be needed here.

"Right," she said. "You can talk. But I'll be there when you do."

"Really, there's no need," said Pascoe. "I was just going to pop into the shed and have a few words while he's cleaning his bike."

"Come on then," said Mrs. Heppelwhite. "I'll show you. Charlie, make a cup of tea."

She strode out of the living room and the others followed, like tugs behind a liner. Heppelwhite and Deirdre Burkill stopped at the kitchen door while Pascoe and Mrs. Heppelwhite moved in silence over the springy lawn toward a substantial shed at the bottom of the garden. A light showed through the single-paned window, but there was no sound of tinkering within, and Pascoe had a premonition that Clint somehow become aware of his presence and made off.

But when Mrs. Heppelwhite flung open the shed door, he realized he couldn't have been more wrong.

Clint Heppelwhite was there all right, but not tinkering with his bike.

He lay on the floor on some old sacking, his jeans unbelted and pushed down over his buttocks. Alongside him lay a girl with her blouse opened and her bra pushed up over her breasts. She was holding the youth's penis in her left hand while his right hand lay between her legs. She turned her round attractive face toward the door and for a brief moment regarded the intruders with Chinese inscrutability. Pascoe saw the family resemblance instantly.

Then she started screaming. Clint pushed himself to his feet, his face slack with shock. His mother, after a moment of utter stillness, advanced, swinging her fists like a fairground boxer and shouting, "You stupid sod . . . you little cow . . . bitch . . . thick . . . I'll kill you, I'll murder you."

Her blows were being aimed as indiscriminately as her abuse. Pascoe advanced, recognizing a duty to interpose his own body, and discovered that her indiscrimination included him. The two youngsters were attempting to take evasive action, the shed shook and the gleaming motorbike with its front wheel removed and surrounded by oil cans and wrenches, toppled slowly off its stand.

Clint let out a cry of agony and wrath and for a second looked as if he might be going to attack his mother.

Then from the doorway came an outraged cry of "*Sandra*" and everything stopped. Everything except Clint's attempts to right his motorbike and pull up his jeans at the same time. Sandra Burkill made no attempt to adjust her disordered clothing but stood against the furthermost wall, breathing hard and regarding her mother with calm indifference.

"Get yourself fastened up," grated Deirdre Burkill. Her voice was low with repressed anger. Behind her Charlie Heppelwhite's long anxious face moved from side to side to get a better view into the crowded shed. He had one hand on Deirdre's shoulder, though whether in comfort or restraint Pascoe could not decide. If restraint, it wasn't very successful as the next moment proved.

Sandra said, "Keep your sodding hair on," and started up to pull down her bra in a manner which may or may not have been deliberately provocative. Pascoe didn't think there was enough space left in the crowded shed for speedy movement but he was wrong. With a cry of "You stupid little cow!" Deirdre Burkill shouldered aside all intervening bodies as she flung herself forward and delivered a full-blooded slap across her daughter's face.

"Bloody little tart," she went on, punctuating each word with another blow. Sandra crouched low in the face of this onslaught, covering up with her arms, and Mrs. Heppelwhite, having had her role as assailant taken away from her, now assumed that of defender.

"Stop that," Deirdre!" she commanded, grappling with her friend from behind, and Sandra, seeing her chance, scrambled along the floor toward the doorway. Here she paused to yell over her shoulder, "You can fucking talk!" Then as her mother threatened a renewed onslaught, she pushed past Heppelwhite and disappeared into the darkness.

"Don't just stand there looking stupid!" commanded the thin man's wife. "See where the lass goes!"

Charlie nodded but didn't move immediately. Then with a despairing shake of his head, he turned and went in pursuit.

Pascoe's mind was working furiously. Ideally he would have liked to talk to almost everybody, alone, immediately, while their pulses were still racing. Failing that, Clint was as good a place to start as any.

"Mrs. Heppelwhite," he said, "Mrs. Burkill's upset. Why don't you take her up to the house and get her a cup of tea? Make one for us all, eh?"

To his surprise, she made no demur, but put her arm around her friend's shoulders and led her out. Pascoe suspected the respite would not be long, so he turned immediately to the youth, who had now righted both his motorbike and his trousers and said, "So it was you, was it? All the time."

"What?"

"Screwing the Burkill kid. Whose idea was it to blame the dentist?"

"What d'you mean?" demanded Clint.

"Oh come one, Heppelwhite! You were caught at it! With my own eyes, I saw it! Is this where you always met? Handy, eh? Just over the garden hedge!"

"Don't be bloody stupid! You're bloody daft, you are!"

"And you're bloody insane if you think you can get away with talking to me like that!" snapped Pascoe, taking a menacing step toward the youth, who retreated behind his bike in alarm.

"You've got it all wrong," he said in a more moderate tone. "Tonight was the first time I'd touched her. Honest. I was just working on the bike and she came in, dead casual like. Well, she sometimes did. You know how kids are, hanging around. She was just a kid, I'd never thought of her as owt but just a kid."

"Don't give me that! Are you blind? I bet you've mangled your meat many a time over pictures of skinnier lasses that Sandra!" said Pascoe coarsely.

"I never thought of her as owt else but a kid!" insisted Clint. "Not till tonight. But it was different, now I knew—"

"What?"

"That she were in the club. Someone had poked her. I knew that and it made a difference."

The boy spoke defiantly and convincingly, but Pascoe was a long way from being ready to be convinced.

"So you just grabbed her!" He sneered. "And she said OK. Just like that!"

"Just about," said Clint. "We sort of bumped into each other. It's not very big this place. That's how it got started."

Pascoe changed his tack. "Listen, lad," he said confidentially. "There's nothing to be ashamed of, really. No one'll blame you. Don't get me wrong. You're not going to get away with anything, but we've got you now anyway. So why not give us it straight."

"What d'you mean, got me?" demanded Clint.

Pascoe shook his head in mock bewilderment. "What's this all about, lad, but illegal carnal knowledge of a girl under age? I mean, you're not going to deny that, are you? I was here. Your mother was here. Your father was here. *Her* mother was here. We all saw it. It won't help saying you were the second or even the fifty-second. You're the one who's been caught on the job. So why muck up that dentist's life? What've you got against the poor bastard?"

"Nothing. I've got nothing against him!" denied Clint.

"Oh? Is that why you were squirting weed killer over his lawn last night?" asked Pascoe.

"That was because he'd been playing around with Sandra," insisted the youth. "These sods think they can . . ." He tailed off as he became aware of his admission.

"Come on," said Pascoe abruptly.

"Where?"

"Up to the house first. Then down to the station. What did you think? I was going to smack your wrist and send you off to bed without any supper?"

Back in the house, he found the two women sitting in the living room drinking tea. The telly had been switched off.

"What's he been saying to you?" demanded Mrs. Heppelwhite of her son.

Pascoe answered. "I've been questioning your boy about two offenses, Mrs. Heppelwhite. One involves an assault on a girl under the age of consent. The other involves trespass and willful damage, to wit, entering upon the property of Mr. Jack Shorter and applying weed killer to his lawn. This offense he has admitted, the other he can hardly deny."

This reduced Mrs. Heppelwhite to silence momentarily and during the moment, her husband came in.

"Where's Sandra?" asked Deirdre Burkill.

"At home," said Charlie. "It's all right. I made her a cup of tea."

"I'd better go," said the woman.

"Hold on just a second," said Pascoe. "I'll come with you. I'd like a quick word with the girl, if you don't mind."

"I wanted to send for Bri," said Mrs. Heppelwhite to her husband. "But Deirdre wouldn't let me."

"Probably best," said Charlie. "Let things settle first."

"They'll be a while settling," said Pascoe. "I'm taking your son down to the station with me to make a statement."

"You're what?"

"He says something about Colin putting weed killer on that dentist's garden," said Mrs. Heppelwhite.

"Is that right, Clint?"

To Pascoe's relief the boy nodded miserably. If he had started denying it now, it could have made things difficult.

"The dirty bugger had it coming to him," said Deirdre Burkill savagely. "And worse."

"He's got worse," said Pascoe. "His wife could be dead by this time. She took an overdose."

His words turned off all sound as firmly as the television switch.

"Oh God," said Charlie Heppelwhite finally.

"Yes," said Pascoe. "Remember that. There's no way of getting at just one person. Others have to suffer too. Mr. Heppelwhite, I'll leave Clint here with you for a couple of minutes. I'm sure you'll be able to persuade him it'd be pointless and futile to take off. Mrs. Burkill, ready?"

"For what?" said the woman, but she accompanied him out of the house without protest.

There was a gap in the hedge between the two back gardens and after they had pushed through it, Mrs. Burkill stopped and turned to Pascoe. "Is it right what you said about that fellow's wife?" she asked.

"Yes," said Pascoe.

"What'd she do a thing like that for?"

"Who knows?" said Pascoe.

"It makes you bloody wonder, doesn't it?" said the woman wearily. She took a deep breath and looked up at the sky and shook her head. Pascoe looked up too. The stars were at their old confidence trick. As they watched, on the western horizon one fell.

"Make a wish," said Deirdre Burkill and opened her kitchen door.

Sandra was sitting in the living room with the television on. The room was like Burkill's front garden, neat and tidy enough, but untouched by the hand of enthusiasm. The furniture belonged to the early 'fifties and a coal fire burned in the original old black range. Only an onyx clock, presented for fifteen years as secretary at the Westgate Club, brought a touch of modernity to the decor. And it was wrong.

"You all right?" asked Deirdre.

The girl didn't answer and her mother angrily pulled the television plug from its socket.

"I were watching that!" protested Sandra.

Pascoe didn't want another domestic battle and walk-out, so he intervened swiftly. "Sandra, I'm Detective-Inspector Pascoe. I'd like a chat with you if you don't mind."

He sat down beside her on the sofa and wished he had a WPC with him and Mrs. Burkill out of the room. He studied the girl carefully. Apart from her fully developed figure, there was nothing remarkable for her age, and these days even that wasn't very remarkable. She wore no make-up; her hair was long, brown and straight, apparently untouched by rollers and setting lotions; her plain white blouse (now buttoned up) and straight gray skirt belonged in the old tradition of school uniform.

There must be thousands like her, he thought. Except that there *was* something else, a kind of sensuous aura, which he would have dismissed as a simple masculine response to knowledge of her experience and condition (Clint's defense, he recollected) had it not been for his strong sense of the same quality in her mother.

"I want to ask about you and Clint, Sandra," he said gently. "Has it been going on long?"

"Has what?" she said.

"How long's he been playing about with you?" demanded Mrs. Burkill.

"He hasn't!" denied Sandra.

"What the hell was he doing tonight then? Giving you driving lessons?"

"Please, Mrs. Burkill," said Pascoe.

"Please, nothing. You want her to answer questions, don't you? There's only one way with this one. I should know. Come on, girl, or you'll get the back of my hand!"

Pascoe sat back in resignation. What am I doing here? he wondered. Looking for truth? Truth like the light from those sodding stars. By the time it reached you, it had taken so long that it lit up nothing and its source was probably an empty lifeless shell.

"Me and Clint never did anything before," the girl was saying. "It was just tonight, that's all. We were just mucking about."

"Mucking about? Haven't you had enough mucking about to last you? Listen, how far's it gone with him? Has he been all the way with you, Sandra?"

"Don't be daft! I'm telling you—"

"I think it's a pack of lies you're telling me!" shouted Deirdre Burkill. "Do you know that dentist's wife's killed herself? Do you know that? So I'm asking you. Was it Clint put you in the club? Was it? *Was it?*"

"No, no, no, no, no!" screamed the girl. "It wasn't, it wasn't. And don't ask me any more bloody questions!" She jumped up and rammed the television plug back in.

"You wait till your father gets home," threatened her mother.

"Yeah," said Sandra. "I'll wait." And she made that sound like a threat too.

There was nothing more in this for him, Pascoe realized. Mrs. Burkill's approach might have been outside the range of the police training manuals, but she'd put the questions he wanted putting.

He stood up. "I'll say good night then, Sandra."

"'Night," she said.

Deirdre Burkill went with him to the door.

"Thanks for your help," he said, only half ironically.

"I'll get it out of her," she said. "If there's owt to get out."

"Don't press her too much," answered Pascoe. "She must be pretty mixed up inside."

"She'll be mixed up outside if I haven't had some sense from her by the time Brian gets home," she said grimly.

The ultimate deterrent, that was our Bri, thought Pascoe as he stood alone between the two houses and wished he was safe in his bed with a day at the office, or the shop, or the factory, or the classroom to look forward to tomorrow, anything to justify the pain of waking up.

With a sigh, he re-entered the Heppelwhites'.

Nineteen

Next morning was lightly covered with a perfect spring sky, pale blue but vibrant with sunlight and sparsely flecked with puff-ball clouds. It was a sky to make even a Yorkshireman less grimly affirmative than usual that it'd rain before teatime.

Pascoe rang the infirmary as soon as he got up. The news that Emma Shorter was off the critical list confirmed his high spirits and he essayed a few bars of "It Was a Lover and His Lass" in the car on the way to work.

"Morning, sir. Lovely morning," he said to Dalziel, who looked as if he'd been kept waiting three hours.

"It'll pee down before noon," said Dalziel. "You'll see."

"Hey ding a ding a ding," said Pascoe.

"What? You're not going screwy on me, are you, lad? I

began to wonder when I heard you'd brought young Clint Heppelwhite in last night. What's it all about."

Pascoe told him and waited for comment.

"Think it'll get your mate Shorter off the hook, do you?" inquired Dalziel finally.

"I thought it opened up a new possibility," said Pascoe.

"Don't you think it was one of the first things Inspector Trumper checked out? Boyfriends; who might have been having a nibble? Nothing to show."

"Well, there's something to show now," said Pascoe. "I saw it."

"So Clint's the daddy. When he finds out, what's he do?"

"He doesn't want Brian Burkill to know for a start," said Pascoe.

"So what's he *do*?"

"He looks around for someone else to blame."

"And he picks on Shorter? Why?"

"He's read his Sunday papers. He knows that doctors and dentists are easy meat for that kind of accusation."

"And Sandra goes along with this. Why?"

"To protect him," said Pascoe. "And to protect herself. It makes her more the injured innocent than being screwed in the garden shed while your mam's watching telly twenty yards away."

"It's not a bad little plot," said Dalziel. "Clever in a way. You've seen more of this lad than I have. Be honest. Do you think he could think up something like this?"

"It's not *that* complicated," said Pascoe defiantly.

"No, come on, Peter. Do you think he could get much further than putting her in a hot bath with a bottle of gin? Or just jumping on his bike and taking off?"

"I'm not a mind reader!" protested Pascoe.

"Aren't you? I thought that's what they paid us for," said Dalziel. "Any road, we've wasted enough time on this. The Haggard business is more important. You're going to talk to Arany today, are you?"

"I thought I'd put Sergeant Wield on to him while I had another chat with Toms," said Pascoe.

"Right. I'll drop in on God Blengdale then, see what he does with someone his own size. Hop to it, lad! There's work to be done!"

Back in his own room, Pascoe buzzed Sergeant Wield, but he wasn't in, which was annoying as he needed to co-ordinate the approaches to Blengdale, Arany and Toms. Which reminded him, he'd better check where the film director was likely to be that morning.

The phone rang before he could pick it up. He answered it abruptly. "Hello!"

"How busy, how important you sound," said a woman's voice. "If only *we* could learn the secret of sounding so important and so busy."

"Good morning, Ms. Lacewing," said Pascoe. "What can I do for you?"

"I should like to see you . . . *Peter*," she answered. She made his name sound like a verb, he thought.

"You would?"

"Yes. Please."

Was it imagination or were there erotic vibrations in that "please"?

"Could you tell me what this is about Ms. Lacewing?" he asked.

"Honestly, it would be better if we could meet."

"All right. Why don't you come around here at—"

"Oh no. Not *there*. Can't you come to me? Really, it would be so much more . . . convenient."

It was unmistakable now, the sensuous undertone. And interestingly, despite his certainty that she was merely mocking him, Pascoe began to feel himself aroused.

"I could call around at the surgery, I suppose. Let me have a look at my diary."

"Now," she said. "It has to be now. You understand; straightaway. Please. You won't regret it."

Pascoe sat and listened to the burr of the dialing tone for a long moment. Even that sounded sexy. He replaced the receiver, rose and went to the gents. As he washed his hands he looked at himself in the mirror. A strong face without being particularly memorable. Nose long, but not excessively; eyes blue, nicely spaced; a high forehead; well-sculpted brows; good teeth in a good mouth, which took on a rather Puritanical set in repose; chin perhaps a little off center? Well, who's perfect? *L'homme moyen sensuel,* that's what he saw. A good face for a policeman.

Not the face that would inspire Ms. Lacewing to offer her all at eleven o'clock in the morning. No, she was taking the piss, but that meant she really had something to tell him, so he had better go.

Carefully he combed his almost black hair and adjusted the knot in his tie. Then, realizing what he was doing, he pressed his face close to the mirror and said, "Who's a cheeky boy, then?" to the surprise of the uniformed inspector who had just come through the door.

* * *

"Good of you to come," said Ms. Lacewing, very businesslike. She must have been on the watch for him, for she had appeared in the entrance hall as soon as he arrived.

"I hope it's worth my while," said Pascoe.

She grinned at him sardonically. Her hands were thrust deep into the pockets of her white coat. It was unfair, thought Pascoe. Uniforms made men look all the same; but women, certain women anyway, made uniforms variform.

"I'm sorry about the Mae West bit," she said. "It was rather childish. Will you come this way?" She led him into her surgery. "Next door in the office I've got Alice Andover."

"Good God," said Pascoe. "Is she a patient?"

"One of MacCrystal's, but that's not why she's here. No, Alice is a sort of member of WRAG."

Pascoe looked at her in disbelief. "But she's seventy! And more than a bit cracked!"

"Conditions which have failed to disqualify many men from leading their countries," said Ms. Lacewing acidly. "We picketed the Calliope Kinema Club one night. Alice watched us through her window. She was in here visiting MacCrystal the following day and she spotted me. Well, we talked. She was like a child who's been shut in a city house all her life and suddenly discovers the countryside. So I invited her to a meeting. She was a knockout! She tended to ramble a bit, all about the old days, but at least she was now starting to see them for what they were!"

"So, you destroyed an old woman's happy memories," said Pascoe. "Congratulations. Where do I come in?"

"We gave her a new future," retorted Ms. Lacewing. "To continue. Alice was adamant that she didn't want her sister to know what she was doing. Nor would she become involved with any protest aimed at that man Haggard. He was her neighbor and a friend of the family, she said. That was fine, I said. But she made me promise to let her in on any other protest I was organizing."

"Don't tell me," said Pascoe. "She's put itching powder in all the jockstraps at the Rugby Club."

Ms. Lacewing looked at him curiously. "It's interesting how many men fall back on coarseness as a defense weapon," she mused. "It's an attempt to reaffirm the old outmoded sexist relationship, of course."

"Great," said Pascoe. "Now I know what I am, can we get back to Miss Andover."

"Miss Alice Andover," said Ms. Lacewing. "She's the younger sister, remember. She came in here this morning to talk to me. She was a little agitated but in control. I listened, then I advised her to go to the police. She became very agitated then. Such is the confidence you inspire!"

"While people rush joyfully to their dentists. Go on."

"I then offered to get the police here. She named you. For some reason, she seems to suspect you may be human."

"Well, she *is* seventy," said Pascoe. "And what is it that she wants to say to me?"

"It's a confession," said the woman seriously. "Be kind to her. Through here, please." She led him into the office next door.

Alice Andover, wearing an ankle-length black coat and

a little lace-trimmed black hat, was sitting by the desk drinking a cup of tea. As soon as she saw him she began to talk, as if fearful that delay might induce some permanent dumbness.

"Inspector," she said, "it's so kind of you. I am so sorry. I hope that it has not put you to too much—"

"Alice!" said Ms. Lacewing in a commanding voice.

"I'm sorry, my dear. Be forthright, you said. Of course, you're right, I shall be."

She took a deep breath, leaned forward, fixed her faded blue eyes unblinkingly on Pascoe's nose and said, "Inspector, I want to confess. Mr. Haggard's apartment. I did it. No, that's not really forthright, is it? Let me be plain. It was I, Alice Andover, who last Friday night wrecked Gilbert Haggard's apartment. And I should like to make a statement."

"I've never really cared for Mr. Haggard," said Alice.

It was the kind of voice and the kind of sentence with which radio plays used to begin—and perhaps still did for all Pascoe knew. He and the old lady were sitting alone. Thelma Lacewing had gone to make another pot of tea at Alice's insistence and to Pascoe's relief. One liberated woman at a time was quite enough.

"I know he was very kind to us," continued Alice. "How kind I cannot tell. Annabelle has always taken care of our finances, but from what she has let fall, I gather we were greatly in Mr. Haggard's debt. Nevertheless, as far as personal relationships go, she had always been much closer to Mr. Haggard than I. Just how close I did not realize till recently."

She pursed her lips disapprovingly and sipped cold tea.

"You know, of course, that Annabelle used to act as a kind of matron when the school was running. I helped also from time to time. There is a door . . . of course, you have seen it. Mr. Haggard put it in. It led directly into his apartment so that children from the school would be less likely to stray into our house. At least that was the reason he gave. But how long this has been going on, I cannot bring myself to think."

"What?" asked Pascoe.

She ignored him. "It's an old house, ours. Full of noises. And memories. I'm sorry. When you have as many cats as we have, of course, you get used to noise at night. In any case, since the film shows started I have tended to turn off my deaf aid at night. But last Friday night, early Saturday morning, I woke up feeling thirsty, and when I automatically turned my aid on I heard footsteps overhead."

She paused (quite unconsciously, Pascoe guessed) for dramatic effect.

"When I went to my sister's room to tell her there was an intruder in the house, I found her bed empty. It must have been her I'd heard, I decided. Perhaps one of the cats had been shut in upstairs. It sometimes happens. Then they howl and howl till someone lets them out.

"On the other hand, I thought, perhaps there *was* an intruder and Annabelle too had been disturbed by his footsteps. She's so arrogant in many ways. She would never dream of waking me for help. I don't know if you have an elder sister, Mr. Pascoe?"

"No, I haven't," said Pascoe.

"If you had, I'm sure you'd know what I mean. Well, I

returned to my room, took my big pinking scissors from my sewing box just in case it *was* a burglar, and went up to see. Isn't it odd how strange your own house can become? That staircase. How many times must I have climbed it. But now it seemed so steep, so twisting . . . And at the top, on the landing, I could see a light. Not an electric light, but flickering. I realized it was coming from the nursery door, which was ajar. I tiptoed over the landing, though I needn't have worried, for I doubt if I would have been heard.

"And I peered in."

She paused again, shaking her head slowly, as though still disbelieving. Pascoe said nothing. He was now ahead of her and had no way of gauging the effect of such a shock on the woman's sensibility.

"It was hard to grasp what was going on at first. The light was so dim. It was one of those old-fashioned night lights they used to leave by the beds of the children who were afraid of the dark. Annabelle was there. She was wearing our old nurse's uniform. She must have got it from the trunk in the attic. And she had a cane. Mr. Haggard was sprawled across the rocking horse. He had his pajamas on, with the trousers pulled down so that his buttocks were exposed." She stopped. Her face began to crumble slightly.

Pascoe wondered if he should call for Ms. Lacewing. "Please, take it easy, Miss Alice," he said. "It must have been a great shock."

"Yes," she said. "Yes. It was a very great shock." She visibly shook herself now and sat very upright. "Under-

stand me, Inspector," she said in a stronger voice. "I'm
old but I am not innocent. I am not a virgin, you know."

She glared defiantly at him. Pascoe was speechless.
Then she laughed. "There. I've said it. I wouldn't have
been able to say a thing like that before I met Thelma.
She's a marvelous girl, don't you think?"

"Marvelous," said Pascoe.

"And yet," said Alice thoughtfully, "I rather think *she*
may still be a virgin. Now isn't that odd?"

"Very," said Pascoe.

"As I was saying," continued the old woman, "I have
heard of such things. I have always known that Annabelle
was—How shall I put it?—a rough, hard sort of girl. She
should have been a man, really. Our father would have
liked it, I think. And as I've told you, I've always found
something rather distasteful about Mr. Haggard. I cannot
understand why they were doing this thing. I abhor pain
so much myself, giving or feeling it. But it wasn't that. It
was the nursery. That's really all that's left to us of our
childhood, those few old things. I often used to go up
there and sit there by myself and remember, and wonder
how it would have been if I too had had children. There
was a boy, but he . . . well, that was many years ago. So,
you see, it was a very special room to me. Now it was
spoilt, spoilt forever. Do you understand that!"

"Yes," said Pascoe. "I think I do."

"I didn't think it out then, not in the sense of proper
thought. But I suppose what I felt was that he had spoilt
my room, so I would spoil his. I knew what I was doing.
I'm not trying to say that my mind went blank or anything

like that. No. I went through the door into his kitchen and then through the living room and down the corridor to his study. And then, well, you saw what I did. I scratched and I tore and where I was strong enough, I broke. I still had my scissors with me—"

"Pinking shears," said Pascoe suddenly.

"Yes, that's right."

"God. Of course. Those curved edges. I should have guessed! I'm not much of a Sherlock Holmes!"

"I should hope not," she answered. "All those drugs. I broke open his desk, I've seen them do it on television, it's really very easy. And I scattered whatever I found all over the place. Some of the things, such filth, I really did begin to lose control and I don't know what I might not have done if the phone hadn't brought me to my senses."

"The phone."

"Yes. Suddenly it rang. I was paralyzed. Suppose Mr. Haggard heard it and returned. I snatched up the receiver. Luckily I realized it would be fatal to speak. My scissors were in my hand, so I snipped the wire. Just like that. For the first time I felt guilty. Wasn't that odd? I suppose in a way it was public property. The rest of the stuff belonged to Mr. Haggard, but not the telephone."

Pascoe smiled inwardly at the distinction, but he had enough sense to keep the smile very inward. "What happened then, Miss Alice?" he asked.

"I went back to our house as quickly as possible," she said. "I was very frightened."

"Oh," said Pascoe, disappointed. "Then what? You went back to sleep?"

"No! Do you think I could have slept after such an experience even if Archie hadn't been missing."

"Archie?" said Pascoe.

"Yes. I love all my cats, Mr. Pascoe, but Archie seems to love me best. He follows me everywhere. Sometimes he's so desperate for a cuddle that I think he must have had a deprived childhood. And I thought, Suppose he followed me through into Wilkinson House and I'd shut him in there? I had to go back, of course."

"Because if Haggard saw him, he would guess who had wrecked his study."

The old woman looked at him as if he were slightly insane. "That never crossed my mind," she said. "Poor Archie would be so terrified if he found himself alone in a strange place. Of course I had to fetch him. I tiptoed back up the stairs and through the door—"

"Was Mr. Haggard still in the nursery?" interrupted Pascoe.

"I didn't care to look again," said Alice primly. "But there was still a light showing through the door, so I guessed he was. I went straight to the study, but Archie wasn't there. When I saw what I had done, my heart sank. We do terrible things to each other, don't we, Mr. Pascoe?"

"I'm afraid we do," said Pascoe gently. "Did you find Archie?"

"Not a sign. I looked through the whole house—"

"You mean you went downstairs?" asked Pascoe, incredulous at the thought of this old lady tiptoeing through the dark empty house.

"Of course. Archie gets lost very easily. I had to make

sure. Then while I was in the little cinema part, I heard the front door open. I was more frightened that I have ever been, Inspector. It was worse even than the munitions factory during the war."

"Factory?"

"Yes. I made bombs. I mean, I did something to something which went inside a bomb and one day there was a fire. It was in the canteen, quite safe really I suppose. But when the alarm went, they couldn't get the emergency exit open and I thought I should die of terror. But this was worse. I heard footsteps. They paused outside the cinema door. I was down on my hands and knees between the seats, looking for Archie. I held my breath. The door opened. I am not a very devout person, Inspector, but I prayed. It was, I recall, a rather general kind of prayer, taking in most of the accepted religions. I don't know which of them is the True Faith, but one of them worked. The footsteps went on up the stairs. I wonder what Thelma is doing with your tea?"

The bathos was too much for Pascoe, who got up from the desk and took a turn around the room. "What happened then, Miss Alice?" he demanded.

"I told you," she said, surprised. "He went upstairs."

"No, I mean to you. You were still trapped. In the dark. Hiding. What did you do?"

"Oh, I see," said Alice. "I went out of the front door and into our front door. It was quite a mild night and I was only in the open for a few seconds."

"You carry a key in your dressing gown?" said Pascoe.

"Of course not. But we always leave one in a hiding place by the front door in case we ever lock ourselves out.

And ever since the munitions factory, I have refused to have bars or chains on any door."

"I see," said Pascoe weakly. "And that was that?"

"Not quite. There was one thing more. Do you know, when I got into my bedroom, there was Archie, asleep on my pillow!"

Pascoe tried to look suitably astounded at this irony. "Just one other thing, Miss Alice," he said. "When the front door opened, Mr. Haggard's front door, I mean, what kind of noise did you hear? Was it just an ordinary noise, like someone using a key?"

"I suppose so," said the old lady. "What else might it be? Why would he not use his key?"

"He? You mean you saw who it was?"

"Of course I did. I may be a frightened old woman, but I was not going to crouch there with my eyes shut while someone came towards me! No, I saw him clearly in the doorway."

"Who?" asked Pascoe.

"Mr. Arany, of course. The foreign gentleman who works for Mr. Haggard. You don't think I would have refrained from telephoning the police if I had reason to think there were burglars in the house?"

On this note of civic indignation, Thelma Lacewing returned with the tea tray. "How's it going?" she said lightly. "I see no manacles yet, Alice."

"It's going fine," said Pascoe, taking his tea. "Why are you telling me this, Miss Alice. Or rather, why have you waited so long?"

"I was frightened," said the woman simply. "I lay awake all that night. I heard the fire engine and the ambulance and wondered what on earth was happening. Then you called next morning and I thought you'd come to arrest me. That's why I acted so stupid—it's a defense mechanism, I think you call it. When I learned that Mr. Haggard had been attacked and killed, I must admit there was some relief mixed with my shock. How awful that sounds. But at least it seemed as if my sister's relationship with that man need never come out."

"But you have brought it out now," said Pascoe gently.

"Yes. I had to," she said firmly. "It took me some while to realize what I must do. But a man has been murdered. I have no right to stand in the way of justice."

"It was a brave decision," said Pascoe sincerely. "And a right one. Have you told your sister you were going to talk to me, Miss Alice?"

"No. I'm afraid I funked that," said the old woman. "I came and spoke with Thelma, whose advice was that I should speak with you. But now, of course, I must inform Annabelle of what I have done."

"I've assured Alice that Annabelle is in no way involved in anything illegal, Inspector. And that there can be no repercussions and should be no publicity," said Ms. Lacewing.

Now who's beginning to have a bad conscience? thought Pascoe.

"No repercussions certainly. And I shall be discreet," he said, rising. "Thank you both for your help and cooperation."

Miss Alice offered her hand. He took it and pressed it with both his own. Ms. Lacewing smiled insolently at him, tongue moistening her wicked little teeth.

Pascoe grinned amiably back at her. If Alice's estimate was right, Ms. Lacewing knew nothing of the waters she was fishing in. She would have to make a better cast than that to get another rise out of him.

Twenty

Pascoe arrived back at the station to find that Dalziel had just gone out but Wield had just come in.

Quickly he told the sergeant what he'd learned.

"Things are beginning to fall into place," he said. "We're beginning to get some idea of where everyone was and what they were doing."

"You reckon Arany for it now, do you?" asked Wield.

"You sound unhappy about it," said Pascoe.

"Well, I can't see any motive, sir. I was happier at the thought of Blengdale caning him, then going over the top for some reason."

"That's out anyway." Pascoe glanced sharply at Wield. "You're not thinking Miss Annabelle might have . . ."

Wield shrugged. "Nothing's impossible. Not after what I've just heard anyway."

"Whatever happened, we need to talk to Arany. No

more pussyfooting either. I want him here and I want him cautioned. You see to that will you, Sergeant? Toms will have to wait. I'm going after Mr. Dalziel to put him in the picture. Besides, I quite fancy seeing him operate on Blengdale!"

Blengdale's lumber year was fairly central, situated on the west bank of the old canal which ran its deep straight line alongside the shallow curving river. In the flooding which followed the great thaw of 1963 the two waterways had joined up, but the banks of both had been strengthened since then and a new line of trees planted on the isthmus between so that a nature lover strolling through the park on the east bank of the river was hardly aware of the monuments to industry only a couple of hundred yards away.

Not that they too lacked their lovers. Beauty was in the gut of the beholder, thought Pascoe, and though the old wharves, warehouses and barges couldn't give him the kick that he derived from a single stunted tree on a naked fellside, yet there was something in these relics of industrial capitalism which caught at the heart. Perhaps it was pride in the illimitable energies of mankind, and despair at their direction.

Blengdale's yard had originally been nothing more than that—an open space between a mill and a warehouse with its own canal frontage and a kind of dutch barn to protect the stored timber from the worst of the weather. Economy and antiquity had brought about the closure of the mill in the early 'sixties and it had lain derelict till Godfrey Blengdale had breathed new life into the family timber business and diversified into ready-to-assemble whitewood furniture. He had bought the mill for a song (so they said) and (so they said again) sold what remained of the old-fashioned looms and other machinery to a variety of industrial museums for rather more than he had paid for the building. Now, where generations of women had labored for very little in an atmosphere full of fluff and fiber, men moved at half the pace for half the time at fifty times the wage, and the air was full of wood dust and complaints.

The nearest Pascoe had been to the yard before was some years earlier when Blengdale had celebrated something (his first ulcer, perhaps) by holding a party there. The bar had been on a barge strung from bow to stern with Chinese lanterns, and a dance band had played among the stacks of timber while the guests gyrated on the wharf. Pascoe had traveled slowly by in a police boat and felt the disdainful superiority of the guardian to the guarded.

This time he approached by road and the first thing he noticed was Dalziel's car parked outside on a double yellow line. Pascoe squeezed in behind him and entered the building, stepping into an atmosphere heavy with noise and sawdust. He presumed there was order here, but his first impression was of utter chaos. He approached a man who seemed to be in some perturbation of spirit about the relative lengths of two pieces of wood he was carrying.

"Mr. Blengdale? Right over there. Up the stairs. Them's his offices."

"Them" were a line of windows at first-floor level in the

high-ceilinged building. There were figures within, but he couldn't identify anyone at this distance. As he moved away he heard the man with the planks mutter, "Centi-fucking-meters! I told him, centi-fucking-meters!"

He was almost at the foot of the stairs which ran up the wall to the first-floor level when he spotted Charlie Heppelwhite. He was running lengths of wood over a circular saw with a speed and precision which obviously derived from long practice. To Pascoe's untutored eye it seemed that the proximity of spinning blades and soft flesh should demand rather more than 100 per cent concentration, but in Charlie's case automatic expertise was obviously enough, for the man's mind was so far from his surroundings that Pascoe had to shout his name twice before he became aware of his presence.

"Oh, it's you," he said stupidly like a man waking from a bad dream to a worse reality.

"Everything all right?" said Pascoe.

"Why shouldn't it be?" asked Charlie, beginning to recover his poise a little. "What do you want now, Mr. Pascoe?"

"Nothing. Nothing. Just passing through," said Pascoe, realizing how unconvincing it must sound. "Clint here? I don't see him."

"He's out in the yard. Do you want to talk to him again?" asked Heppelwhite.

"No. Not just now. It's your boss I'm after. See you later," said Pascoe.

As he climbed the steep and worn stairs to the office, he thought with regret how impossible it was not to sound threatening when you talked to people who were involved, no matter how innocently, with police business. The staircase was enclosed by an single handrail. At the top he glanced down. Charlie Heppelwhite was looking up at him, but when their gazes met he quickly turned away and resumed his work.

These office had been built in the good old-fashioned tradition by the overseer who quite literally oversaw the work. From here you got a taskmaster's-eye view of what was going on. In the first office he came to, a dark-eyed typist, who looked about ten years younger than the machine she was beating, regarded him with little interest.

"I've come to see Mr. Blengdale," said Pascoe.

"He's in there," said the weary child.

"He's not engaged, I hope," said Pascoe.

"Through there," said the girl, as if to an idiot.

"I mean, is there anyone with him?" persisted Pascoe.

"Yeah," said the girl. And returned to her work.

Pascoe smiled to himself. It made a change to meet a secretary who didn't read the kind of women's magazine which preached that the only acceptable alternatives to mothering your family was mothering your boss. He opened the door.

"Oh God!" said Blengdale. "Here's another of 'em!"

He was sitting at a desk piled so high with paper that Pascoe felt a pang of sympathy for a fellow sufferer.

Standing in front of him as though being interviewed by a headmaster was his wife. She wore a light blue suit with a skirt long enough to be fashionable but not long enough to be trendy. A small square of blue silk sat elegantly on her sculpted locks (like a gay judge passing the death sentence, thought Pascoe gruesomely) and she wore a pair of chamois leather gloves, also in blue, which needed no label to declare they were made (probably) in Italy and had cost (certainly) fifty pounds.

Behind her in a suit so shiny that his nails scarred the glaze as they scratched his left buttock was Dalziel.

"Good. You've got here, Inspector," he said as if Pascoe was the first person in the world he expected to see.

He advanced on Pascoe and forced him into a corner. "I'm getting nowhere with this bugger," he muttered. "Say something about Haggard."

"What?" whispered Pascoe.

"Anything. Come on, lad!"

"Alice Andover caught her sister beating Haggard," he murmured.

"Louder, for Christ's sake!" said Dalziel. "His name louder."

"Haggard," said Pascoe. "She saw *Haggard* being whipped."

Dalziel nodded vigorously, turned his head and shot a baleful glance at Blengdale, who was observing them angrily. "I mayn't be able to trip the bugger, but by God! I'll scare him," muttered Dalziel.

"Superintendent!" said Blengdale. "I'm a busy man. I'm always a busy man. This morning I'm so busy, I don't think I'll catch up with myself for a month!"

"Business troubles?" said Dalziel with that spurious sympathy which Pascoe so admired. "Cash flow problems? Hard times, hard times."

"No. For Christ's sake, don't go saying things like that. That's how rumors start," said Blengdale in alarm. "Truth

is, business is too good. It's meeting the demand that's my
problem. I'm up to my eyes, and what happens? You turn
up, Gwen turns up, your sidekick turns up. The only one
who doesn't turn up's my bloody foreman and he's the
only one who can be any good to me!"

"Brian Burkill, you mean?" said Dalziel.

"Aye. Of course, you'll know him. No word. Just doesn't
appear. Trouble at home, that'll be his excuse. Show me
someone who doesn't have trouble at home! I've got trouble at home, but I've got to come in!"

"Not to worry," said Dalziel, looking out of the big
window down onto the work floor. "One of your worries
is over. There's Burkill now."

"Where?" demanded Blengdale as if he didn't trust
Dalziel. He came out from behind his desk and they all
stood in line and stared through the window.

It was indeed Burkill, threading his way across the
floor toward the office stairs. But there was something not
quite right about him, thought Pascoe. Of course—it was
his clothes. Everyone else wore overalls of some description, but Burkill was dressed in the brown checked suit
he'd been wearing at the Westgate Club the night before
last. He was walking slowly, as if uncertain where he was.
Finally he reached the bench at which Charlie Heppelwhite was working and here he stopped; Heppelwhite
turned around leaving a length of wood to be chewed at
will by the spinning blade; the two men talked; Burkill
emphasized what he was saying with hammerlike taps of
his forefinger into the other man's chest; Heppelwhite
seemed to be expostulating with him; he made nervous

waving movements with his hands; Burkill's face was thrust only a few inches from the other man's; workers at neighboring benches looked around at them curiously.

Then Blengdale opened the window, leaned out and shouted, "Burkill! Get yourself up here this bloody instant!"

Brian Burkill looked up. He hadn't shaved that morning. Whether he saw them all or only Blengdale it was hard to say. In fact, thought Pascoe, so stretched and tight was his face with some emotion, it was difficult to tell if he even saw his employer. A fork-lift truck with a load of doors came rolling down the aisle between the machines and benches. There was plenty of clearance, but to those above it seemed as if Burkill jerked away from its approach, instinctively stepping backward and turning as he did so. Or perhaps he wasn't seeing the truck either.

His shoulder caught Charlie Heppelwhite full in the chest, knocking him backward. Charlie put out his right hand to steady himself. It rested on the piece of wood he had left in the saw. The pressure of his hand was enough to drive it through the spinning blade like a piece of cheese being split by a wire.

And his hand offered even less resistance than the wood.

For a second there was no noise, or at least no noise other than the whining of the machines, the general clatter of work. Something lay on the surface of the bench and a jet of blood pumped from the end of Heppelwhite's arm, striking the whirling saw and fountaining off in all directions. Heppelwhite raised his other hand to his face as though to ward off the spray.

Then someone screamed.

It was Gwen Blengdale, standing next to Pascoe. One gloved hand was in her mouth, her eyes were wide and unblinking as she stared at the scene below.

And now everybody was moving and shouting.

Blengdale went pounding out of the office. Dalziel grabbed the telephone, dialed 999 and tersely gave instructions for an ambulance. Pascoe couldn't move. Gwen Blengdale was learning against him, her body shaking, her eyes riveted to the scene below. She had chewed the stitching loose from the glove at her mouth.

Heppelwhite had slumped to the ground now, his back against the bench. Blengdale knelt beside him. Workmates hovered around with the helplessness of the unprepared. Burkill had half turned and looked as if he would have moved away from the spot if the press of people had not prevented him. But no press was tight enough to prevent Dalziel from getting through. His tie was off and in his hand. Pushing Blengdale aside, he knelt and with a swift efficiency applied a tourniquet.

Satisfied with his handiwork, he stood up and looked around. "Belt up!" he yelled. "Bloody well belt up!"

The hubbub of talk faced away.

"Switch off them machines!" he commanded next. "And when you've done that, I want everyone out in the yard. *Go on!* You're just in the bloody way!"

What a gift for man-management he had! thought Pascoe, his arms around the still throbbing woman.

The workers slowly moved away, stunned by the accident and the way Dalziel had spoken to them. Dalziel turned to Blengdale. "You've got a stretcher? Right, fetch it!"

Blengdale looked for a second as if he was going to give an argument, then set off at the trot. Dalziel looked up at the window and made an imperious gesture of summons. Pascoe tried to ease Gwen Blengdale to a seat, but finding that her unchewed hand was gripping the sill so firmly that he could not pry it loose, he left her to the mercies of the tired typist.

Chivalry was not dead but it went into hiding whenever Dalziel put in a challenge.

Pascoe arrived by the injured man at the same time as Blengdale. The little round man was carrying an old canvas stretcher, a first-aid box and a blanket. He was puffing hard.

As they eased Heppelwhite onto the stretcher, someone cried, "Dad!" and Pascoe looked up to see Clint Heppelwhite forcing his way against the flow of men going into the yard.

The boy was paler than his father, who looked up at him and essayed a smile.

"All right, lad," he said. "All right. Tell you mam . . . not to worry."

"Dad, what happened? Oh fucking hell!" gasped the youth as he saw the bloodstains spreading through the rough bandage that Dalziel was winding loosely around the injured hand.

"He'll be fine, lad, fine," assured the fat man. "Listen. There's the ambulance. Get him to the door. The quicker he gets to the infirmary, the better."

The ill-omened clang of the ambulance bell was coming near. Blengdale picked up one end of the stretcher and

Pascoe would have picked up the other if Dalziel hadn't stopped him.

"Clint, you take it, lad," he commanded. "You'll want to go to the infirmary with your dad."

Uncertainly, the boy took the strain, staggered weakly for a couple of steps, then stiffened his legs and the stretcher moved swiftly away.

"Is that wise?" asked Pascoe. "He could drop it."

"Better he has something to do. Listen, someone's got to tell his wife. You know her, don't you? Right, you get round there and get her to the infirmary."

"Right," said Pascoe, moved by his boss's humanity.

"And while you're there, keep your eyes skinned for Burkill."

"Burkill? But he's here . . ." said Pascoe, looking around. There was no sign of the man.

"He's long gone. Wouldn't you be? Mebbe he'll head for home. Mebbe not. Depends what's bugging him."

"Jesus Christ," said Pascoe. "You're not saying this wasn't an accident?"

"I'm saying nowt and you're saying a bloody sight too much. You may have stirred up more shit than you thought last night, so get round there and have a look-see while Mrs. Heppelwhite's taking her pinny off. Oh Jesus wept!"

Dalziel was glowering at the bench top. "They've forgot the bloody fingers!" he said. "They can fix 'em back on sometimes."

He unfolded a huge khaki handkerchief, carefully scooped up the red-stained flesh and handed the bundle to Pascoe. "Give it to the ambulance driver on your way out," said Dalziel. "Go on. Move!"

Pascoe looked down at the grisly package, looked up to the office window, where he could see quite clearly the staring eyes and set face of Gwen Blengdale and the fatigued indifference of the young typist, turned away and set off at the trot after the stretcher.

Twenty-one

There was a Panda car parked outside Heppelwhite's house. On the doorstep stood Betsy Heppelwhite confronting a uniformed constable. Pascoe's first thought was that his mission was being performed for him and he felt the usual human mingling of relief and disappointment at not being the first with bad news.

Then he realized that it would have been almost impossible for the constable to have got there before him; and in addition they formed a tableau which didn't fit the thesis. The constable was doing the listening, nodding his head sagaciously from time to time, while the woman spoke volubly, square jaw falling and rising like a steam hammer. Her arms were folded firmly as a shelf for her heavy bosom which at regular intervals she heaved gently upward in time with little jerks of her head toward the house next door.

They both recognized him at the same time and when he asked, "What's up?" they both started answering, but the constable quickly abandoned the uneven struggle.

"It's her next door," said Betsy. "Deirdre. I went down to the shops about half ten and I have her a knock to see if there was owt I could fetch her. There was no answer and milk was still on the step. So I went off. When I came back I tried again. The same. So I got to worrying. I don't like to stick my nose in where it's not wanted, but you've got a responsibility."

"So you called the police?" said Pascoe.

"Don't be bloody daft!" she said. "I'm not that worried. Yet."

"I just came along to check on Mr. Burkill, sir," said the uniformed man. "I was patrolling along Arnhem Road when the caretaker at the Westgate Social gave me a wave. When he'd turned up this morning to open the club for the cleaners, he'd found the side door unlocked. Nothing had been taken or damaged, so he just put it down to forgetfulness. Then a bit later in the morning, someone told him Mr. Burkill's car was round the back. It looked as if it had just been left there with its lights on and engine running and naturally it was out of petrol and the battery was flat. The caretaker thought it was odd, but not odd enough to do anything about till he saw me. I called round to check and like Mrs. Heppelwhite here couldn't get any answer."

"So I called him over for a chat," said the woman. "What about you? Why've you come? Has he done something daft."

"Who?"

"Bri Burkill, of course. There was a hell of a barney late on last night when he got back from the club."

"What time would that be?" inquired Pascoe.

"Don't know, but I was woke up about two o'clock. There was shouting and screaming and God knows what. It must have been bad for us to hear it. These walls are right thick, not like them sheets of hardboard on the new estate. Well, a bit later we heard Bri's car start up in the road outside and off he went. He wasn't back this morning. Charlie had to go to work on the back of our Colin's bike."

"But you didn't go around till you were going out shopping?" said Pascoe.

Something of bewilderment in his intonation must have got through.

"Listen, Inspector," she said grimly. "You don't stick your nose in, not unless you're asked. But when she doesn't open the door to the police, I begin to wonder. That's all. But you still haven't said why *you're* here."

"Oh God. I'm sorry," said Pascoe, acutely embarrassed. "All this distracted me. Look, Mrs. Heppelwhite, it's bad news I'm afraid. There's been an accident at Blengdale's."

"Our Colin?" she said, arms unfolding, hands rising to her cheeks.

"No. Charlie. He's cut himself on one of their saws. Look, it's all right. I mean he's not in danger. They've taken him to the infirmary. Clint—Colin's with him."

"What's he cut, for God's sake?" she demanded.

"It's his hand."

"His hand? You've not come round here to tell me Charlie's cut his hand!" she said disbelievingly.

"It's a serious cut," said Pascoe. "What I mean is, his fingers . . ." Now it got to her and that strong square face went rhomboid in shock.

"Cut off? Oh my God! Why didn't you say? Oh God!"

Pascoe put out a comforting arm but she shook herself back to something like normality, pushed it aside, and, saying, "I'll get my coat on," she disappeared into the house.

Pascoe turned to the constable. "You take Mrs. Heppelwhite to the infirmary, will you? I'll stop here and have a look around next door."

With a small sigh which said all that needed to be said about the relativities of detective-inspectors and Panda drivers, the constable took out his personal radio and explained the situation to his control.

Pascoe watched them into the car and waited till they'd disappeared around the corner before opening the Burkill gate. As he walked up the narrow concrete path he had a premonition of something nasty waiting for him within. Childe Roland to the dark tower came.

Perhaps he was just being overimaginative, he thought as he banged on the door. But he hadn't imagined what he had just heard about Burkill's departure in the night, nor about the discovery of his abandoned car. And he hadn't imagined the haggard, unshaven face he had seen that morning. The more striking image of the mutilated hand had temporarily blotted out that pale set face, but it came back to him now and he hammered on the door with greater vigor.

Still no answer.

He looked closely at the lock. If necessary, and if the

door were not bolted, he could fiddle his way past that easily enough. On the other hand, if last night had been packed full of excitement, household routine had likely gone by the board . . .

He poked his fingers through the letter box. He was right. There was a key on a string behind the door and last night it hadn't been wound around the doorknob in its "secure" position. He pulled it out, fitted it, turned it.

There were no bolts fastened either. The door swung easily open. He went in and closed it behind him. For a moment he stood very still in the gloomy hall and listened. Nothing.

"Hello!" he called. "Anybody at home?"

The silence shrugged his words off effortlessly without even giving them the acknowledgment of an echo.

Pascoe began to search. The front room was cold and dead. Old-fashioned furniture, but so little used throughout the years that it might have been genuine reproduction, if anyone were yet genuinely reproducing uncut-moquette discount suites of the 'fifties. There were chairs for sitting upright in and making formal conversation. Pascoe felt a sudden twinge of memory. He had had his first touch of female pubic hair in such a room as this, sitting in such a chair. He had been pretty upright too.

The living room was different. It was a mess; not the deliberately destructive mess which Alice Andover had made of Haggard's study, but an incidental mess. The fire had been allowed to die in the grate and not cleared out. There were unwashed teacups on the table.

But it went further than simple neglect.

A chair was overturned. The onyx-framed clock lay on

the carpet by the door, its green stone cracked and its innards spilling out. Above it on the wall was a dent where it had struck with some force. The fire-iron stand had been overturned and the poker lay some distance away. Pascoe stooped and examined it carefully but he did not touch it.

The kitchen was just untidy. There was a cupboard under the stairs. Pascoe peered in there too, with difficulty suppressing a whistle to keep his spirits up. It contained mops, brushes and leftover pieces of carpet preserved against an irremovable stain or irreparable burns.

That just left upstairs.

As he slowly mounted the narrow staircase Pascoe found himself thinking of the private eye in *Psycho* searching the household. A quick rushing attack from a maniac wouldn't give him much chance of defense. Best would be to turn his inferior situation to advantage and, instead of retreating, bend his shoulder into his assailant's belly and hurl his body down the stairs. They did it all the time in cowboy films.

But he reached the landing without trouble. It was only a few feet square with four doors leading off it. Three of them were ajar.

Those first, thought Pascoe.

A bedroom, single bed, all the insignia of modern girlhood: viz., cuddly toys; a pink-panther nightgown holder; posters of three pop groups Pascoe had never heard of; a red plastic record player; ditto transistor radio; comic-strip magazines; a wardrobe; cheap clothes but plenty of them; three pairs of suicidal Wedgies. All the evidence of parental indulgence, thought Pascoe, mentally totting up costs. The bed had been lain on but not slept in.

Twenty-two

The first rule was to look without touching.

The woman was lying diagonally across the bed, face down, her left arm dangling over the edge. Her fingers pointed to a wide stain on the pink carpet. Her legs were bent away beneath her. A shoe remained on her right foot, while the other was bare. There were spatters of blood on the pillow.

Pascoe let out his breath in a deep sigh and slowly approached.

At the bedside he knelt on one knee to made identification positive. It was Deirdre Burkill all right even though he could only see the back of her head, half a cheek and one eye.

A waste, he thought. It ends like this. All that hope. The world lay all before them. The future is terror.

He put his hand over his eyes and rubbed his brow as if to eradicate the thought.

When he took it away, the single eye had opened and was watching him. Pascoe fell backward in his fright.

"You a priest as well as a policeman?" said Deirdre Burkill, rolling over on her back. "It's a doctor I need, thank you very much."

She wasn't joking. Her face was badly bruised and grazed. The other eye couldn't have opened, so swollen was the surrounding flesh. Her nose had been bleeding and flakes of congealed blood still clung to her upper lip, while the lower lip had a nasty split, and from the way she clasped her arms around her ribs, Pascoe surmised she was in pain there too, either from bruising or a fracture.

Her breath stank of vodka. The half-empty bottle had fallen from her dangling hand and rolled beneath the bed, leaving the sinister stain on the carpet.

"I'll get an ambulance," said Pascoe.

"No you bloody well won't," said Deirdre. "I'm not going anywhere looking like this. Oh God, I feel right sick. You couldn't make us a cup of tea?"

Pascoe went downstairs to the kitchen. While the kettle was boiling, he went quietly out to his car and reported in, asking Control to get word of what he'd found to Dalziel.

When he went back upstairs with the tea tray, he found the woman had washed her face and was sitting in front of her dressing-table mirror trying to conceal the damage with make-up.

"For God's sake!" he expostulated. "It's antiseptic you want, not powder."

"Got to look right," she said. "That's all you sods'll let us have, our faces."

Pascoe poured the tea. "I've got a doctor coming," he said. "If you want your own doctor, I'll arrange for that too. But I thought the sooner we had you looked at the better."

She shrugged indifferently and winced.

"Brian did this?" said Pascoe casually.

"It weren't self-inflicted," she answered.

"Where's Sandra, Mrs. Burkill?" pursued Pascoe.

"Out. At a friend's, I expect. She'll be all right, that one."

"When did she go out?"

"Last night. This morning. If I'd any sense I'd have made a run for it too. But I've never seen reason for running from what you don't respect." She laughed bitterly.

"Would you like to tell me exactly what happened?" asked Pascoe gently.

She lit a cigarette from a packet in the dressing-table drawer and coughed raucously. "Why not?" she said. "I don't mind much who knows. You were here last night. You know the state you left us in. Well, I calmed down after a bit, I don't know why I got so upset. Kids, you should expect it of them nowadays. Me, I was sixteen before I even kissed a lad. I've made up for it since, but what you do when you're grown up's your own business. They've no childhood now. Babies one minute, talking mucky the next. I don't know."

She sipped her tea reflectively, wincing as the hot cup touched her swollen lip.

"There she was, pregnant. All right, so she'd been se-
duced or led astray or whatever you like to call it. But unless they hold you down, you've still got to lie there and
let it happen. Well, I kept my temper then, I had to. Brian
would have killed her if he'd got going. When I saw her
last night, though, with that Clint, it were too much. But
for all that I'd made up my mind to say nowt to Brian. But
when he came in about one o'clock, he knew summat
was up."

"How?" asked Pascoe.

"You do nowt round here without every bugger knowing," said Deirdre Burkill. "Someone in the street'd go
down to the club later on and mention, dead casual like,
that they'd seen the rozzers at our door. Well, I just said
you'd wanted a word with Sandra, check her statement.
Up he goes to her room, all indignant."

"Surely she'd be asleep."

"Not her. She was lying on her bed, playing records.
When her dad came in looking annoyed, she must have
thought I'd told him about her and Clint. Well, she jumps
up and starts shouting the odds, silly little fool, and Bri
soon catches on. He really goes wild now. He's always
spoiled her rotten and he'd even convinced himself that
she'd got put in the club all innocent like. But he couldn't
see his way round this. So he clouted her. Just the once.
But it were enough."

"Enough for what?" prompted Pascoe.

"Enough to make her start blabbing," said Deirdre. "I
didn't know she knew. I'd always been that careful."

"About what?"

"She blamed me, you see. Thought I'd set her dad on her. So she told him. I can't blame her."

"For what?" demanded Pascoe in exasperation.

"For telling Bri about me and Charlie," snapped the woman.

"Telling him *what* about you and Charlie?" asked Pascoe stupidly.

She looked at him in surprise, turning first to amusement and then to pain as her smile stretched her battered flesh.

"You and Charlie? Charlie *Heppelwhite?*" said Pascoe, incredulous.

"I don't mean Chaplin," said the woman wearily. "Yes, me and Charlie Heppelwhite. Long thin Charlie. Poor old Charlie. Poor old Deirdre."

She began to cry.

Dalziel arrived with the doctor, who was the same one summoned to attend Shorter.

"What happens to people when you're around?" he asked.

"Oh, an attack of this, an attack of that," said Pascoe.

He and Dalziel went into the cold unwelcoming front parlor.

"Takes me back," said Dalziel looking around.

You too, thought Pascoe. Is nothing sacred?

"What's up then?" asked the fat man, sprawling on the sofa and scratching his groin with an expression of sensuous reminiscence on his face. It disappeared as Pascoe spoke.

"So, he found out at last," said Dalziel. "That explains why he's gone missing."

"At last?" said Pascoe, raising his eyebrows.

"Aye. Didn't you know? I thought everyone knew! Everyone save Bri and Betsy, of course, and I'm not sure about her. Well, it figures, doesn't it? You don't leave an active, handsome woman like that to her own devices night after night, not unless you've fitted a time lock. What did she tell you?"

Deirdre had offered no explanations or analysis—why should she?—but the picture had emerged quite clearly. Night after night, her husband would be off down to the club. Charlie Heppelwhite would come around to say would she like a lift. And when they got back, Charlie would see her safely into the house. Probably Charlie used to moan about it at first, always having her along, and Betsy probably gave him the rough side of her tongue whenever he moaned. Until one day . . . How do these things happen? Who decided? Who cares! Whenever Charlie went around, there would be contact from then on. A kiss or a caress, if it was just a matter of saying the car was ready. But doubtless there were other things to do, the coals to bring in, a shelf to fix, a fridge to repair, little neighborly things, little unremembered acts. Ah, how ingenious is the human mind in pursuit of pleasure!

"So what exactly happened after Sandra had blown the whistle?" asked Dalziel.

"Deirdre heard it all from the bottom of the stairs. She should have got out if she'd got any sense, but she didn't. She's a brave woman in a funny kind of way. Burkill came downstairs and she backed off into the living room. He was right on the edge, but oddly enough I think what got to her in the end was that he didn't *want* to believe it, not because of her, but because of Charlie. So it ended up with her almost having to persuade him that she'd been unfaithful. Well, she succeeded. He went berserk; you saw the room. She made it upstairs to the bedroom, Sandra was screaming and shouting, she remembers, then Burkill really laid one on her and knocked her out. When she woke up the house was empty. She crawled downstairs and poured some vodka into her. Then she staggered back upstairs and drank some more to wash down some tranquilizers to deaden the pain."

"Had Sandra gone with her dad?" asked Dalziel.

"She doesn't know. After what happened, she didn't much care. The pills and the booze combined soon put her to sleep."

"Till the brave prince came and woke her with a caution," said Dalziel.

"That's it," said Pascoe. "There was something else, though. I got a pretty full version of the speech she made to Bri before the thumping got properly under way."

"And?"

"Among other things he'd been screaming at her that she was no fit mother for Sandra and that it was no wonder the girl had got into trouble. So she retaliated by telling him about the lass and Clint in the garden shed."

"That was natural," observed Dalziel.

"Yes, but she went on to suggest that as Charlie had been coming around to bang her regularly, what was to stop him having a go at Sandra too?"

"She said that?" asked Dalziel. "My God!"

"Yes. She was sorry she'd said it, mind you. Partly because she thought after it wasn't fair to Charlie, but mainly because that's what really started the thumping, but I've been thinking ever since she talked to me and . . ."

"Go on," prompted Dalziel.

"Well, suppose it was true."

"Well, well, well," said Dalziel. "I'm with you. So now it's not Clint who's framed your mate Shorter. It's his dad!"

"Yes. Look, it makes a lot more sense," urged Pascoe. "All right, I admit Clint might not have the gumption to try to pass the buck like that, but Charlie Heppelwhite's a different kettle of fish. He'd know that anything was better than getting Bri Burkill on his track."

"Hang on a minute," said Dalziel ponderously. "Let's just make sure we know exactly where we are. Burkill beats up Deirdre because she admits his best friend's been screwing her. He then starts believing the same friend may have been having a go at his daughter. So what now? If I read you right, you reckon Burkill goes down to the club, lets himself in, sits brooding and boozing till morning, finds he's left his lights on and his battery's flat, so off he walks to Blengdale's to chat with Charlie?"

"Right," said Pascoe.

"Except," said Dalziel. And paused.

There was something splendidly Ciceronian about Dalziel's "except." A single word left hanging, ungrammatically, in the air. And amidst the serried ranks of senators a small sough of intaken breath, then utter silence as they concentrated all their attention on the next eloquent weighty sentence to emerge from that eloquent weighty figure, statuesque at the center of the tessellated floor.

"Except it's all balls," said Dalziel.

Riot in the forum! Secretaries scribbling like mad on their tablets so that generations of unborn schoolboys may experience the profit and delight of translating this wisdom, one stumbling word after another.

Pascoe's face showed nothing of his fantasy. "In which particular respect?" he inquired courteously.

"In every fucking respect," replied Dalziel cheerfully. "Because it's daft in the first respect. I know our Bri. The natural thing for him to do when he heard what he heard was to go right round the next door and stamp on Charlie a bit. I'd have done the same myself. Anyone who's not a sodding civilized intellectual would. Kick the door till someone comes or it falls in. Then, whumph!"

Dalziel nodded in agreement with himself, an expression of savage righteousness on his face. It was many years since his wife had left him and he had once confided to Pascoe in his cups that she had broken the news by telegram. A woman blessed with wisdom, thought Pascoe.

"He sorted Heppelwhite out later," said Pascoe. "Perhaps he just wanted to plan out his course of action."

"For Christ's sake, he's not the Count of Monte bloody Cristo!" said Dalziel scornfully. "No, if Bri didn't go right round next door to remold Charlie's face, there was a reason. We'd best find Sandra. Happen she can help."

The doctor appeared in the doorway. "Nasty," he said laconically. "She's really been thumped. Husband caught her on the job, did he? I've got the name of her GP so I'll make sure he knows what's happened. What brings you two out here, anyway? A bit high-powered for wife beating, aren't you?"

"Same as you, Doc," said Dalziel. "Makes a change from brain surgery, doesn't it? Thanks a lot. We'll have a drink sometime."

Pascoe looked at his watch as the doctor left. "Dinnertime," he said. "You know, sir, the doctor's right in a way. Basically this *is* just a domestic job."

Dalziel shook his head. "Not till choirs of angels tell me Shorter's in the clear, it's not. There's a girl missing too. We'd best find her. And don't forget that Charlie Heppelwhite's lying in hospital. And where's Burkill? No, there's a bit of mileage in this yet."

"I'm sure, sir. But I've got to go and talk to friend Toms this afternoon. And I'm still keen to have a long chat with Mr. Maurice Arany. You have any joy with Blengdale before we were interrupted, sir?"

"I hadn't really got going," said Dalziel. "I think he was more worried than he cared to let on, but his missus turned up at the same time as me, so I couldn't really turn the screw."

"Which reminds me," said Pascoe slowly. "Mrs. Blengdale—"

"Not a bad-looking woman," said Dalziel. "Mind you, it'd be a bit like screwing a statue of the Queen."

"Perhaps not," said Pascoe. "I was beside her when we saw Heppelwhite fall onto that saw."

"Aye, I noticed you doing a bit of nifty supportive work," said Dalziel lasciviously.

"Yes," said Pascoe. "But it didn't feel like supporting a

sensitive lady knocked over by shock. No, if anything, I'd say the sight of Charlie Heppelwhite's fingers on the bench turned Mrs. Blengdale on rather than switched her off."

Dalziel rolled his eyes heavenwards in what was doubtless intended as an expression of bewildered piety but came out more like a lecherous peek up God's skirts.

Before he could speak, a constable came in. "Excuse me, sir," he said. "Message for Mr. Pascoe from Sergeant Wield. Would you meet him at Maurice Arany's flat as soon as possible, please."

Pascoe looked at Dalziel, who nodded.

"Off you go," he said. "Yon ugly bugger doesn't send out summonses without cause. He's just the partner for you."

"You mean because of my beauty," simpered Pascoe.

"I mean because *he* believes in facts," said Dalziel. "Now bugger off. But keep me informed!"

Twenty-three

There were no sounds of life in Arany's flat and as Pascoe pressed the bell button, he wondered if Wield had moved on. He turned the door handle on the off chance that it was unlocked, and was dragged into the room as the door was flung open with great force.

"Oh," said Wield, his face close to Pascoe's. "It's you, sir."

"What were you about to do if it wasn't?" wondered Pascoe.

"Depends," said Wield grimly.

"You'd better tell me about your morning, Sergeant," said Pascoe.

"I went to Arany's agency," said Wield. "Told the girl I was really a female impersonator just pretending to be a policeman. Won her confidence. She said Arany hadn't been in the office that morning. But he'd telephoned her shortly after she'd got in and asked her to make a purchase and deliver it to his flat."

Now came the narrative pause, inviting the question.

"Get on with it," said Pascoe.

"Girl's clothes. Sweater, jeans, sandals."

"So," said Pascoe. "What then?"

"I came round here. There was no reply. So I went back to the station to report in. You weren't back, of course. Gradually news began to get back about what happened at Blengdale's. Soon as I heard Burkill's name, I began to wonder. Then I heard from Control what was going on at Burkill's house and I got round here fast."

"Finding the door open, of course," said Pascoe ironically.

"No," said Wield evenly. "I broke in. No one's going to complain. The place was empty, but I found this."

He led Pascoe out of the living room into a bedroom. On top of the ruffled counterpane was a blue nylon nightie, decorated with pink panthers.

"It's Sandra's. Got a name tab in it. For school trips and things, I suppose. Her mother must be a careful woman."

"Not careful enough," said Pascoe.

"That's not all, sir," said Wield. "I had a poke around. Through here."

He went back into the living room and stopped in front of a dark oak bureau which with a bit of restoration work wouldn't have been out of place amidst the expensive antiques of Priory Farm.

"There was one drawer locked. I had to fiddle a bit," said Wield. He pulled the drawer open.

"Take a look," he said.

Pascoe removed the plain buff envelope which was all the drawer contained and took a look. "Oh," he said.

They were half-plate photographs of a naked girl and two naked men. They formed a sequence. The girl was Sandra Burkill.

"Film stills, I shouldn't wonder," said Wield.

"Let's go look for Uncle Maurice," said Pascoe.

"We'd best take a stretcher," said Wield. "In case Bri Burkill's found him first."

Pascoe left Wield in the flat till he could send someone else to keep an eye on it in case either Arany or Sandra returned.

As he returned to the station, he worked out a scenario in his mind. Sandra changing from a gawky nine-year-old to a fleshy fully developed woman in the space of three years; Uncle Maurice watching, waiting—No! that implied an element of premeditation too monstrous to be considered even in this melange of monstrosities. But a moment had arrived when something happened, a first step. Arany would have taken it, though, perhaps even the girl . . . adolescent pash, surprise, the delight, at the power of her newly formed body; Arany full of guilt (why is it, wondered Pascoe, that despite what I see in my job, I cannot imagine a world in which a man wouldn't feel guilty at seducing a child?); but guilt that was just the initiate fear. Behind the lecher stood the pornographer. There was a market for schoolgirl films. As for Sandra, did she need to be coaxed? tricked? bribed?

I don't know, thought Pascoe adding aloud as he entered his office, "And I don't want to know."

He'd checked Dalziel's office. The fat man hadn't returned. Pascoe sat down wearily.

Dalziel had been right, thought Pascoe. Burkill had indeed discovered something that had taken his mind temporarily off his wife's infidelity. Perhaps he'd beaten Sandra, too. Perhaps, tired of all this hysterical indignation from adults whose example and actions had helped her to where she was, Sandra had blurted out the whole business just to shut him up.

Then what? Sandra, grabbing a coat to pull on over her nightie, dashes off into the night. Where does he go? Where else but to Arany?

And Burkill's destination is equally obvious. He makes for the one place he is sure of himself, the place where he is king. The Westgate Social Club.

There he thinks and drinks. Drinks till he stops thinking. Sleeps. Wakes. Goes in search of Arany, who had by now got clothes for Sandra and taken off.

So, his prime target having evaded him, he now makes for his secondary—poor old Charlie Heppelwhite. And having fettled him, where now?

Arany again, thought Pascoe. It wouldn't be a bad idea to let Burkill catch up with him either. In fact, unless he came up with some clever notion of Arany's possible movements, it could well be that Burkill got there first.

"Fool!" said Pascoe, reaching for his telephone. There was an obvious place for Arany to make for. He wasn't in this alone, and self-interest would suggest warning his confederates. It was probably too late already, but no harm in checking.

"Detective-Inspector Crabtree," he said. "Ray? Hello, Peter Pascoe again. Look, there've been developments."

Briefly he sketched out what had happened. "Now there's a possibility that Arany will turn up at Homeric. Eventually, if I'm right and they did film the girl, we're going to really turn them upside down and shake them till their change jingles, but meanwhile can you do a check, see if there's any sign of him about the place? Be discreet, but if he's got there before you, or if there's any sign of people packing up, take a grip and let no one move till we rustle up a warrant."

"Got you," said Crabtree. "I'll get right on it."

"Hold on," said Pascoe. "You'll need Arany's description. And you'd better have Burkill's too in case he's somehow got himself over there."

Quickly he described the two men.

"Fine," said Crabtree. "Hey, is the Thin Man in on this?"

"Who?"

"Grosseteste. The talking balloon. Dalziel."

"He will be when he gets in. Don't worry, young fellow. Daddy won't be angry with you."

"Ha ha," said Crabtree. "I'll get back to you. 'Bye."

It was only five minutes till Dalziel appeared. Pascoe told him about the discoveries in Arany's flat and laid out his scenario for inspection, humbly acknowledging his superior's acumen in guessing that Burkill must have had a very strong reason for not dealing with Heppelwhite immediately. To his surprise, this humility did not produce the anticipated revolting smugness.

"That's how it looks to you," Dalziel said slowly. It was difficult to work out if this were a question or not.

"That's how it looks," said Pascoe.

"It's your case," said Dalziel. "You've got a call out on Arany?"

"Oh yes. And I've been on to Harrogate to get them to check Homeric in case he makes for there."

"Have you now? Your mate Crabtree, I suppose."

"That's right," said Pascoe.

Dalziel scratched the folds of his chin. It was like the finger of God running along the Grand Canyon.

The pictures were spread out on the desk before them.

"It's certainly our Sandra," said Dalziel. "Do the men look familiar?"

Pascoe shook his head without even looking at the photographs.

"Can't see much of their faces anyway," said Dalziel. "Film stills, you say? Why not just a sequence of snapshots?"

"Why not?" echoed Pascoe. He felt very tired and despondent. Perhaps even Galahad had on occasion felt like saying "Sod the Grail" and going off home for a tatie-pot supper and an early night.

"Well, look at the things, will you?" demanded Dalziel. "God, if you'd got hold of these when you were fifteen, you'd not have let them out of your sight for a fortnight!"

Pascoe looked. Looked away. Looked back.

"What?" said Dalziel.

"That fireplace. Here, you just see a corner of it. But I'm sure—"

"What?"

"It's at Hay Hall. That's where Homeric do their filming. I'm sure it's the same one. Damn! That's where they'll all be! Probably no one in the Harrogate office. I'll get on to Crabtree and tell him." He reached for the phone.

"No," said Dalziel. "I've a sudden fancy to see these people for myself. Do they have a phone out there."

"I don't think so," said Pascoe. "No power supply, certainly."

"Then if Arany wanted to see Toms, he'd have to go in person? Good. Peter, get Sergeant Wield back from Arany's flat. No one's going to turn up there. Send Inspector Trumper in to see me. I've got a few phone calls to make, so give me five minutes, will you? Then . . ."

He looked speculatively at Pascoe, who felt that the fat man was debating whether to tell him something.

"Then?" he prompted.

"Then," said Dalziel. "Then it's heigh-ho for Hay Hall!"

Twenty-four

As they turned into the green tunnel which was the drive of Hay Hall, Dalziel asked, "How far's the house?"

"Quarter of a mile. Less," said Pascoe.

"Good. We'll walk. Do us good. Just stop here. *Here*, I said!"

"I was trying to pull off the driveway," explained Pascoe. "Otherwise it'll be blocked."

"Never mind that. Sergeant, you stay with the car. Commune with nature and any other bugger who comes this way. Come on, Peter. You youngsters are all the same. You've forgotten what your feet are for!"

Pascoe looked at the fat behind he was following and remembered wistfully one thing a foot was for.

"What's that noise?" asked Dalziel.

Pascoe listened. It was a throbbing mechanical sound.

"The generator truck," he guessed. "They have to provide their own power source."

"Doesn't the noise get on the sound track?" asked Dalziel.

"I suppose they park it at the far side of the house, use directional mikes, that sort of thing."

"Aye. Any road, I suppose it'll be like the music at the Ball of Kirriemuir."

"What?"

"You couldn't hear it for the swishing of the pricks. Sorry, I keep forgetting you're a soccer man. 'EE-ay-adeeo we're going to win the cup.' No fucking art."

The Hall came into sight. Half a dozen cars ranging from an antique mini to a shiny Jaguar were parked in front of the main entrance. The generator truck was tucked away around the side as Pascoe had surmised.

"Straight in?" said Pascoe.

Dalziel considered. "You go straight in," he said. "I'll have a stroll around. I'm enjoying the air. They know you, they'll likely make you very welcome."

"I'm sorry, sir," said Pascoe. "I'm not quite clear about our strategy."

"Strategy? We're thief takers, not generals, lad. If it moves, arrest it; if it stands still, suspect it. What's your main concern in this business?"

"I suppose," said Pascoe slowly, "to protect the girl, make sure it can never happen again."

"Never? You're a knight in shining armor right enough, Peter. Get yourself in there and clank around a bit. I'll be with you soon." The fat man moved into the trees.

"And good night, Chingachgook," murmured Pascoe as he resumed his approach to the house.

The front door was slightly ajar. Cautiously he pushed it. Suddenly the slow movement accelerated as the door was pulled open from within and Pascoe was dragged forward off balance. He had time to think, Second time today! as a pair of strong hands gripped his lapels and a knee came up between his legs. Instinctively he twisted sideways to avoid the blow, but he was too unready. His testicles would have been badly crushed if the knee hadn't decelerated, as though the assailant had had second thoughts. Even so, contact was still made and Pascoe cried out in pain as his attacker released his jacket and stepped back.

"Peter!" he said. "For God's sake. I didn't realize—Are you all right?" It was Ray Crabtree.

"Great, great," gasped Pascoe. "I think there's one of them not quite flat, and we can always adopt."

"Come and sit down," said Crabtree, full of concern. "There must be something to drink in this place. Penny, where do you keep the booze?"

Penelope Latimer had appeared in the hallway. She was wearing a tight-fitting silver lamé trouser suit. Nothing could hope to reduce her bulk, but this gear accentuated it to a point where, strangely, it almost disappeared. The material shot out wires of light like the sky at night, and like the sky at night it made the gazer aware of his own insignificance rather than the vastness of what he regarded.

"What's happened?" she asked.

"A bit of an accident," said Crabtree.

"I'm OK, really," said Pascoe manfully, not caring to nurse his crutch in front of a woman. "It just came as a surprise. Ray, what the hell are you doing here?"

Crabtree's eyes flickered warningly toward Penny. "*Is* there any chance of a drink, love?" he asked. "Or a cup of strong sweet tea?"

"Sure," said the woman. "I'll go fix it." She left them, hesitating in the doorway and glancing back before she finally disappeared.

"Can't be too careful," said Crabtree, "though I dare say they've guessed something's up now you've arrived. What happened was, after you rang I remembered that all the Homeric lot would be out here, not in town. So out I came. I played it low-key, told them that something had come up on the break-in at the Calli and asked if they'd seen Arany."

"They admitted to knowing who you were talking about?" interrupted Pascoe.

Crabtree laughed. "I didn't give them a chance to deny it. Anyway, no one's laid eyes on him, they claim. So I had a stroll around inside just to check, then I thought I'd glance over the grounds just in case that lad—whatsisname?—Burkill, should be lurking, though it didn't seem likely. I was crossing the hall when I saw the door begin to open, all slow and furtive, and I thought to myself, Ray lad, you're wrong. Here comes Burkill looking for Arany or anyone else he can get his hands on. And so—"

"So you decided to damage him for life," said Pascoe.

"No! But you did say he was a tough customer, Peter,

and likely to be a bit demented. I just didn't want to take any chances. I've said I'm sorry. You needn't think I'm going to kiss it better!"

"You've been here too long," said Pascoe. "Where's that drink?"

Crabtree led him across the hall into the room in which he had first met Toms on his last visit here. The room was empty now, though the atmosphere was heavy with cigarette smoke and the smell of human beings.

"Penny'll be along shortly, I should think," said Crabtree. "She's a good provider, that one. Look, Peter, you weren't very clear on the phone. Do you reckon that Homeric have really been up to something nasty? And I mean, nowadays nasty has really got to be nasty, right? I mean, we all like it! It's just a matter of degree."

"I've told you everything I know," said Pascoe.

"Which brings it down to the girl. Couldn't this fellow Arany just have some private thing going? Dirty photos to sell round the clubs. I mean, you don't know for sure there was a film, and even if there is, you don't know that Homeric have got anything to do with it."

"You seem pretty reluctant to tie in Homeric," said Pascoe. "For God's sake, pornography's their business!"

"Even the law recognizes degrees, Peter," said Crabtree seriously. "Toms I don't know well enough to judge, but I can't see Penny Latimer being mixed up with anything really harmful."

"What's this? What's this? Unsolicited testimonials?" said the woman coming through the door carrying a tray with some paper cups, a thermos flask and a half of Scotch on it.

The men didn't answer, so she put the tray down and poured tea from the flask into the paper cups.

"Tea or Scotch?" she said to Pascoe. "Oh, and we've got no milk."

"I'd better stick to Scotch then," said Pascoe. "Thank you. Cheers."

"Cheers," said Penny. "And now, my boys, why don't you come clean and tell old Penny the truth, or the time, or whatever policemen are best at telling?"

Pascoe considered the question carefully while he enjoyed the Scotch. "All right," he said.

"Oh good," said the woman. "Telling the truth. Take one. Action."

"Not the truth," corrected Pascoe. "Just the time. You did give me the alternative. And I'll gladly tell you what time it is. It's time you and Mr. Toms and all your associates packed up your bags and crawled out of this county, and out of this country, until you get back under whatever stone you crawled out from in the first place." He spoke far more emphatically than he had intended.

Interestingly, Crabtree reacted more strongly than the woman. "Hang about, Peter," he said. "You can't talk—"

"Hold it, Ray," said Penny Latimer quietly. "I'm not a bad judge of character, and Peter here doesn't strike me as being one of the Mrs. Grundy brigade. In fact, if he can be as rude as that while he's drinking my whisky, he must reckon he's got something to be rude about. You're not still on this snuff-film tack, are you?"

"I haven't put it out of my mind," said Pascoe. He might as well have said he couldn't, and never would. He reached into his jacket pocket and pulled out the envelope which contained the photos of Sandra Burkill. Selecting one, he passed it over to the woman.

She glanced at it without curiosity or revulsion. "It's further than we go," she said. "But it's up to the lawyers to draw lines."

"The girl is twelve years old," said Pascoe.

Now she made a moue of distaste.

Pascoe continued, "And that's a line the lawyers *have* drawn, even if your spastic conscience can't quite manage it."

"What the hell do you mean, *my* conscience?" demanded the woman.

"Oh, have a look at the pictures, dearie," said Pascoe. "I've got a good memory for details. I reckon it'll be easy to prove that that was taken in your shooting room in Hay Hall."

She looked again and her face blanked over. "I know nothing about this," she said.

"Really? Don't tell me; it's the corrupt fuzz fitting you up, right? That's one of our policewomen and the fellow on the left's the Chief Constable."

"Don't get too indignant, sweetie," she replied. "It'll give you crow's-feet round the eyes."

She was right, thought Pascoe. This indignation might be aging; it was certainly addictive. And it would get him nowhere. "Let's go see Mr. Toms," he said.

Retrieving the picture from Penny, he strode out of the room and across the vestibule, following the power cables which snaked from the generator truck via some side window across the scarred oak floor.

The cameras were rolling, as were the actors. Toms

stood looking down on the tangle of limbs with the worried frown of a senior English master considering whether he ought not to expunge the word "bastard" from the school production of *King Lear*.

"Cut," said Pascoe.

Toms turned around. "What the hell do you think you're doing?" he demanded.

Pascoe approached and spoke softly in his ear. "I've come for an audition," he said. "I'm going to screw you up."

The actors had disentangled themselves and were rising to their feet. There was not, Pascoe observed, an erection in sight.

"You can bugger off out of here," instructed Toms. "I've got work to do. You've ruined this shot already. That costs money."

"Gerry, I think you should listen to the Inspector," said Penelope Latimer.

"You do? Oh all right. We might as well take a break. Five minutes, boys and girls. And try to come back looking a bit less like evacuees from the geriatric ward!"

The cast left, pulling on an assortment of dressing gowns and bathrobes.

"Now, Inspector, perhaps you'll start explaining."

"Perhaps you will," said Pascoe. "The girl in this picture. When did you see last see her?"

Toms glanced at the photo. "That's easy. I've never seen her in my life," he said confidently.

"Never? How odd. It looks to me as if this very room is the setting for this picture. Wouldn't you agree?"

Toms examined the photograph once more, pursing his

lips as he ostentatiously switched his gaze from the picture to the fireplace.

"It's certainly a *similar* fireplace," he said. "But the design is not uncommon and I dare say you can buy something very like that in marbled plastic at any DIY shop. But tell me, Inspector, what does the girl say?"

Pascoe's first reaction was that Toms was mocking him, safe in the knowledge that the girl had been spirited away, God knows where, by Arany. But there was something in the man's intonation, a sense of effort to remain casual, that made him decide to treat the question as genuine.

"When I spoke to her last night," he said carefully, "she seemed ready to change her story."

This noncommittal answer seemed to give Toms new confidence. "It seems an extraordinary thing, Inspector, that you should feel able to come here with your slanderous accusations based on no more than a rather poorly defined film still!"

"Slanderous?" said Pascoe. "How have I slandered you? You do take pictures, don't you? Nude pictures, pornographic pictures?"

"Within the law," said Toms, very morally superior. "When you start accusing me of conniving at the sexual molestation of a twelve-year-old you're saying I've committed a crime. And *that's* slanderous."

"You're right," said Pascoe. "You're so right. Now I wonder how you manage to be so right?"

"What?"

"What I mean is how do you happen know that the girl

in the picture, whom you have never seen before, is only twelve years old?"

Toms looked blank for a second, then slowly smiled and ran his fingers through his tousled hair. "Did I say twelve years old? Well, so what? I used the term generally, not particularly. She's obviously a kid, else why all the fuss? I really am sorry to spoil your Perry Mason moment, Inspector, but I'm not about to be tricked into one of your nasty cells just to please your puritan conscience. I see your game. You don't like the modern liberating spirit abroad in the arts, no policeman does, so you desperately look around for some method of getting at the artist."

"Save it," said Pascoe wearily. "I've seen the film of the matchbox cover. Let's stop mucking about."

"Yes, let's," interrupted Penny Latimer. "You've been all round the houses. Now it's time to spell it out, baby."

Pascoe looked at the other three people in the room. Curiously, of them all, Ray Crabtree was the only one who looked at all ill at ease. Understandably so, in a way. No policeman likes to have another pointing out what's been going on under his nose. Toms was affecting boredom fairly successfully, while the woman looked alert and interested, which might not be the worst way of concealing guilt.

Where the hell was Dalziel? wondered Pascoe. How would he want this played?

Carefully, was the only answer.

"Let's sit down, Mr. Toms, shall we? There are one or two more questions I want to ask."

"Oh God! Ask if you must. I need a drink."

So saying, Toms headed out into the hallway, presumably in search of Penny's bottle.

Pascoe followed, still talking because he was beginning to feel that if he stopped talking, he might thump somebody. "You made several telephone calls from the Candida Hotel last Friday night," he said.

"Yes. I told you. I rang Penny to say I was stranded."

"I know that, Mr. Toms," said Pascoe. "It's the other calls I'm interested in."

"Other calls?" said Toms, halting, "What others?"

"To Mr. Godfrey Blengdale, for a start," said Pascoe.

"Blengdale?" said Toms. "I don't recollect the name." He sounded completely confident in his ability to deny all knowledge of Blengdale.

Pascoe attempted to match his confidence. "You mean, you don't know your own partner's name?" he asked "Perhaps I misunderstood Miss Latimer, but I thought she implied that Mr. Blengdale owned a third of Homeric?"

The lie sent a shiver of indignation over Penny's frame. Toms glared at her angrily. Pascoe regarded them with an expression of mock bewilderment which would have done credit to Dalziel, and somewhere some god of mischief chortled in delight, flicked a few pieces hither and thither and sat back to enjoy the perfect moment he had created.

The front door opened. A short round figure half stepped, half fell in. One arm hung useless at his side, the other was raised in a vain effort to stanch the flow of blood from a broad gash across his brow.

"Why, here's Mr. Blengdale himself come to resolve

all problems," said Pascoe cheerfully. "My compliments to the make-up man. That looks *really* convincing!"

No one made a move toward the now recumbent figure which had slid to the floor like a medieval outlaw crossing a church threshold to sanctuary.

But the drama was far from over.

"Mr. Toms!" called a sepulchrally deep voice from outside. "There's someone out here would like to talk to you!"

Slowly, ignoring Blengdale, Toms moved through the doorway. Pascoe followed.

The spring sun was low in the sky now and he had to shade his eyes against it before the blur of figures at the far side of the driveway sharpened to identifiability.

Dalziel was there, hands thrust deep into his coat pockets, bulky and menacing as an Easter Island statue. Wield was there too, his harsh and angled face set like a witch doctor's mask. Between them, with the sergeant's broad left hand firmly grasping his right forearm, was Brian Burkill.

Suddenly Pascoe was sure his guess about Blengdale's financial involvement with Homeric was right. Somehow Burkill had found out too. It had been Blengdale that Burkill had been in pursuit of at the yard this morning. Poor Charlie Heppelwhite had merely got in the way. And presumably after Blengdale came Toms. And then Arany. Though perhaps the Hungarian was already lying battered and bleeding somewhere on Burkill's trail.

"Who are those men?" said Penny Latimer over Pascoe's shoulder.

"Two of my colleagues," said Pascoe. "And the one in

the middle's called Burkill. It was his daughter in the photograph."

She drew in her breath sharply and Toms reacted too with an involuntary twitch of the shoulders. But he held his ground as the trio of men slowly approached.

"Mr. Toms? It is Mr. Toms?" said Dalziel in his best meet-the-nobs voice. "I'm Detective-Superintendent Dalziel. I'd have come in with Mr. Pascoe here, only I thought I recognized Mr. Blengdale's car out front and knowing how much he likes a breath of air, I took a chance on finding him somewhere in the grounds."

Burkill's clothes were in the same disarray and he was flushed and perspiring as from some hard physical effort. But his unblinking gaze never left Toms's face.

"Well, I was right. I found him," continued Dalziel. "Only he wasn't alone. He was with Mr. Burkill here. I joined in the conversation. Some very funny things Mr. Blengdale was saying about you, Mr. Toms."

"Was he?" said Toms. "That's odd. I don't know the man."

"Really? He said he was some kind of associate of yours, but then he was a bit upset and I may have picked him up wrong. So, Mr. Blengdale's not known to you? Or Mr. Burkill either? This is Mr. Burkill here."

"I know nothing of these people," said Toms.

"Then I'm sorry we've bothered you. Must be a mistake somewhere. Sergeant, a word with you."

Dalziel took a few steps to one side. Wield let go his grip on Burkill and followed him, leaving Burkill and Toms about two yards apart facing each other.

Behind him, Pascoe heard the front door slam shut. Blengdale must have been listening and decided that he'd seen enough of Brian Burkill for one day. At the sound, Toms looked quickly around, his face twisted as he saw his retreat shut off.

Then Burkill moved. His large hands descended on the film man's shoulders and it looked as if his sheer strength would force Toms into submission at a single blow. But as the slight man went down, he thrust his elbow desperately into Burkill's groin, slipped out of that terrible grasp, and set off along the front of the house, scarcely in his panic taking time to rise into an upright position.

Burkill pursued. Pascoe glanced at Dalziel, who was deep in conversation with Wield. Beside him Penny Latimer said, "He'll kill him!"

Pascoe agreed and took a couple of uncertain steps after the fleeing pair.

"Peter!" said Dalziel. "Do you have a moment?"

He halted, turned, looked back at Burkill and Toms. Dalziel followed his gaze as if this was the first he knew of any trouble.

"Inspector Crabtree," he said. "It is Inspector Crabtree isn't it? Long time since we met. Perhaps you'd go and sort out that bit of bother."

Crabtree, who was lurking behind one of the pillars of the portico, showed no great enthusiasm for the task but obediently lumbered in pursuit.

Burkill was not gaining on Toms, whose fitness or fear was producing a good turn of speed. He was heading across the narrow lawn now toward the concealment of the unkempt shrubbery.

"Can't you stop them?" demanded Penny of Pascoe. "This is monstrous! That fat man did it on purpose."

"Miss Latimer, isn't it?" said Dalziel genially. "I'm just a simple bobby and when people say they don't know each other, I take them at their word. Any road, your Mr. Toms will be safe in a moment."

But as Toms reached the sanctuary of the shrubbery, a third figure detached itself from the ragged blackness of an overgrown rhododendron clump.

"Now who would that be?" wondered Dalziel.

"It's Arany," said Pascoe.

Toms had halted before the newcomer. Presumably now with this reinforcement he would feel emboldened to turn and face his pursuer and for a moment it looked as if this was what was happening.

Burkill arrived. Crabtree was still some way behind. The triangle of men stood quite still for a second. Burkill raised his fist. Arany reached up and laid a restraining hand on it. Then the Hungarian turned to Toms and taking him by the shoulders gave him a devastating triple knee: first the crutch; then, as he folded, the belly; and finally, as he bent double, the face, which straightened him out again and flung him full length backward on the lawn.

"Oh dear," said Dalziel with something of admiration in his voice.

The two men still standing spoke together for a moment. Then Arany turned and blended with the bushes again. Crabtree, who had just arrived, made as if to pursue him. Burkill seized him by the collar, and when the Inspector tried to struggle around to face him, he contemptuously pushed him aside so that he stumbled and fell across the recumbent Toms.

Pascoe put on the intelligently alert look of one who doesn't understand a bloody thing and looked inquiringly at Dalziel, who smiled back at him in a condescendingly amiable manner and stepped forward to meet the returning Burkill as though he'd just arrived for a vicarage garden party.

"Man of your age shouldn't be running around like that, Bri," he said.

"Man of my age can learn a lot of things, Mr. Dalziel," said Burkill grimly. "I'm off to see our Sandra now."

"That'd be best. Maurice left her at Mrs. Abbott's, did he?"

"Aye."

"Sergeant Wield'll go with you. There may be some difficulty in getting out, else."

Pascoe didn't understand this either, till the sound of approaching vehicles made him turn, and a stream of police cars began to emerge from the green tunnel of the driveway.

"Now I dare say one of these gents has got a search warrant," said Dalziel. "Miss Latimer, perhaps as an interested party representing Homeric Films you would care to be present during this search."

"All I want is to contact my solicitor," said Penny.

"Contact away," said Dalziel.

"There's no phone here," said the woman.

"Then you'll just have to shout very loud," answered Dalziel. "Inspector Trumper."

"Sir," said Trumper, who had just emerged from the leading car.

"You have the warrant? Good, get things organized, quickly as you like. Take your time on the search, though. We've got all week if we want."

"Excuse me, Mr. Dalziel," said Burkill.

"You still here, Brian?"

"Maurice said to look behind the chimney in the main bedroom."

"Did he now? You hear that, Inspector? I must thank Mr. Arany when I see him, which should be shortly unless your men are sleeping."

"They're not sleeping, sir," assured Trumper.

"Good. Well, let's get to it. Sergeant Wield, before you go, give Control a shout, tell 'em we need a doctor."

"Right, sir."

"And that's about it, I reckon," said Dalziel. He went under the portico and stood by the door, which was open once more, looking, thought Pascoe, like some nineteenth-century industrial parvenue who'd just built his first mansion.

"Just one thing more," said Dalziel. "I almost forgot. Inspector Crabtree."

"Sir," said Crabtree, who had just arrived holding one side of Gerry Toms, who looked to be in a bad way.

"Inspector Crabtree," said Dalziel ponderously, "you are suspended from your duties pending investigation of certain allegations which have been made into your conduct as a police officer. You will remain here until a senior officer from your force arrives who will accompany you to your home, where a search will be made in your presence. You understand me, Inspector?"

"Yes, sir," said Crabtree without emotion.

"Good," said Dalziel and went into the house.

Crabtree let Toms slip to the ground and pulled a pack of cigarettes out of his pocket.

Pascoe stared at him uncomprehendingly. "Ray," he said.

Crabtree smiled and shrugged. "I've a complete answer to all the charges," he said. "It's 'Go fuck yourself.' Better push off, Peter, before master gets impatient."

"Inspector Pascoe!" bellowed Dalziel from within.

Crabtree's smile broadened.

Pascoe went into the house.

Twenty-five

Dalziel hit him across the face.

"Peter! Peter!" he said.

"Get stuffed," choked Pascoe.

"You OK? Here, have a drink of water."

"I'm OK, I'm OK," said Pascoe.

"I'll get you something stronger just now. For Christ's sake, lad, you've seen worse than that, and in the flesh too."

"I know it, I know it," said Pascoe.

He had too. He had seen bruised and battered flesh, shotgun wounds like spoon holes in a bramble pie, bodies ballooned with long immersion or devoured by long decay. But these he had somehow dealt with, somehow reduced to facts, somehow eventually controlled with his intellect. But this girl dying silently on the screen in the half-light of the Calli viewing room had slipped through his defenses as though they didn't exist.

"OK now?" repeated Dalziel. "If you're going to honk, do it under the carpet. I'll get back and tell that lot in there you were caught short. Can't have them thinking you're soft. Though it might not harm. There's some as reckons the ACC's as bent as a Boxing Day turd." Dalziel went out.

Thanks, mouthed Pascoe after him. He meant it. He'd sat through as much of the film as he could, but in the end he'd had to make for the exit. Once through, he had relaxed the effort of will which had carried him thus far and folded up into the arms of Dalziel, who'd followed him out.

He rose now and went to the window. Wilkinson Square looked peaceful and well ordered in the spring dusk. If the vigilantes knew what had just been shown in the Calliope Kinema Club, they would surely have come running out to tear the place down brick by brick. At least Pascoe hoped they would. But there was no certainty. "We all like it," Ray Crabtree had said. "It's just a matter of degree." Well, that was just special pleading, Pascoe now recognized. But for any plea whatsoever to be possible in defense of *this* made a mockery of civilization.

Crabtree. He shook his head wearily, but was glad to have something else to concentrate his thoughts on. Dalziel had used him there. Sooner or later there must be a confrontation about that, but Pascoe could already map out the route via which he would be conveyed to a state of indignant impotence.

It was clear now that Crabtree and Homeric had been under investigation for some time. Normally when suspi-

cion falls upon a police officer, action is swift and open.
Fellow officers are naturally reluctant to become involved
in any clandestine investigation of one of their own number. Whose turn will it be next? But when a neighboring
task force in the process of closing down its own local
pornography industry had chanced on a trail which led to
Homeric and eventually to Crabtree, it had been decided
to keep things very quiet till the full extent of the business
could be seen.

"Great thing about Homeric is that they admit pornography's their business," Dalziel had said as they drove
away from Hay Hall. "Disarming, that. 'Please, sir, tell us
if we go too far.' "

"How far's too far?" Pascoe had asked.

"Not for me to say, lad," said Dalziel grimly. "But if
there is a 'too far,' then Homeric must be going it, for we
reckoned they were going all the way."

He turned in his seat as he spoke and looked at Pascoe.
"I don't really mean *we*," he said. "Not my investigation,
you understand that? I had to know, of course. But I
wasn't running things."

When Pascoe had come along with Shorter's story,
Dalziel had tried to wet-blanket it. In any case it seemed
too farfetched to be possible. But once Pascoe had struck
out on his own by contacting Homeric direct, Dalziel had
pushed him on.

"I knew if you went to Harrogate, you'd start chatting
to Crabtree. Now, the Homeric lot would be having a go at
him too, asking what the hell was going on. There had to
be something for him to say. Old mate P. Pascoe being a
bit overconscientious—that fitted the book nicely."

"You could have told me," said Pascoe sourly.

"Would you have done it?"

Pascoe considered.

"In any case," continued Dalziel, "you might have turned something up. You certainly stirred something up. At the Calli."

The connection between Homeric and the Calli had been vague.

"We knew that Arany was tied up with Homeric in some way, but you've got to remember that they were openly in the porn game. Arany was an agent. Also he had got a share in a film club. So what was more natural? But just how much he was mixed up in the under-the-counter stuff we didn't know. All that fuss by the fuddy-duddies gave us an excuse to take a close look at the Calli and old Gilbert. But it was looking pretty well OK till two things happened. Miss Alice and you."

"Look, sir," said Pascoe. "Can we just get two things straight. Who killed Haggard?"

"Arany, of course," said Dalziel in exasperation. "I don't think he meant to, but he did. And those stupid sods let him slip through."

This was the only fly in his ointment. Despite Trumper's assurances, Arany had got out of the grounds of Hay Hall with no bother at all. On the credit side, his tip about the fireplace had proved very helpful and the boot of the car was laden with material they had found stored away there.

"Second thing," said Pascoe. "Why doesn't Burkill want to mangle Arany? They acted like old mates."

"They are," said Dalziel. "Thing is, Arany knew nothing about Sandra doing that film, though he was instrumental in getting her involved. She'd met Toms and the Homeric lot a couple of times when Arany had taken her out to Hay Hall to see some filming in process. The clean bits, let me add. He was very careful of her morals, poor bastard. Toms spotted her potential, though. I suspect she very much played the little girl with Uncle Maurice. You know how ruthless kids can be, milking him for all he was worth. But with other men she could be very different. And Toms, the big film man, all that glamour—well, it was a crazy thing to do on both sides, but they did it, made the film, then she came along and said she'd got herself knocked up."

"Who by?" asked Pascoe.

"Who knows?" said Dalziel. "She made it clear that if the balloon went up, she'd blame Toms or her fellow stars. He promised to fix up an abortion. Then her mother cottoned on."

"So she dropped Shorter in it?"

"Aye. That might have been a fail-safe story devised by Toms. Probably was."

Pascoe nodded vigorously and assumed an I-told-you-so expression.

"Don't get too cocky, Peter," warned Dalziel. "Ask yourself why they concocted that particular story."

"For God's sake!" snapped Pascoe. "You're not going to go on with that business, are you?"

"Of course not. No jury on earth'd convict him when this other lot came out," said Dalziel. "But that doesn't make him innocent. But where was I? Oh aye. You start probing. Toms rings Penny Latimer, who's far from clean, but I don't think she's in the muck much beyond her thighs. Christ, can you imagine them thighs? One of those across you and you wouldn't be up for breakfast."

"So Toms rings," said Pascoe impatiently.

"Right. Penny tells him about you sniffing around. Toms is worried. First of all the film *Droit de Seigneur* does have something in it that he didn't think anyone would notice. He's evidently a great one for patching things together—"

"I told you that," said Pascoe.

"So you did. Also he's worried about the actual film. Now Blengdale had it."

"How do you know."

The fat man chortled in glee. "It's surprising how much he was able to spill out just for me keeping Brian Burkill from working him over again."

This then was the explanation of Dalziel's long delay at Hay Hall. A little torture session in the woods. Pascoe knew he ought to feel disgusted.

"Next Toms rings Haggard. No answer. Alice cuts the wire. Finally he rings Arany, tells him what's up, says he's worried something may be going on at the Calli, would he slip round and take a look."

Suddenly Pascoe comprehended. "Ah!" he said. "Miss Alice said, 'Some of the things I found there. Such filth!' I thought it was just an old woman's generalization!"

"She doesn't sound like the type to generalize," said Dalziel. "No, there were pictures. Blengdale had been looking at them that night. Pictures of Sandra. A kind of trailer. Or perhaps when we get close to it, we might even find that Blengdale himself was joining in the fun. Any-

way Arany goes upstairs, finds the wrecked study, won-
ders what the hell's going on. Then he spots the photos.
Sandra's like a daughter to him. He thinks of her as a
child—"

"Which she is," said Pascoe.

"Yeah," said Dalziel. "Arany goes a bit crazy, looks for
Haggard, can't find him but guesses where he is. We can
be pretty sure he knew all Haggard's little quirks. So he
does a bit of wrecking off his own bat just to make it look
good."

"But he doesn't touch the kitchen, because he doesn't
want Haggard to get scared before he's right in the flat,"
said Pascoe.

"I bet you're great at Friday's crossword puzzles on
Saturday," said Dalziel. "Haggard comes in, all fresh and
glowing, at least his bum is. And bang! the ceiling falls in
on him. Arany doesn't mean to kill him—he'd have finished him there and then if he had—but I don't expect he's
much bothered when the old pervert dies. But of course
he doesn't know just who or what's involved, though he's
got a pretty good idea. So he keeps a low profile, tells Toms
some story about finding the Calli wrecked and Haggard
dying when he got there, blames a gang of tearaways or
something. Toms is worried, but ready to believe. After
all, the only other people interested in Haggard and the
Calli are the police, and we're not likely to behave like
that. Are we?"

"Not so near Easter," said Pascoe.

"Right. He doesn't care to see Sandra, can't even bring
himself to deliver her birthday present. Then she turns up,
all hysterical in the early hours of this morning. It all

comes out, about her being pregnant and everything. He dosed her with some pills and went out in search of Burkill, guessing he'd find him at the club. They swapped information. This morning after his secretary had brought her some clothes, Arany took Sandra off to that woman, Abbott, in Leeds. The one you went to see. Very conventional in some ways, these pornographers. A child needs a woman's care."

"She was a good choice," said Pascoe.

"Mebbe. I reckon the idea was also to clear the decks for a bit of the old wild justice. But Burkill, who was probably sleeping it off, didn't want to wait when he woke up. He set out for a chat with Blengdale."

"Yes, I'd worked that out," said Pascoe. "You reckon Heppelwhite was an accident then?"

"Oh yes," said Dalziel. "I mean, when Bri Burkill finally got round to Charlie, he wouldn't have stopped at a couple of fingers, he'd have pulled the whole arm off and hit him with the soggy end.

"Well, Arany finds Bri's jumped the gun, guesses he'll have headed for Hay Hall (God knows how he got out there!) and goes in pursuit. I think we saw most of the rest. Not a bad day's work, if they can lay hands on that Hungarian sod. He'll sing like a drunken Irishman, I reckon. Still with a bit of luck we've got enough in the boot to sort them all out. By God, it should be a good evening's entertainment going through this lot!"

It had seemed a not unamusing irony that Dalziel had picked on the Calli as the place for viewing their booty from Hay Hall. The officers gathered there had been in high spirits as news of the successful completion of other stages in this multi-force operation came through and there had also been something of anticipated pleasure in the air, which only Dalziel had the honesty or the insensitivity to express openly.

But when the first film they showed proved to be the original from which the snippet in *Droit de Seigneur* had been taken, the atmosphere had quickly changed. Pascoe had tried to think of other, pleasant things, of Ellie waiting for him at home, of the bank of spring flowers he passed on his way to work every morning, of his holiday plans for the summer; but the best he could manage was Haggard bleeding to death internally, Emma Shorter swallowing pill after pill, Gwen Blengdale biting the stitching from her gloves as she peered through the breath-hazed window. And even with his eyes firmly closed, the images from the screen had still come through.

But now he was out of it. For someone else it might be a case. Track down the maker, the actors, the distributor. Perhaps Toms was at the center of things, perhaps he was just peripheral. But for Pascoe it was over. A few loose ends, and then all over.

He checked the time. Still early enough to start some tying up. Let Dalziel and the brass think what they might. He had no stomach for any more of this evening's entertainment.

Outside in the square he paused and glanced up at the Andover sisters' house. He thought he glimpsed a pale movement behind an upstairs pane. It might have been a face. Perhaps just a cat. He waved just in case and went on.

First he went to the infirmary.

Charlie Heppelwhite, they told him, was doing well. He had lost two fingers but the third had been stitched back on, so Dalziel's quick thinking had not been in vain. A nurse showed him to the ward. She was young and Irish, with a bright little face of a melodic line of chatter like a song thrush in a hedgerow. Pascoe liked listening to her, though he took in hardly a word of what she said.

It was visiting time and the ward was full of fruit and Lucozade and bright repetitive conversation punctuated by smiling desperate silences.

Charlie Heppelwhite had three visitors: Clint, Betsy, and Deirdre Burkill.

The last was patched and plastered and looked rather worse than when Pascoe had last seen her.

"Hello," said Pascoe genially. "I was up here so I thought I'd look in."

"Nice of you," said Charlie. On the whole he looked the healthiest of the bunch. Clint had a sullen, closed, pale look and Betsy's face had an unnatural feverish flush.

Does she know? wondered Pascoe, looking from Heppelwhite to Deirdre Burkill. "You OK?" he said inanely.

Heppelwhite held up his bandaged hand. "I won't be much use at the washing up for a while," he said.

"You never were," said Betsy without force.

"I'm going to do Blengdale for every penny I can get," continued Charlie. "Never took notice when we complained about lack of safety precautions. The sod hasn't been anywhere near me since it happened, do you know that? Well, when he does, he'll find out he's got real troubles."

"He might have called round," agreed his wife.

Oh, he was busy elsewhere, thought Pascoe. As soon as he realized what Burkill's late arrival at the yard meant, he must have tried to get hold of Toms. Then when he couldn't, he'd made the mistake of going out to Hay Hall himself.

It suddenly struck Pascoe that his approach up the drive must have been spotted from the house, precipitating Blengdale's flight.

And Crabtree's delaying tactics. His crutch ached at the memory. The sod had known bloody well who it was on the other side of the door!

"Mrs. Burkill," he said, "Sandra's all right. I thought you might like to know."

"Thanks," she said indifferently.

"And Brian too."

This time she didn't thank him.

At the reception desk he made inquiries about Emma Shorter and discovered that she had discharged herself that afternoon.

"It was against doctor's orders," said the receptionist. "But we can't keep them in if they don't want to stay." She sounded disapproving, as though, had she the running of the place, there'd be a stop to this softness.

Pascoe begged the use of a phone and dialed Shorter's number. He deserved to know that the case against him was almost certain to be dropped.

There was no reply. Pascoe stood by the phone and

wondered. If Emma Shorter had left just this afternoon, you'd have thought there'd be someone in the house this evening.

"Thanks," he said to the receptionist and went out to his car.

He wanted to go home. He felt almost desperate for home. But instead he swung west in a wide arc which eventually took him by a series of social degrees from houses that reflected the dignity of labor to villas that proclaimed the delight of wealth, and ultimately to Acornboar Mount.

Shorter's lawn was beginning to burn where Clint had sprayed the weed killer, but the dentist's water treatment had blurred the edges of the word so that it was almost illegible. There were two cars in the drive, Shorter's Rover and a battered mini.

Pascoe put his finger to the doorbell and leaned on it till he heard footsteps in the hall.

"For God's sake—Oh, it's you," said Shorter ungraciously.

"Sorry, Jack, but if you can't hear your phone, I thought I'd better make sure you heard your doorbell," said Pascoe. "Can I come in?"

Shorter looked less than enthusiastic, but Pascoe was moving forward with a policeman's majestic instancy and it would have taken a physical barrier to prevent him.

"In here, is it? Great," said Pascoe, pushing open the lounge door.

Emma Shorter, pale-faced but with something more of her calm self-possession and elegant grooming than the last time Pascoe had seen her, sat in one of the tubular steel chairs. At the other side of the room, looking both physically and mentally uncomfortable, Alison Parfitt perched on the edge of the hanging basket. She was wearing a red raincoat with the belt pulled tight in a casual knot to reveal the generous curves of her bust and behind. And to counter the somewhat overstudied calm of the other woman's demeanor, the young nurse had a determined set of the jaw and shoulders which gave promise that her unease would not make her an easy target.

"Peter!" said Emma. "Come in. Do you know Miss Parfitt, John's nurse? We were just going to have a sherry. Won't you join us?"

"Come on, love!" exclaimed Shorter. "Yes, he knows Alison. And he'll know a bloody sight more besides. They'll have been conning my private life pretty thoroughly, so we don't need to make up stories to preserve the decencies. All right, Peter. Here we are, nicely mounted for your detective microscope. There's my wife who's had such a nasty shock to her standards and values that she took an overdose. Though I suspect it was an even nastier shock for her to realize just how much of an overdose she'd taken. Next, here's my mistress, come to have things out in the open and stake her claim. And finally, there's me. On the edge of professional ruin, jail even. But I must be all right deep down inside, else why should these two virtuous ladies squabble over me?"

How odd, thought Pascoe. I hadn't noticed. Of the three of them, it's Shorter who's by far in the worst condition.

"I'm not squabbling, my dear," observed Emma. "I invited Miss Parfitt around here to talk sensibly about our plans, not to compete for you."

"You knew about . . . *this*, then?" said Pascoe.

"About them all, even when I haven't been able to put names to them," said Emma Shorter. "I'd adjusted my life to include them, I suppose. This other thing was just too much. I couldn't fit it in. I suppose that's why I took the pills. John is right, but only partially so—his usual degree of success. I meant to kill myself. But I regained consciousness while they were doing all kinds of unpleasant things in an effort to revive me, and when I realized from what I could pick up that there was a real chance they wouldn't succeed, *then* I suddenly felt frightened. And angry! But you know what I felt in the end? When I opened my eyes yesterday morning and knew that they'd succeeded and saw John sitting all baggy-eyed at the end of the bed?

"I felt vastly amused! I was too exhausted to laugh out loud, but I laughed inside. And I've been laughing inside ever since. I'd almost done him the biggest favor of his life, but it hadn't come off and the poor dear would just have to keep a stiff upper lip and hide his disappointment!"

"Perhaps," said Shorter grimly, "perhaps I won't bother."

"What about you, Alison?" asked Pascoe gently. "What do you feel about all this?"

"I love him," said the girl, adding angrily in response to Emma's small but eloquent raising of her eyebrows, "Yes, I do. And I love him enough to stand by him. That's what loving means."

"Is it, now?" murmured Emma Shorter. "I suppose it is. Well, I'm about to *sit* by him from now on. I've decided to leave things in the hands of the law. If he gets convicted, I shall divorce him. Otherwise I see no reason why we shouldn't continue our charade, except that from now on he will know I know it's a charade."

She is ashamed, thought Pascoe. Ashamed that she could do what she did. Odd. And Alison on the other hand is rather proud of herself. She's seeing herself as the heroine of the hour. Hence am I, little me, declaring my love for and loyalty to this worthless man, in his own house in front of his wife. It's like something out of . . .

"It's like something out of Noel Coward!" said Shorter desperately. "I think I'd rather be in jail!"

"That's your best bet too, my dear," said his wife to Alison. "Then I'll divorce hm. Why not turn witness for the prosecution?"

"I'll stick by him whatever happens," swore Alison. "Whatever!"

Oh dear, thought Pascoe. He coughed gently. It was time to change their lives.

"I just dropped in to tell you, Jack, that there probably won't be any charges now. That's unofficial, OK? But I reckon you're in the clear."

He left them in a silence unbroken by the popping of champagne corks, the ring of merry laughter, the tears of joyous relief. He left them in a three-cornered trap in a thirty-thousand-pound house in a three-quarter-acre garden with a four-letter word burned on the lawn.

Perhaps like seaside rock candy it went all the way through.

Twenty-six

"I'm home," he said.

"Not before time," said Ellie. She gave him a big kiss, then stepped back and regarded him with a kind of twisted smile which could only be described as a smirk. "Good day?" she asked.

"Mixed," he said. "No. Good really, only it's knocked me out a bit. Shorter's off the hook."

"What?"

"Yes. No case. I'll tell you all about it later."

"Good," she said without conviction. "Are you still going to go to him?"

"As a dentist you mean? I don't know. I suppose so. After all, he knows my fantasies."

"Yes. I dare say Ms. Lacewing can make a pretty good guess at them too."

"Good lord," he said. "Can one liberated woman be jealous of another?"

"Of course not. But being liberated, I'll thump her on the nose if I catch her making eyes at you again."

"Making eyes?" said Pascoe, astounded.

"That's what it comes down to," said Ellie. "I know a rival when I see one."

"Do you? You know, perhaps I've been wrong about that girl. Ask her around to dinner some night. Preferably some night when you've got a committee meeting."

"Ha ha."

"Which reminds me," said Pascoe, accepting gratefully the drink which Ellie offered him. She must be a mind reader, he thought as he assessed that its length and strength were just what he needed. He sank half of it in a swallow.

"Reminds you what?"

"Your committee. It shouldn't be such hard going. I think God Blengdale's going to have other things on his plate."

Ellie laughed. "Haven't you heard? It's out of God's hands."

"What is!"

"The whole business. He just wanted to bring us into town, release the site for his nasty country club. Well, on the news tonight they read out a list of colleges which the Department of Education want to close completely as surplus to requirements. And lo! there we are at the top."

"Good Lord," said Pascoe. "Can't you appeal?"

"Oh, never fear. There'll be a lot of bloody fighting

before the axe falls. But I doubt if we'll talk our way out of this one."

"Another drink?" said Pascoe. "I must say, you're taking it all with exemplary calm."

"Well, to tell the truth, I've been getting a bit sick of it all," said Ellie. "I've been thinking how nice it would be to give it all up, retire for a bit, start a family, perhaps."

"Well, that would need thinking about," said Pascoe cautiously. "Starting when, for instance!"

"Oh, I should say, starting about three weeks last Wednesday when we got back from that birthday party and I didn't have time to get to the bathroom cabinet and you said it didn't matter as what was good enough for the Pope was good enough for you."

"Good Lord," said Pascoe. "Well, well, well."

"Is that *all* you can say? Aren't you pleased?"

"Hold on," said Pascoe. "Let me see. That'll be . . . October, November, December. That's great! We won't have to go to your mother's for Christmas! Darling, I'm delighted. Come here so I can learn that smirk from an expert."

The phone started ringing five minutes later, but they ignored it. It rang on and on and on, but they paid no heed. Finally it stopped.

"You see," said Ellie, "if you pay the nasty world no attention, it goes away."

"Yes," said Pascoe.

But Shorter had tried not to answer the telephone today and much good it had done him. Though in his case, perhaps the nasty world was there already. There was no doubt in Pascoe's mind that Sandra Burkill's accusation was a fail-safe device. But could Toms have invented such a mass of circumstantial detail?

He recalled the old adage: If you want to tell a lie, tell the truth.

"Peter," said Ellie warningly. "The nasty world has gone away. Forget it."

"I will, I will," he said fervently.

The phone began to ring again.

About the Author

REGINALD HILL has been widely published both in England and in the United States and has been justly compared with P. D. James and Ruth Rendell. He received Britain's most coveted mystery writers award, the Cartier Diamond Dagger Award, as well as the Golden Dagger, for his Dalziel/Pascoe series. Reginald Hill writes thrillers under the name of Patrick Ruell. He lives with his wife in Cumbria, England.